THE
GOOD
SON

Carolyn Huizinga Mills

THE
GOOD
SON

a novel

Cormorant Books

The publisher gratefully acknowledges the support of the Canada Council
for the Arts and the Ontario Arts Council for its publishing program.
We acknowledge the financial support of the Government of Canada through
the Canada Book Fund (CBF) for our publishing activities, and the Government of
Ontario through Ontario Creates, an agency of the Ontario Ministry of Culture,
and the Ontario Book Publishing Tax Credit Program.

LIBRARY AND ARCHIVES CANADA CATALOGUING IN PUBLICATION

Title: The good son / a novel by Carolyn Huizinga Mills.
Names: Mills, Carolyn Huizinga, author.
Identifiers: Canadiana (print) 20200238418 | Canadiana (ebook) 20200238426 |
ISBN 9781770865921 (softcover) | ISBN 9781770865938 (HTML)
Classification: LCC PS8626.I4563 G66 2021 | DDC C813/.6—dc23

Cover photo and design: Angel Guerra / Archetype
Interior text design: Tannice Goddard, tannicegdesigns.ca
Printer: Friesens

Printed and bound in Canada.

CORMORANT BOOKS INC.
260 Spadina Avenue, Suite 502, Toronto, ON M5T 2E4
www.cormorantbooks.com

To Scott — for encouraging me, always,
to follow my dreams.

THE
GOOD
SON

PART
ONE

CHAPTER ONE

·

I DIDN'T ALWAYS HATE MY big brother. There was a period of my life, in fact, when I looked up to him with something close to admiration. But I was a little girl then and it was easy to be impressed by him. Ricky's fooled a lot of people in his forty-six years — just ask any of the other pissed-off women in his life. We make a surprisingly long list.

NOW THAT WE'RE ADULTS, I generally avoid talking to him, which isn't hard given the fact that he lives in Toronto, over a hundred kilometres away; but, since today is his birthday, I have done the sisterly thing and called him. Already, I regret it. He is describing some woman named Dee Dee. And as I listen to him explain how amazing she is, I have an overwhelming desire to tell him that he's boring me to the edge of violence, to the point of wanting to punch him. Lucky for him, I have plans tonight, so he's safe — he always is — ensconced in his swanky townhouse, far removed from Dunford and all his secrets hidden here.

I switch the phone to my other ear and glance at Jason to see if he's annoyed with how long this call is taking, but he's sitting on my couch, quite relaxed, flipping through last month's edition of *Maclean's*. If he's feeling at all impatient, he's doing a good job hiding it. We were just getting ready to head out the door when I remembered I hadn't acknowledged Ricky's birthday, so I decided to make what was meant to be a quick call just to get it out of the way. And now Ricky seems to think I should be just as excited as he is about Dee Dee, even while he insists things are "still fine" with Brenda, his wife. What kind of name is Dee Dee anyway? It sounds like a stage name for a stripper.

"I hate to cut this short, Ricky," I say, "but Jason and I were just about to step out." At the mention of his name, Jason looks up and smiles. I do my best to smile back, but from the way my lips refuse to cooperate, I'm guessing it comes across more like a grimace. I'd been looking forward to going out for dinner with him tonight, but this conversation with my brother is ruining my appetite.

"Oh, hey, no problem," Ricky replies. "Thanks for the call, eh?"

"Sorry," I say to Jason, after I hang up. "I didn't think he would talk for so long."

Jason shrugs. "No worries. You ready to go?"

The fact that Jason doesn't easily get bothered is one of the things I like about him, but at times he can come across as indifferent. Not that I'd want him to be overly attentive or affectionate — I don't do the whole affectionate thing all that well myself. We're a good match on multiple levels. Our personalities are similar and we don't demand too much of each other. Jason is tall, six-one to my five-eight, with an athletic build. He has dark hair, just starting to thin a bit at the crown. My natural hair colour is a mousy brown, but after years of highlights, I prefer to think of myself as an ashy blonde, with a few streaks of copper thrown in for good measure. I have an okay body, nothing that would stop anyone in their tracks, but for a thirty-eight-year-old, I'm in decent shape.

Jason is forty-one, with a seven-year-old kid he sees every other weekend, and an ex-wife who teaches Pilates for a living. It's probably a good thing I don't have stellar abs or a killer body, because then I'd just remind him of her. At least that's how I like to look at it.

Mom, for one, would love it if I finally settled down and married Jason already. "You're not getting any younger, Zoe," she's reminded me on more than one occasion.

Even more than tying the knot with Jason, I think what Mom would really love is if I got back together with Amir. She never really let go of that little fantasy. I have to be honest, the thought does give me goosebumps, which is completely unfair to Jason, but in reality, there's no danger of Amir and I ever reuniting. None whatsoever. I haven't spoken to him in years; I don't even know where he lives now. And I can pretty much guarantee that if we did happen to cross paths, he wouldn't give me the time of day, much less entertain any ideas of linking himself romantically to me again.

Still, every now and again Mom brings up Amir's name with this wistful look on her face, even though I've clearly moved on. And the fact that I'm with Jason is proof, isn't it, that I've moved on?

JASON TAKES MY HAND AS we walk into town. We're heading to The Crow's Nest, which is only a few blocks from my bungalow on Pine Street, and one of the few decent restaurants in Dunford. It's where we usually go. Incidentally, it's also where we had our first date, almost two years ago, which gives you an idea about how spontaneous we are as a couple. The restaurant had just opened then, in what used to be Wilson's Hardware. The new owners kept the rough wooden plank flooring and incorporated bits and pieces from the hardware store into their décor. Beside the cash register at the front there's a container full of mismatched screws and bolts, and in the women's bathroom, there's an old tin watering can sprouting fake flowers by the sink. The best part though, is the former lumberyard, which was converted into a sprawling outdoor patio facing the southern bank of the Still River.

I'm guessing the patio won't be open tonight, despite how nice it is outside. The last few days have been unseasonably warm, with the temperatures climbing into the teens, which is crazy for this early in March. As much as I'm enjoying the bizarre spring-like weather, I also know how a sudden melt affects the water quality in the river, which in turn makes things extra busy at the Water Treatment Plant. I can just imagine the turbidity levels sky-rocketing over the weekend. But I'm not going to think about work tonight. I want to enjoy myself.

"Anything new with your brother?" Jason asks, squeezing my hand as we walk along Main Street, past the faded storefronts and torn awnings of downtown Dunford. Is it just me, or does everything look a little extra dingy now that the last traces of snow have disappeared?

"Nah," I say, wondering whether or not I should mention Dee Dee. Jason is touchy about affairs. His ex left him for a guy she met online when their son, Parker, was just a toddler.

Jason looks at me quizzically and I decide he's expecting more than the non-answer I'd hoped to get away with. "He's taking Leah to a play next weekend," I offer. "They're going to see *Sleeping Beauty* or maybe it was *Beauty and the Beast*."

"That sounds nice," Jason says. And I can't help but think that my brother has him fooled, too.

Leah is my brother's eleven-year-old daughter from his second wife. The wife before Brenda. And as much as he seems to be a decent dad, I honestly don't know how he can look at that sweet girl and live with himself. Because I know I couldn't. In fact, if it weren't for Leah, I might never have broken things off with Amir. At the time, I couldn't bear the thought of him being connected to me, to my brother, and to that innocent, innocent little girl.

CHAPTER
TWO

·

JUST AS I PREDICTED, THE patio at The Crow's Nest is closed. The outdoor tables are still piled against the side wall of the restaurant, stacked on top of each other like toy furniture. I'm vaguely disappointed; it would have been nice to eat outside tonight. Perhaps with a bit of fresh air and open space my unsettled thoughts about my brother would simply float away.

Jason lets go of my hand while we wait in the dim vestibule of the restaurant to be seated and I run my fingers over the scarred piece of oak left over from the original front counter of Wilson's Hardware. As always, I request a table at the back, by the large windows looking out onto the Still River. We follow the hostess obediently through the dining room, threading our way through the low murmur of voices around us, and I try to push the conversation with Ricky from my mind.

Once Jason and I are seated, I watch him study the menu as if he doesn't already know exactly what he's going to order. Neither one of us needs a menu — we both have the same thing every time we come here. Steak sandwich for Jason, chicken parm for me.

Jason seems a bit jittery and I notice, for the first time, that he's wearing what must be a new shirt, or at least not one I've seen before. He looks oddly formal given that it's a polo shirt — navy with thin white stripes — especially compared to the T-shirts I'm used to seeing him in. It looks good on him, though. I wonder, suddenly, if my brother dresses up to see the amazing Dee Dee, or is it the opposite for him? Does he consider it slumming when he's out cheating on his wife? Brenda must know. Or at least, she must know it's always been a possibility; Ricky doesn't exactly have a glowing track record when it comes to being faithful.

"Zoe?" Jason is looking at me, eyebrows raised. "Are you ready to order?"

A waitress is standing at our table, pad and pen in hand, and she gives me a tight smile as I order the chicken parm.

"I might try something different tonight," Jason says. "Just to liven things up." His voice is too loud, too enthusiastic, and I can't figure out why he's acting so strange.

He vacillates between ribs and fish, before settling on the haddock. When he hands the waitress his menu, his hand is shaking. And suddenly, I know. Or I think I know. He's going to propose. Oh god. That would explain the shirt.

My hands are sweating. I should be excited; obviously I like him, but just the idea of someone slipping a ring on my finger makes me nauseous.

When the waitress returns with our wine, we toast and I try to think of something to say. He wouldn't do it here, in the restaurant, would he? Jason sets his glass down and reaches for my hand across the table. "Zoe —" he says, but I interrupt him before he can go any further.

"What made you decide to get the fish?" I ask. I tug my hand back and straighten my cutlery.

Jason holds my eyes with his. "I wanted tonight to be different."

"Not me," I say quickly, feigning a little laugh. "I like things to stay the same."

"Zoe —"

"Like, you know how we've talked about moving in together?" This is mean. Moving in together has been a mild source of contention between us recently. It's like I'm trying to pick a fight. "I was thinking about it again the other day, and I know it makes sense financially, but I don't think I'm ready."

I watch as he sits back, absorbing the implication of what I'm saying. I've ruined the moment. When our food arrives, I try to make up for being such a jerk on what should've been a nice night out.

"I'm not saying I won't ever be convinced," I say. "You were pretty convincing last night, actually."

He doesn't even smile. "Zoe, I don't want to argue. Let's talk about something else."

I nod, and I know, as I take another bite of chicken, that my nervousness is a direct reaction to my phone call with Ricky.

Most of my life has been a reaction to Ricky. Which is only part of the reason I hate him.

I SOMETIMES WONDER WHAT IT was like for Ricky after I was born. He had been an only child for such a long time — eight years — that he must have resented the attention that unexpectedly shifted from him to me. Was he gentle with me when I was a baby? Did Mom have to remind him constantly to be careful, to be quiet, to be a good big brother?

Knowing how he was while I was growing up, it seems likely that he was already a jerk as an eight-year-old. I imagine him crashing around the house, jolting me awake while I lay uneasily behind the bars of my crib. I can picture him playing with me too roughly, scaring or even hurting me, then watching from wherever he'd been sent to sit quietly while Mom consoled me, all of her attention and kisses raining down on my little head.

According to Mom, I was an overly sensitive baby. Particularly to noise. She used to make my dad open his beer cans in the bathroom with the door closed because the slight pop and hiss when the tab lifted was enough to wake me from a dead sleep. Ricky said he ripped a piece of paper in front of me once, and the sound caused me to burst into tears. I can hardly blame him then, if he found my presence an unwelcome intrusion. A baby sister who cries at the sound of paper tearing. At this age, thinking about it, even I find the idea a bit pathetic.

Although, I also think Ricky liked how easy it was to scare me. I have a vivid memory of him pulling me down the sidewalk in our red Radio Flyer wagon, zigzagging wildly past the houses on our street, while my pudgy toddler fingers clutched the sides of the wagon in terror. He probably relished my fear, breathing it in like an expensive cologne: the scent of my powerlessness.

Mom insists I can't possibly remember anything from when I was that young. She's also quick to dismiss the notion that Ricky would have gone out of his way to scare me. "He was always good to you as a baby," she says. "He loved you."

And yet other memories surface. Like the time he led me into our parents' bedroom and set me on the top of their tall wooden dresser. My legs dangled over the edge, and while I might not have understood the danger of how high up I was, I knew enough to understand I was stuck there.

"Don't move," he instructed me solemnly, before walking out of the room.

I sat perfectly still, waiting and waiting for him to come back.

I must have been scared. Even now I can't figure out why he left me up there like that. Was he hoping I would cry out for him? Did he want me to fall? Whatever his intentions, I remember reaching out my arms to him in relief when he finally came back to lift me down.

If he was disappointed that day by my silent brand of terror, secretly wishing for a more vocal manifestation of panic, he didn't show it. He simply wrapped his spindly arms around my quivering body and set me gently on the floor.

"Don't tell Mom," he probably said. Or maybe I already instinctively knew enough not to.

WHEN MOM WAS UPSET WITH Ricky, it was as if the whole house suddenly became wobbly. There was something deeply unsettling about hearing her yell at him, asking him why he had to give her so much trouble, all while he looked at the floor so she wouldn't see him smiling. Later, he could casually stroll into the living room and ask her for twenty bucks, and she'd hand it over. As he folded the money into his wallet, he'd look at me and wink.

Once, after a particularly big blow-up, Ricky left and returned with a rose bush in a black, plastic bucket. He carried it to the backyard, took a shovel from the shed, and started digging a hole.

Mom came outside just as he was watering the newly planted rose bush and said, "What's this?"

"A surprise for you," Ricky replied.

Mom smiled. That night she made fish cakes for supper and I knew Ricky had been forgiven. He was always forgiven.

PERHAPS BECAUSE I WAS SO sensitive, or because I was her last baby, or simply because I was a girl, Mom coddled me. I'm sure she only wanted to protect me, but looking back, I sometimes wonder — if

Mom had paid more attention to Ricky, would it have made any difference? I doubt it. If our dad hadn't gone and killed himself by falling off a roof, would that have changed anything? It's hard to say. I don't remember much about my dad. I was only four when he died, but Ricky was twelve and it must have hit him pretty hard. Sometimes it still makes me jealous that my brother got to have a dad for at least part of his life. Mom has albums full of pictures of the two of them doing stuff together: building a tree fort in the backyard, fishing off the pier in Boelen, standing with their arms around each other in front of our putty-coloured brick bungalow. And while I'm in some of those pictures, I'm just a side-bar. The baby in the background. There is one photo of Dad holding me on an ugly gold and brown sofa, but even in that picture his eyes are on my brother who is standing on the cushion beside him, with one arm thrust into the air like Superman. So, when it comes to our dad, Ricky is the one with all the memories.

LATER, WHEN I WAS IN grade one and I wanted to play with the big kids after school, I felt, maybe for the first time, my father's absence in a concrete way. Not his actual absence, because I didn't remember enough about him for that, but the fact of his absence.

I'd grabbed my bike to join a game of cops and robbers that was starting, but quickly discovered I couldn't keep up because of my training wheels. I couldn't figure out why other kids my age knew how to ride a two-wheeler when I didn't. Tina Martin told me. Her dad had taught her over the summer. Brian Lowther's dad had taught him too, and the unfairness of that simple fact hit me like a kick in the ribs.

Ricky found me in the backyard with a screwdriver, where I was trying, with all of the determined concentration of a six-year-old, to take the training wheels off my bike.

"What're you doing?" Ricky asked, sinking onto the grass beside me.

"I want to play cops and robbers," I told him. I attacked the bolts on my training wheels with renewed energy, banging the screwdriver uselessly against them.

"You can't use that," Ricky said, taking the screwdriver gently from my hand. "You need a wrench."

He disappeared inside and returned carrying a hard, black case. He opened it to reveal a collection of metallic tubes and one long handle. "It's a socket wrench set," he explained. "See all the different sizes?" I hugged my knees to my chest as I watched my big brother remove my training wheels using our dead dad's tools. When he was done, we both stood up and I gripped my bike by the handle bars.

"Come on," Ricky said, leading me through the front gate to the sidewalk. "I'll teach you."

You can see how easy it was back then to be fooled by him. He wasn't just my big brother; in many ways he was my hero.

THE REST OF MY DINNER with Jason at The Crow's Nest turns out to be a subdued affair. He's polite enough, but distracted. I feel bad for bringing up the whole moving-in-together thing. For constructing a wall like that. Now I'm worried that I've discouraged him completely. The strained silence between us makes me uneasy.

"How's the fish?" I ask lightly.

"Fine."

"Maybe I'll try it next time. Is the batter thick?"

Jason sets down his fork. He studies me for a minute. "You're worried about your interview, aren't you?"

"No," I say, but even as I say it, I know I'm lying. I've worked at the Dunford Water Treatment Plant for almost twenty years, and in January the township sold the plant to a private company. Now the entire staff has to sit through an interview with the new owners, Crystal Clear Solutions, or CCS for short, and while we've been assured that the whole process is merely a formality, there's also been talk about CCS wanting to make changes. Downsizing. Cuts. So as much as the process is being touted as a formality, people are understandably nervous. My interview is on Friday and it's been weighing on my mind like a stone.

"You'll be fine," Jason says, "you're the only female Operator in Charge. They're not going to fire you. The optics would be bad."

"They're not going to fire anyone. At least that's not what they'll call it when they give your job to someone else. They have their own people they want to bring in and I highly doubt they'll give two craps about the fact that I'm female."

Jason takes a sip of his wine. "Okay," he says slowly, drawing out the syllables. "You're in a fine mood tonight, aren't you?"

I wish we could go back to how things were this afternoon, before I talked to Ricky, before everything became awkward. A few hours ago, I was stretched out on my couch with my feet in Jason's lap, laughing while he attempted to massage my toes. As the tension at our table lingers, I become hungry for signs of reassurance. Maybe we should've stayed in tonight. I could have made Jason dinner and then he would have spent the night with me before slipping away in the early morning to get ready for work at the body shop. I have a feeling that tonight, after dinner, he'll head back to his place, alone. I can't say I blame him.

When we first started dating, we used to spend almost every night together, either at his place or mine, except for the weekends that he had Parker. But even then, when Tammy came by to collect Parker on the Sunday night, I would sometimes already be there, in Jason's condo, anxious to have him to myself again.

"Can I get you some dessert?" our waitress asks, and I look at Jason, in case he's planning to change things up and order something random instead of the cheesecake we usually get.

"I think we'll share a chocolate cheesecake," Jason replies. He raises an eyebrow at me and I nod in agreement. Good. No more surprises.

The plate sits in the middle of the table and we take turns cutting off bite-sized pieces of the rich, creamy cake. I drag each chunk through the raspberry sauce that's been drizzled on the edges of the plate, and when the slice is gone, I sit back to enjoy my decaffeinated tea while Jason has a coffee. I watch him closely in case it suddenly looks like he's about to drop to one knee.

He pulls out his phone and scans it, even though he was the one who came up with the rule that we shouldn't have our phones out at meals.

"Just checking the time," he tells me. He signals for our bill and we are quiet again.

On the short walk back to my house, I am relieved when Jason reaches for my hand. Feeling his fingers wrapped loosely around mine eases some of the anxiety that has been steadily building in my gut over the past hour. The sun is sinking slowly, and as it rests momentarily against the roofline of the Royal Bank, it spills golden light down the once-impressive building's chipped bricks. I wish I had my camera.

Dunford wasn't always so run-down and depressing. In the halls of the Municipal Office, I've seen black and white photographs from when the town was thriving. In those pictures, the Royal Bank rises majestically from the corner of Main Street, and the thick pillars that flank the steps to the front doors give the whole building an air of grandeur. The King's Tavern, across the street, looks like it used to be a decent hotel, instead of a seedy bar attached to a bunch of low-rent apartments. It's as if, over time, the whole town has sunk into a kind of slovenly disgrace; a slow decay. I've occasionally thought about doing a photo montage depicting Dunford's past and present, juxtaposing current images of the buildings against their black and white counterparts, matching, as best I can, the distance and the angles from which the originals were taken.

I do wonder sometimes why I stayed here. I mean besides the obvious reasons like my job, and being close to Mom. Maybe Ricky had the right idea. He hightailed it out of Dunford the minute he finished high school.

Jason squeezes my hand. "You're awful quiet," he says.

We're passing the library now, an Edwardian mansion converted years ago after the original library went up in flames. Mom used to work at the old library and when it burned down, she was upset for days. I squeeze Jason's hand back. "Just tired." I want to explain what happened to me at dinner, but I can't very well admit that I panicked at the thought of him proposing. It's easier to let him believe I'm just worried about my job, which is partially true. Besides, just because Jason wore a new shirt doesn't mean he was about to pop the question. I need to get a hold of myself.

My street is only one block away and already I'm lonely. I know that when we get to my house, Jason will come inside just long enough to grab his things, then he'll drive away and I'll be left alone inside my empty bungalow.

And Ricky, goddamned Ricky, will probably be out celebrating his birthday with Brenda, pretending he isn't thinking about Dee Dee the whole time.

So, for tonight, I will carry the weight of that indiscretion for him too.

CHAPTER THREE

.

AFTER OUR DAD DIED, RICKY starting getting into all kinds of trouble. Mom refers to this period as his "acting out" phase, and when she talks about it now, she makes it sound like it was all a bit of a joke, but I remember loud confrontations between the two of them that were anything but funny.

On one afternoon I was sitting at our kitchen table with my Rainbow Brite colouring book when the phone rang. Mom hurried over and partway through the conversation, something in her voice made me pause in my colouring and watch her. She had closed her eyes, like she was so tired she was going to fall asleep right there, leaning against the counter. After she hung up, I sat there, waiting for her to look at me and smile and go back to normal. But she didn't.

She picked up an empty glass from the counter and slammed it into the sink. The sound of breaking glass sent a spasm of fear down my spine and I started to cry. She looked at me then.

"It was an accident, Zoe," she said. "You don't need to cry."

I wanted to believe her, but watching her pick the shards of glass out of the sink made my stomach hurt.

When Ricky got home from school, he tossed his backpack on the floor and started down the hall toward his bedroom without saying a word to either of us. Mom called him back using all four of his names.

"Richard Joshua Martin Emmerson, you come back here this minute!"

He turned around slowly and made his way toward Mom. I scuttled past him into my bedroom, but even from behind the closed door I could hear the angry accusations ricocheting off the walls of our living room. I couldn't make out very much of what they were saying, but I remember squeezing my eyes shut at the sheer meanness in their voices.

"You think I'm acting crazy?" I heard Mom shriek. "Who do you think is going to pay for the damage?"

I couldn't hear Ricky's reply.

Mom said something in a low, menacing tone and whatever it was it set Ricky off.

"Why are you such a — a witch?" he shouted. "Why do you always have to make such a big deal out of everything? Just leave me alone!"

"You don't even care, do you?" Mom yelled, right before I heard the bedroom door next to mine slam.

I peeked out of my room and saw Mom leaning forward, one hand on her chest. Her eyes were closed again and she was biting her lip. She stood, shoulders hunched, for a few seconds before straightening up and taking a deep breath.

I found out later from Ricky what he'd done. He'd written the word SHIT with a thick black marker on the wall in the boys' bathroom. And he'd smashed one of the mirrors above the sinks with his foot.

"Why did you do that?" I whispered.

"I was mad."

At the time, I couldn't comprehend that kind of violent anger. That urge to strike out, to cause damage, to hurt someone or something.

I BECAME A PLEASER. AT home, at school, anytime I was around other people, I went out of my way to be helpful and polite. It's possible I was just a nice kid, but I seem to remember making a concerted effort to be good, to not cause any trouble.

Once, at recess, I picked up an empty juice box and a Kit Kat wrapper that was blowing around on the tarmac. When I carried them over to a garbage can by the door, Mrs. Smith, my grade two teacher, gave me a beaming smile. "Why thank you, Zoe!" she said. "We could use more helpers like you!"

The next day, on my way outside for recess, I reached into one of the garbage cans in the hall and pulled out some crumpled wrappers and a damp Kleenex. I quickly stuffed them in my pocket, planning to repeat my little garbage hero performance when it was time to come inside.

As I was straightening up, I heard snickering behind me. "Garbage-picker! Garbage-picker! Zoe is a garbage-picker!"

Ashley Ridowski and Jennifer Palmer were both pointing at me, their faces scrunched up with exaggerated disgust. I stared at them, my mouth hanging open in an 'O' of surprise, then turned and fled. Later, at home, I pulled the wrappers and the soggy Kleenex from my pocket and dumped them in our kitchen garbage under the sink, where no one could see.

RICKY'S SHENANIGANS, AS MOM NAIVELY refers to them now, only got worse when he went to high school and started hanging around with Darius. The two of them were trouble. I never liked

Darius, not from the first time I met him. He had greasy hair that hung in his eyes and this hunched way of walking that I'm sure he thought was cool, but that really made him look like he was too lazy to stand up straight. Mostly Darius ignored me when he was at our house, which was fine by me because I didn't like talking to my brother's friends.

I woke up one morning to the sound of Mom crying as she asked Ricky over and over, "What were you thinking? Oh Ricky, what on earth were you thinking?" I couldn't hear his reply, so I imagined him shrugging at her the way he so often did when she wanted an explanation. His reaction to pretty much everything at that time was casual indifference. Shrugging us off.

I was used to Mom being angry with Ricky, but I wasn't used to hearing her cry. Whatever Ricky had done this time, I knew it was a different kind of bad. I sat cross-legged on my bed, listening to the barely-controlled fury in Mom's voice, absorbing the fog of anger and disappointment that permeated the air.

Ricky slammed out of the house and I snuck into the kitchen. Mom pasted on a smile, but her eyes were still red-rimmed and puffy. I made myself an Eggo waffle in the toaster, being careful not to use too much syrup. While I was eating, Mom sat at the table with her hands wrapped around her coffee mug, staring past me at a spot on the wall. When I was done, I carried my dishes to the sink and went back to my room. I sat on the floor and began sorting through my bins of hand-me-down Lego. Most of it used to be Ricky's. The day he gave me all his Lego stands out in my mind as one of a few golden moments.

"Hey, Zoe," he'd said, stopping at my bedroom door. "You want my Lego? You like building stuff, don't you?" He set a large grey bin on my floor saying, "I have more. You can have all of it."

His generosity that day made me feel like floating. I ran over and hugged him and he patted my back awkwardly.

The morning that he slammed out of the house, as I raked my hand through one of my bins, the sound of the Lego pieces jostling together distracted me from the hollow silence in the rest of the house. I organized the pieces by size, creating neat piles in a circle around me.

While I sat on my green bedroom carpet, focusing on finding all the square two-by-twos, Mom called her friend, Linda. Through my open door, I overheard enough of their conversation to understand why she was so upset.

"It was his friend's dad's car. They were racing it down the Old Canal Road and a rabbit jumped out of the bushes. I guess the dog was right behind it." Pause. "No! Neither of them has their licence yet. I know. I know." A long, shaky inhalation. "Linda, he could have been charged! That poor man. He comes around the corner and there's his dog, lying on the road." Another pause. "Yes, it was dead."

My heart was hammering. Ricky had killed a dog? He'd driven a car down Old Canal Road? It was more of a dirt track than an actual road, but still. I'd ridden my bike down it many times and could easily enough picture a rabbit and a dog appearing out of nowhere. One of the things I didn't like about the road was that it was lined with overgrown shrubs that in the summer held swarms of mosquitoes. Whenever I was biking down it, I felt closed in, hidden from everything that was safe.

As Mom continued talking to Linda, I climbed onto my bed and buried my face in my pillow. What was happening to my brother? I pictured the owner of the dog sinking to his knees on the dirt road while Ricky and whatever friend he'd been with — although I suspected it must have been Darius — stood by helplessly. I couldn't stop the sobs that shuddered from my small body, and

I ended up biting my pillow just to muffle the sound of my anguish.

Later, I tiptoed around the house, putting away my toys, trying to avoid doing or saying anything that might upset Mom. I became invisible, drifting in and out of rooms on noiseless feet. I put on my pyjamas without being asked and brushed my teeth. When I went to Mom in her reading chair beside the living room window in order to say goodnight, she held me for a long time, not saying anything. Her breath smelled like lemons, from her after-dinner tea, and as I hugged her, that lemon-scent seemed to me to be infused with a desperate sort of sadness.

MOM MAINTAINS THAT DURING THOSE years Ricky was simply going through a difficult period when he didn't know how to handle the emotions of losing his father. She still makes excuses for him, but then, I guess I do too.

Just more reluctantly.

CHAPTER
FOUR
·

JASON DOESN'T HANG AROUND LONG after we get back from The Crow's Nest. When he leaves, the remaining evening hours loom before me. I briefly consider calling Mom and telling her about Dee Dee — it would serve Ricky right and she'd be hard-pressed to make excuses for him this time. However, if I really wanted to destroy her image of her precious first-born, there are other, much worse, suspicions I could divulge. It's better to keep quiet. Better for all of us.

I waver between watching Netflix and heading downstairs to my darkroom. Amir built the darkroom for me, turning one corner of my unfinished basement into a sanctuary where hours can slip by unnoticed. When I'm in the darkroom, bathed in a soft red glow, breathing in the scent of developer, watching my photos slowly take shape, I am at my most relaxed. Whatever stresses exist outside of that room seem to dissipate the minute I step inside.

Recently, I've been working on a collection of ten-by-ten black-and-white prints for Parker. It's his birthday next month and I've tried to capture all the places around Dunford he loves: the park, the baseball diamond, Ice Cream Island. My goal was to take each shot from a unique perspective so while the place itself is identifiable, the viewpoint is unexpected. One of my favourite photos is the baseball diamond. I shot it through the chain-link fence, using a wide-frame angle, and it just has this endless feel to it. The bases look so stretched out, like the diamond has warped and expanded, but in a good way. It makes me think of long, lazy afternoons.

Before I make up my mind about whether to head downstairs or just sprawl on the couch to watch an episode of *Suits*, my phone rings. It's Mom, wanting to know if I remembered to call Ricky.

"I talked to him earlier, before Jason and I went out for dinner."

"I wish he would visit more often. I feel like I hardly ever get to see Leah. Do you think he and Brenda will have any kids?"

I hate it when my mom does this. She's always trying to gossip with me, like I'm one of her girlfriends, as if I have opinions about my brother and his sex life. "I have no idea," I say to her, but what I'm thinking is: Maybe he'll accidentally knock up Dee Dee and give you another grandchild that way. Would that make you happy? "Isn't Brenda kind of old to have kids?" I venture.

"Old! She's not even forty-five, is she? I know plenty of women in their forties who have had children. But she's not getting any younger, that's for sure."

"Well, I guess you should ask them then. Because it's not something Ricky and I really talk about."

I know exactly where this line of questioning is headed. What about me and Jason? Am I going to settle down and start a family before it's too late and my eggs shrivel up or do I plan on stringing Jason along indefinitely? "You're not getting any younger either, Zoe." Yeah, yeah. I could mention that I have a sneaking suspicion Jason's getting ready to propose. Although, even then,

Mom would likely have flashbacks to the whole Amir thing and wouldn't really rest until after Jason and I had been proclaimed man and wife under the watchful eye of a hundred guests.

"How's Parker doing?" Mom asks.

"I don't know. This wasn't Jason's weekend. Ask me next Sunday."

"He's a nice kid. I wouldn't mind having him for a grandson, you know."

"Yeah, I know. I gotta go, Mom. I'll talk to you soon, okay?" I don't like cutting my mom off like this, but sometimes I just can't get into it with her. After hanging up, I head downstairs and sequester myself in the tiny darkroom. It's too late to work on any prints, but sometimes I just like puttering in the space. There's no light source other than the safelight, so even when I'm not developing, the room is layered in shadows and dimly lit a muted red.

A series of grey-toned prints are strung across the drying line and I pull them down one by one. They're all the same image: the pilings from the old bridge that used to span the Still River before the township built a new one with a pedestrian path. I shot the crumbling structures on a misty morning when they rose from the water like concrete ghosts. In some of the photos, a network of skeletal branches loom in the foreground. The effect is haunting. I've taken lots of shots over the years that I'm proud of, but these images are probably some of my best work.

I slip the prints into an envelope — I'll decide later what to do with them, which ones to keep working on or to frame — then absentmindedly rearrange the bottles of chemicals on the wooden shelf above my long work counter. By the time I've wiped down the enlarger, including all the lenses, and dusted the storage shelves with a damp cloth, it's late. I have to be up early for work, but as I'm lying in bed, thinking about the prints I still need to develop for Parker and how much it will cost to have them custom-framed in time for his birthday, I realize with a small jolt that he'll be eight this year. In Dunford, turning eight is a big deal. It means you're finally old enough to compete in your first official Dunford Classic, the town's annual go-kart race. Jason isn't originally from around here, so he might not understand the significance of the Classic, but I do.

EVERY YEAR, ON THE THIRD Saturday in May, the entire town shows up to cheer on the racers. Swarms of people line the perimeter of the course, a short section of downhill road starting at Pineview Lodge, Dunford's one and only retirement home, and ending in front of the Pentecostal Church, where the parking lot is converted into a bazaar with vendors, hotdog stands, balloons, and carnival games.

My own eighth birthday fell two months after the Classic, so I had to wait almost a full year for my first race. One of my presents that summer was a board game called Sorry! and Mom told Ricky he had to play it with me. We set it up on the coffee table in the living room and I knelt on the floor across from Ricky, who was sitting on the couch. The first time I bumped one of his pawns back to the start, he glared at me, but in a teasing way. He was still wearing the party hat Mom had set beside our plates of cake.

"Oh, is that how it's going to be?" he said after I'd issued my gleeful "Sorry!" and moved his pawn.

Partway through the game, he tossed his party hat onto the couch. On his next move, he landed on a slide and knocked off one of my pawns. "Not sorry," he said, looking me right in the eye.

I tugged at the elastic chin strap on my party hat. It was digging into my skin. The pawn he'd just bumped was four spaces away from my Safety Zone. It would have been my first pawn home.

I was more careful after that. I made a point of being nice, of sparing his pawns if I had the choice. Ricky showed no mercy, and in the end, he won. "Sorry I beat you on your birthday," he told me. Then he raised his hands as if to say he was helpless to stop himself.

He didn't stay to help me put the game away; instead, he strutted from the room with a satisfied smirk on his face. I gathered up the cards and the little plastic pawns, silently cursing my cruel brother.

As the months rolled by, and my inaugural Dunford Classic loomed on the horizon, I became increasingly excited. I couldn't stop daydreaming about crossing the finish line to the cheers of my family. Ricky was uncharacteristically enthusiastic about my first race as well and he promised to help me with my kart. Over our March Break we dug through the shed in the backyard, pulling out anything we thought might be useful. Ricky found a set of wheels from one of his old karts, but he said they were too small to be any good so we ended up dismantling the red Radio Flyer wagon and using those wheels.

We dragged everything we had collected to the basement, where our dad's tools were still neatly stored at his workbench, and Ricky brought down his ghetto blaster. We spent whole days down there, listening to Def Leppard while tinkering with the design of my go-kart, which Ricky had dubbed the "Zo-kart." Those hours in the dusty basement with my brother were magical. Even now, whenever I hear the song "Bringin' On the Heartbreak," I feel like that little girl again, brimming with enthusiasm and hope.

Darius would stop by occasionally while we were working and Ricky would toss out a series of instructions for me before the two of them took off. Darius had just got his licence, so they'd clamber into his dad's light blue Thunderbird and head to Boelen or Leeville or Port Sitsworth. Anywhere that wasn't Dunford.

I didn't have a name then for the bad feeling that crept up on me whenever I saw Darius and Ricky together, but looking back, I think it was simple distrust. Watching Ricky climb into that car reminded me of the time the two of them had taken it without permission and run over the dog on Old Canal Road. (It had been Darius that day, just like I'd thought.) For some reason, Darius always squealed the tires as they rounded the corner at the end of our street and the sound of the rubber screeching made me cringe. I didn't know what they were trying to prove, if anything, but when they were together, I could feel my stomach tighten.

By the end of March Break, my go-kart was almost done. The steering was a little wobbly, but Ricky said he could fix it and I believed him. I imagined us continuing to work side-by-side in the basement until the kart was completely finished, at which point we would emerge triumphantly to present the Zo-kart to Mom. Together.

That didn't happen. Ricky's interest in the project evaporated as soon as we were back at school. He went out almost every night, leaving me to work on my Zo-kart alone. I didn't do much. I sat in the basement, toying with it, not making any real changes, listening to Ricky's Def Leppard cassette.

Then, only two days before the Dunford Classic, Ricky announced it was time to test the kart.

"Dad showed me the best place to practise," he said. "The path that runs down to the ravine from the overpass has the perfect slope. Come on, let's go."

I pushed my kart to the end of our street where it abutted the ravine, then followed Ricky along the narrow path that led to the overpass.

"Steering is the most important thing," Ricky warned me. "If you can't steer, you'll wind up driving off the course. Trust me, half the kids won't be able to steer. It doesn't matter how fast your kart goes. What matters is that you can keep it in a straight line and make it to the finish line."

As stupid as it seems to me now, that day I wanted so badly to make Ricky proud. My legs shook as I climbed into the kart. I was worried about the wobbly steering since Ricky never did get around to helping me fix it, and when he gave my kart a gentle shove, I gripped the steering wheel so tightly my knuckles hurt. I concentrated on keeping the kart in a straight line, knowing that the second my wheels hit the grass on either side of the path, I would roll to a stop.

I could hear Ricky yelling behind me, "Keep it straight. Keep it straight!"

As the ground levelled out at the bottom of the ravine, I slowed to a natural stop and turned to find Ricky grinning at me. He ran up to me and slapped my hand in a high-five. I forgave him in that moment for everything — all the fights with Mom, all the times he ignored me, even killing the dog — all of it.

It felt so good to bask in his approval.

A GROUP OF KIDS WERE skipping rope when we got back to our street. "I love coffee, I love tea," they chanted as the long rope turned and turned. "I love the boys, and the boys love me." One of our neighbours, a little girl named Amy, was jumping alongside a redhead from a few blocks over. Their matching pigtails bounced up and down. A young boy stood on the sidewalk waving a bubble wand back and forth in front of his face, sending cascades of glistening bubbles into the air.

"I can take the kart home if you want to play," Ricky said.

I shook my head. "They're all little kids." I reached out my index finger and popped a bubble as it drifted past.

Ricky laughed. "If you say so. You're like, what, two years older than them?"

I shrugged, and as we continued down the street, the words of their silly song echoed behind us. "Yes, no, maybe so." Their child-ish voices, along with all those shimmering bubbles, drifted up and away.

THE MORNING OF MY FIRST Dunford Classic dawned clear and bright, with just a hint of a breeze rippling through the warm air. High Street was cordoned off by police cars with flashing lights and the sidewalks along the route were lined with animated crowds. I stood on trembling legs at the starting line with the other racers in front of Pineview Lodge. I had no idea where Ricky and Mom were along the route or if they were even together. An organizer wearing a bright orange vest was arranging the racers into four groups. "You," she said, tapping me on the arm, "over here. You're in the second group. Stand back and don't move into position until I say."

The first group lined up and when the starter gun went off, the racers gave their karts a quick shove before jumping in and rolling down High Street. Only two of the six kids made it to the finish line. Three of them drove off the course, and one kid's wheel fell off in the first fifteen seconds. The corner of his kart scraped the pavement with a sickening screech before the whole thing ground to a lopsided halt.

The woman in the orange vest motioned my group forward. I moved to the starting line. All I could think about, standing beside my kart with my heart pounding, was steering straight. Then, all of a sudden, the starter gun rang out and I was push-ing my kart forward and clambering over the side, grasping my wobbly steering wheel with every muscle in my scrawny arms.

My front wheels were zigzagging like crazy as the steering wheel jerked from left to right in my hands. There were two people ahead of me, but I wasn't worried about them. I just wanted to keep the Zo-kart on the course right to the end.

When I lurched across the finish line, I looked around excitedly for Ricky, but before I had even finished scanning the faces of the crowd, I was being told to clear the way for the next group.

"Move along, move along! Get your karts out of the way!"

I stumbled to the side.

"Good job, Zoe!" a voice called out. I looked up to see Mom pushing her way toward me. "You made it!"

I nodded, still scanning the crowd for my brother. The third group of racers were on their way down the hill, with one kart way in front of the others. Someone let out a piercing whistle followed by an enthusiastic holler, "Go Steven!" I stood to the side with my mom, watching as Steven crossed the finish line in his bright blue kart. It had a giant yellow 'S' painted on the side and I suddenly wished that I'd done a bit more to spruce up my kart. I could have written *Zo-kart* on the side, although part of me didn't want anyone else to know about that nickname. It belonged to me and Ricky and to our afternoons in the basement with Def Leppard blasting from the stereo.

After the fourth group of racers came teetering down the street, the winner of each group prepared for the final race-off in our age category. I still hadn't found Ricky. Not surprisingly, Steven, the boy with the bright blue kart, won the final race and I watched with envy as his whole family surrounded him at the finish line.

I tugged on Mom's arm. "We should put this in the car," I said, motioning to my rickety, unpainted kart.

"Don't you want to see the older kids race?"

I didn't, but I couldn't come up with a good reason not to stay and watch. For the past three years, I'd begged Mom to take me to the races where I'd eagerly watched every group of karts roll down the hill and across the finish line. The older kids were more aggressive; they sometimes tried to force each other off the course, which usually resulted in them veering out of bounds themselves. But today, I didn't want to watch them; I just wanted to find Ricky.

"Yeah, I guess," I said to my mom, because it seemed simpler than putting my disappointment into words.

She gave me a sympathetic smile. "Are you sad that you didn't win?"

I shrugged. "At least I made it to the finish line."

The bazaar in the Pentecostal Church parking lot was crawling with people. I stared into the crowd until I finally spotted Ricky standing beside a girl who was holding a bag of pink and blue cotton candy.

"Can you watch my kart?" I said to Mom, before dashing past tables of knitted hats and home-made jam toward my big brother.

The girl pulled out a chunk of pink cotton candy and offered it to Ricky, who leaned over and ate it out of her hand. She laughed as he wrapped his mouth around her fingers. I stood absolutely still, but Ricky had seen me.

"Zoe!" he called. The girl glanced in my direction, then wiped her hand on her jeans.

"Did you see my race?" I asked. "I kept it straight the whole time. I made it all the way!"

"Awesome," Ricky said. He lifted his palm in a high-five and I reached up to smack it.

Only later did it occur to me that Ricky hadn't answered my

question and that quite possibly he hadn't bothered to watch my race at all. I couldn't compete with a girl who was willing to let him suck cotton candy off her fingers in the middle of a crowded church parking lot.

I was upset with Ricky that day, but my disappointment was nothing compared to what would follow in just a few short months — when everything good I believed about my brother came crashing down around me.

CHAPTER
FIVE

·

ON MONDAY MORNING, I NOTICE right away that the temperature has dropped. No double digits for us today. Instead, a thin sheen of frost coats my windshield, and even with my car's heat on high, the coldness seeps into my skin as I drive to the Water Treatment Plant. Once I'm there, I can't get warm. The inside of the plant is always chilly, but I'm actually shivering as I complete a jar test in the make-shift lab. Later, when I wash my hands under a stream of almost-scalding water, I don't want to turn off the tap because the hot water feels so good against my skin. I'm already wearing a fleece pullover, but I grab a goose-down vest from my locker as well, hoping the extra layer will warm me up.

I sit down next to Roger Hoekstra in what passes for our lunch-room, which is really just a cramped rectangular room with two fridges, a microwave balanced on milk crates, and a coffee maker that someone brought in from home. A series of narrow windows line one wall, looking out onto the parking lot. Roger grunts at me and resumes eating his sandwich. He has the same lunch every day: a ham sandwich on white bread, a piece of fruit (either an apple or a banana), two yogurts, and a thermos of soup. I don't know if Roger is such a creature of habit that he wants the same thing every day, or if his wife makes his lunch for him and he has no say in the matter. I've met Beatrice, and she is most definitely a creature of habit. So much so that I get the sense she wouldn't let Roger muddle around in the kitchen, getting crumbs on the counter, so even if he wanted to make his own lunch, he's probably not allowed.

I rub my hands together. "It's cold today."

"Supposed to go down to minus thirteen by this afternoon," Roger informs me. "We're not done with winter yet. At least it'll stave off some of the run-off we've had the past few days. Damn turbidity levels are all over the place."

I nod sympathetically. I'm glad I wasn't working on the weekend. The above-average temperatures and the subsequent snow melt would have stirred up all kinds of sediment in the river. I bet the water coming in through the intake pumps was murky as hell. I know from experience it was no picnic for the operators who would have had to adjust the alum dosages constantly.

I watch as Roger slowly pours some soup into the lid of his thermos; the steam curls into the air and I wish I'd thought to pack something hot today. My tuna sandwich is too dry — not enough mayonnaise — so I end up washing it down with swigs of lukewarm coffee.

When I first started working at the Water Treatment Plant, fresh out of high school, Roger was the one who trained me. He's quite a bit older than I am — he must be in his mid-sixties by now — and yet there's something in his quiet personality that I was drawn to from the start. He was a patient teacher, never seeming to mind when he had to explain things to me more than once or had to show me how to do something that he'd already demonstrated multiple times before. He also didn't care that I was a girl, and I can't say the same was true for the other men at the plant. When I first started, it was very much a boys' club; it still is, to some extent, but at least now I'm not the only female. There are three of us, which isn't exactly a sweeping majority, but it beats being the lone set of boobs in a building full of beer bellies.

Roger's even more pissed off than I am about the plant being privatized, mostly because he's so close to retirement. Even though the upcoming interviews with CCS are weighing on my mind, I decide not to mention them. Instead, Roger and I eat in companionable silence while I steal jealous glances at his steaming spoonfuls of soup.

Eventually, my mind drifts back to last night. Was I imagining Jason's nervousness? As much as I said I wasn't ready for us to move in together, if I lose my job, his arguments about saving money by combining our households will make even more sense. And when it comes right down to it, I don't believe for a second that Crystal Clear Solutions is truly planning on retaining all of us. They can't be. Why else would they bother with this whole interview farce? And if I did suddenly become unemployed, would Jason think twice about proposing or would it spur him on? Maybe he'd jump at the chance to play the rescuing hero; he's done it before. It's how we met.

"How're those pictures you're making for Parker coming along?" Roger asks. He's finished his soup and is screwing the lid back on his thermos.

"They're coming," I say. I almost tell him that I thought Jason was going to propose last night. It seems like something I would have told him, before; but for some reason, I don't mention it. Roger is more like a father-figure to me than anyone else and he's listened to his fair share of my drama-infused tribulations over the years, but I'm not ready to admit my foolish suspicions out loud. Partly because then I'd also have to admit how I ruined the moment, if there was, in fact, about to be a moment.

I used to spend more time than I do now with Roger and his wife. I still have dinner at their house every now and again, although I would be lying if I didn't admit it was more fun when Amir was around. I'd be willing to bet that even Roger misses Amir. He didn't ask any questions when things went south; all he said when I told him was, "I guess it's none of my business." That's basically our motto with each other. For example: Roger and Beatrice never had any kids and while I have my own theories about why, I've never once broached the subject with Roger, because really, it is none of my business. Amir, though, he couldn't seem to wrap his head around their childless state.

"Do you think Roger is disappointed that he never had any kids?" Amir asked me once, after we'd spent an afternoon decorating Easter eggs with Roger and Beatrice. I was standing at the sink, rinsing a handful of radishes for a salad.

"No," I said, turning off the tap and setting the radishes on a paper towel. "Why would he be disappointed? My guess is he didn't want kids."

Amir poured himself a beer and sat down at the table. "I bet Beatrice did. That would explain why she's so uptight about everything in her house. It's the one thing over which she has complete control."

I slid a cutting board in front of him, along with the radishes. "Don't slice them too thin," I warned him. Amir probably assumed that, like him, everyone else wanted kids, and that if a couple like Roger and Beatrice didn't have any, it must be because they couldn't, not because they simply chose not to.

I didn't know the real reasons behind Roger and Beatrice being childless, but I, for one, completely understood the instinct not to have children. I just never shared that small fact with Amir. Not that it matters now.

In the two years that I've been dating Jason, we've only been to Roger and Beatrice's house a handful of times. Generally speaking, we don't do a whole lot of socializing as a couple — not like how it was with Amir. There was an occasion, however, when Jason and I invited Roger and Beatrice to play cards at my house, and while they were over, Mom stopped by. At first, I thought the reason she was acting all weird was because I hadn't invited her to our little card party. Later, I realized she was just surprised that Jason and I were interacting with other people. She said as much when I tried to apologize.

"Oh, don't worry about me," she replied. "I still have plenty of friends."

WITH JASON, THINGS ARE JUST different than they were with Amir. I don't usually compare the two; in fact, I try to make it a point not to, but now that I've got it stuck in my head that Jason is ready to propose, I can't help but think about the last time I agreed to marry somebody. Amir was one-of-a-kind: sweet, thoughtful, gentle, and surprisingly funny. He wasn't too hard to look at either. Besides being physically attractive, he had an almost hypnotic charm that drew people to him. Jason is sweet too, but he's more withdrawn. Possibly because his ex-wife shit all over the life they'd built and brutally abused his trust. I wonder if Amir became more withdrawn after I broke off our engagement. If losing me took some of the air out of his sails. There are times I'd like to know how he's doing, but then I remember that I have no one to ask, not to mention, no right to ask.

I have convinced myself that Jason and I are better suited to each other than Amir and I ever were. Amir deserves someone uncomplicated and wholly emotionally available, not a closed-off iceberg like me. Jason, on the other hand, doesn't seem to mind my occasional coldness. At least I don't think he does, and anyways, he can be just as distant. We give each other space; that's why we work. Although, if that's really true, then why was I so freaked out at the thought of him proposing? I concentrate on swallowing the last bites of my dry tuna sandwich, noticing as I chew, that my jaw has started to ache. I try to imagine Jason and I exchanging vows, but it's hard to concentrate because it's not just my jaw that hurts, it's my whole damn head.

Next week, I decide, after my interview is done and over with and if I still have a job, I will seriously entertain the thought of talking to Jason about moving in together. We've already agreed my house is the better option since I have a yard and a garage, not to mention my darkroom. Hell, even if I don't have a job, I'm going to tell him I'm ready, because if I can't wrap my head around us living together, I'll never be able to contemplate marriage. And I don't want to scare him off. I don't want him to give up on me. I do believe, in my heart of hearts, that I am his second chance. He is certainly mine.

AFTER WORK, I STAND IN the shower for a long time, trying to get warm. I can't shake the feeling that I set something irreparable into motion when I blurted out at the restaurant that I wasn't ready for Jason to move in. How did I expect him to react? And how will he react when out of the blue I appear to have suddenly changed my mind? Which also begs the question: have I really changed my mind?

My weird little outburst at the restaurant is Ricky's fault, I think irrationally. If he hadn't just divulged the fact that he was once again about to royally fuck up his marriage, I wouldn't have been so defensive, so freaked out by the idea of Jason proposing. I bet this Dee Dee chick has big boobs. I remember one Christmas when Ricky said, right in front of Brenda, that he'd be willing to pay for her to get a boob job if she ever wanted one.

"I mean, that's an investment I'd be happy to make," he said, grinning around the table at the rest of us.

She'd slapped him playfully on the arm, but I'd been embarrassed for her. And pissed off. Thinking about his comment now, I'm reminded of the time I was rooting through Ricky's closet looking for his old baseball cleats when I came across a rolled-up magazine stuffed inside a sock. I pulled it out and was shocked to discover page after page of naked women, brazenly showing off what seemed to me to be impossibly huge breasts. Although I was still a kid, Ricky was seventeen, and I couldn't fathom why he would want to have something like that. Still, I knew enough to understand that it was a secret. Mom wouldn't like it one bit if she found out.

I stuffed the magazine back in the sock and left his room empty-handed. I asked him later about the cleats, but I didn't admit that I'd gone through his closet. By then, I was smart enough to keep a few secrets of my own.

I started sneaking into his room after that, looking for things he might be trying to hide. I stumbled upon all kinds of stuff that made my stomach twist: a pack of cigarettes tucked away in the bottom drawer of his nightstand; a pair of lacy pink underwear in a shoe box under his bed; and strangely, a pair of earrings that I recognized as Mom's, pinned to a small square of velvet that he had hidden under the corner of his mattress. I was digging through the stuff in his closet again when I found a lumpy plastic bag tucked away in the back corner, buried under a Toronto Maple Leafs jersey. My heart was pounding as I lifted the bag onto my lap. The handles had been tied in a loose knot and it took me a few minutes to tease them apart.

At first, I wasn't sure what I was looking at. Then, slowly, I realized that the plastic limbs at the bottom of the bag were naked Barbies. When I pulled one of the dolls out to examine it, I saw that someone, Ricky most likely, had used a black marker to draw between the Barbie's legs. I fished out another one. Same thing. And this one's head had been pulled off. Something hot and angry burned in my chest. These were my dolls. How dare he draw on them! Did he think I wouldn't recognize them because they weren't wearing any clothes? I'd noticed three of them were missing weeks ago, but since I had pretty much stopped playing with my Barbies, I hadn't bothered looking for them.

Footsteps sounded in the hall. I crammed the plastic bag of Barbies under the jersey. My heart thudded with fear as I tried to come up with a good reason for being in Ricky's room. The footsteps continued past his bedroom door. I breathed out in relief.

Back in the safety of my own room, I rearranged the cushions on my bed and counted my breaths until I felt calm. I didn't know how to describe the way I felt about seeing the scribbled black lines on my Barbies, but for days, I couldn't stop thinking about those naked dolls.

I didn't hear him come home the day he walked in and caught me digging through his sock drawer. Before he could say anything, I held up some sort of glass tube with a spout sticking out the side. "What's this?" I asked, trying my best to sound innocently curious.

"Gimme that," Ricky said. He grabbed the tube, which I now know was a bong, and shoved it back in the drawer. "What the hell are you doing in here?"

"Nothing. I just wanted to see —"

"Stay out of my room."

It took me weeks to summon up the nerve to sneak in there again. He must have known I'd come back though, because I don't remember finding anything good after that.

And I looked. I especially looked for that bag of Barbies. I wanted to wash off the black marker between their legs; I wanted to make them clean again. I thought I could fix what Ricky had done.

The police probably would have been interested in those Barbies, but, by the time I made the connection, it was too late.

CHAPTER
SIX

.

MY EXTRA-LONG SHOWER DOES at least temporarily take the chill out of my bones. As I'm towelling off, I glance at my phone and notice that I have a missed call from Jason. I'm anxious to talk to him because I don't want the weirdness from last night to linger, but first I need something to eat; I'm feeling light-headed.

I decide on an omelette. I don't have the energy to make anything more ambitious. I'm dicing a green pepper, half-listening to the news on the TV in the living room, when I hear a name that stops me cold. Still gripping my paring knife, I stand on the threshold to the living room, staring in stunned silence at the image of six-year-old Amy Nessor on the screen.

It's the same school photo they used when she went missing twenty-nine years ago, with her uneven blonde pigtails and her impish smile showing off the gap where her front tooth used to be. I remember this picture all too well — the slight tilt to her head, the plaid dress and lace collar — although I haven't seen it since I was a kid. My heart races as the news anchor explains in his ultra-calm voice that Amy Nessor's case is being re-opened. New evidence has emerged. There aren't many more details than that and the anchor quickly, too quickly, moves on to the next story. Amy's sweet, unsuspecting face is replaced by a protest taking place somewhere else in the world. People are shouting and punching the air, but I don't register any of it. The knife slips from my hand and as the handle strikes my foot, I'm jolted out of my stupor. I bend down to pick up the knife. Does Ricky know? What is he doing right now? He must be freaking out. I think of my mom and feel bile rise in my throat. This is going to kill her. This is absolutely going to kill her. With a rasping grunt that tears through my ribcage I jam the thin blade of my paring knife into the kitchen doorframe. It wobbles there for an instant, like an accusation, before I pull it out and return to the kitchen where I drop the knife into the sink before collapsing onto a chair. My body has turned to Jell-O, but as much as I can't seem to stop shaking, a tiny part of me is relieved.

LINDELL DRIVE, THE STREET WHERE I grew up and where my mom still lives, is a quiet street that butts up against the north end of the ravine. There weren't many kids sharing that short stretch of road during my childhood — just me and Ricky, the Nessor girls, and the Kinzie's baby. Later, there were twin boys, but I never knew their names. Most of the kids in our neighbourhood lived behind Lindell Drive, in the subdivision closer to the school, where the streets loop in cul de sacs, and where I used to play cops and robbers, although I stopped playing after Derek Weberson's accident.

The two of us were pedaling furiously down the same street, hearts pumping, when Derek veered toward the side of the road and crashed into the back of a parked pick-up truck. I watched him hit it and for a split second, there was no sound other than the echoing clash of metal on metal. Then Derek started to howl. In between wails, he took great shuddering breaths that terrified me more than the sound of his crying. I skidded to a stop and ran over to where he was lying sprawled on the asphalt, but I didn't know what to do.

"Are you okay?" I asked.

He didn't answer; he just kept screaming.

I tried to lift his bike off him, but he screamed even louder as soon as I touched it, so I backed up and stared at him, waiting for someone else to come and help. It didn't take long. Mrs. Thompson, who lived on the corner, came scurrying toward us with a tea towel thrown over her shoulder. She scooped up Derek's bike so quickly he didn't have time to protest. Then she sent Mike and Tommy, who had just come tearing around the corner on their own bikes, to get Derek's mom.

"What happened?" she said, turning to me.

"He ran into the back of the truck. He turned around to look behind us, then —"

"You're okay, you're okay," she said to Derek, who was still sprawled on the road. He hadn't even tried to sit up.

As more kids began to crowd around, Mrs. Thompson ordered everyone away. "Get on home," she said. "He doesn't need you gawking. Go on now!"

Derek's mom came racing down the sidewalk in her socks. "Is he okay? Oh god, please tell me he's okay." Mrs. Weberson knelt beside her son and smoothed his hair away from his forehead. At her touch, Derek began howling again and the sound swirled inside my head, making me dizzy.

I sank down onto the curb.

"The boys said he'd been hit by a truck," Mrs. Weberson said. She swung her head toward me, eyes frantic.

"No, no," Mrs. Thompson interceded. "He hit the truck. Right, Zoe?"

I nodded. I could feel hot tears dribbling noiselessly down my cheeks.

Mrs. Thompson helped Mrs. Weberson lift Derek into a sitting position and I watched as they hoisted him to his feet. His arms, which I later learned were both broken, dangled at his sides and he made the most pitiful sound as he stood. Mrs. Thompson steered Derek's bike to her lawn and laid it gently on the grass.

"You can come back for this later," she told him. "Or one of the other boys can bring it to you."

No one asked anything more of me. I waited until after Derek and his mother had gone before rising from the curb and walking my own bike home with the sound of Derek's pain-filled shrieks reverberating in my ears.

My bike was getting too small for me anyway so it was easy to pretend that was the real reason I stopped playing cops and robbers. Instead, when I was outside, I spent most of my time hanging out on Lindell Drive, collecting rocks or bouncing a ball against the side of our house or just watching the neighbours from the safety of our porch.

The Nessors lived three doors down from us. They had two girls, Amy and Sabrina, who were both younger than I was and, as a result, not very interesting. I often saw Amy playing on her front lawn, or riding her tricycle down the sidewalk, while her mom sat on their front step bouncing Sabrina on her lap. If Amy hadn't been so little, I might have made more of an effort to get to know her, to play with her, even. I might have paid more attention. And if I had? Would that have changed anything?

By the time Amy started grade one, I was in grade four. We both followed the same short route to school and back, but we never walked together. I might have been too shy, or maybe she was; whatever the case, I usually ended up trailing a few paces behind her as she sashayed down the street, her blonde pigtails swinging.

ON THE TUESDAY BEFORE THE Thanksgiving weekend, when I was walking home from school, Amy was about half a block ahead of me. Certain details about that afternoon are etched permanently into my brain; I remember that it was gloriously warm outside. As I meandered down the sidewalk, the sun shone hard and bright, turning the trees that lined the street into a brilliant canopy of fiery colour: orange and red and glowing yellow. I was clutching a paper turkey that I'd made at school using a tracing of my left hand with my thumb as the turkey's head and my four fingers as feathers. On each of the fingers we had written something we were thankful for. I was excited to see Mom's reaction when she saw her name on one of those fingers, carefully spelled out in my best printing.

Amy Nessor strolled ahead of me, braids swishing. I lost sight of her momentarily when she turned onto Lindell Drive, but as I came around the corner, I saw her again, walking up to a light blue car that was parked between our houses. As soon as I saw the car, my throat constricted with a spasm of disappointment because it meant that Darius was over and he and Ricky were probably going somewhere. I wanted to show Ricky my turkey, too, because I'd put his name on my pinky finger and I thought it would make him happy. But then Amy pulled open the back door of the car and climbed in and I was flushed with the momentary relief that it wasn't Darius after all and that Ricky would get to see my turkey.

Except when I walked into the house, Ricky wasn't home. It was just my mom, setting out a snack for me. I handed her my special turkey and waited. She glanced at it without saying anything, then stuck it to the door of the fridge under a real estate magnet that covered more than half of the turkey's body. She asked about my day, absentmindedly, while peeling potatoes at the sink. I don't know if she even looked at what I'd written on those turkey feathers.

I decided I would point them out to her later, when Ricky was back. Then Mom would smile and tell me how sweet I was and I would fall asleep that night with her words brushing against my skin like a soft blanket.

After I'd had my cup of milk and a cookie, Mom sent me outside to play. The air was warm and still. I sat on our front step with my baseball glove in my lap hoping that when Ricky got back he'd agree to play catch. It wasn't often anymore that he spent time with me, but the afternoon was so nice, the weather so dazzlingly perfect, I thought there was a chance it just might happen.

It sickens me now to think about how much I prized those snatches of time spent with my brother, about how much his attention mattered. Especially how, even if it was just briefly, I considered him something to be thankful for.

Lindell Drive was particularly quiet that day as I sat outside waiting for my brother. Even old Mr. Lowell, who I usually saw out walking after school, whacking anything that was in his way with his cane, was nowhere in sight. He once sent my Hula Hoop sailing right into the middle of the road. "What's this thing doing here?" he'd yelled. "Waiting to trip me up? Keep your blasted toys off the sidewalk!"

Because the afternoon was so perfect, I expected more people to be out. Mrs. Kinzie, perhaps, pushing her stroller. Someone sweeping their steps. Mr. Lowell, definitely, shuffling along with his cane. Yet, on that particular Tuesday, it seemed there was no one outside but me. When Mrs. Nessor came out of her house calling Amy's name, it rang out loud and clear down the empty street.

Her call was met with silence. Spying me on the front step, my ball glove balanced on my knees, Mrs. Nessor walked over.

"Have you seen Amy?" she asked.

"She went in a car."

"She went in a car? What car? What do you mean?" Mrs. Nessor's eyes squinted in confusion.

"I saw her — I saw her get in a car," I repeated.

"Today? You saw her get in a car today?"

I wanted desperately to stand up and go inside. Mrs. Nessor's questions were too sharp and quick. I could feel tears springing to my eyes. "When I came home," I whispered.

"What?" Her eyes widened in alarm. Many of the details that followed have blurred over time, but I remember her eyes. Her frightened eyes searching my face, silently begging me to unsay what I'd seen. Her hands began flailing at her sides as she looked wildly up and down the empty street, and I watched her fingers as they fluttered then fell. "Zoe, what are you talking about? When did she get in a car?"

The front door opened and suddenly my mom was standing on the porch behind me. "Is everything okay, Janet?" she asked. I stood up quickly and tried to sneak past her into the house, but she stopped me with a firm hand on my shoulder.

"No." Mrs. Nessor's voice came out high-pitched and shaky. "I can't find Amy. And Zoe says ... Zoe said she saw her get into a car."

Mrs. Nessor had moved her hands to her face now, where they rested on her cheeks as she stared at my mother helplessly. Fear wafted from her eyes and mouth, furling around my feet, rooting me in place.

"Okay, okay," Mom said, and her voice sounded so calm, so confident. "Don't worry. We'll find her." Then, turning to me, she asked, "What did you see?"

LATER, AFTER THE POLICE HAD asked me over and over again to describe the car, to explain how exactly Amy had climbed into it — Could I remember anything about the driver? — and long after Mrs. Nessor had been escorted back to her house, I heard Ricky come home. I had told the police everything I remembered, except for one tiny detail. Not once did I mention, that for the briefest of moments, I'd been convinced that the car I saw belonged to my brother's best friend.

CHAPTER
SEVEN

·

I SIT ON THE WOODEN chair in my kitchen for a long time, trying to sort out my emotions about Amy Nessor's case being re-opened. What new information could possibly have come to light all these years later? When my phone rings beside me, I ignore it. I don't even look to see who it is.

Eventually, I start moving again. I put away the eggs and the peppers and the cheese that I took out for my omelette. I hand-wash the paring knife and the cutting board, drying them slowly and methodically. The knife doesn't seem any worse for wear after being gouged into the doorframe, although the blade might be a little crooked. I place my unused plate back in the cupboard and wipe down the counters. I scrub the sink for no good reason. I return to the living room where I watch, with an odd churning sensation in my gut, for more news about Amy's case, but each time they come back to the story, the information is the same: the investigation is being re-opened due to the emergence of new information which the police have reason to believe is credible at this time. That's all they say. They give away nothing.

THE DAY THAT AMY WENT missing, that long, long ago Tuesday, Ricky came home late at night. Dusk had settled over the street hours earlier, while I stood at the living room window peering into the shadows. When Ricky got home, there were still two police cars parked in front of the Nessors' house and our sink was filled with dirty dishes. I remember the dishes because even more than the police cars outside, those unwashed cups and plates signalled something menacing to me. Amy's disappearance had crept right into our kitchen and laid its cold hands on my mom, preventing her from washing up like she did every night.

I wasn't really worried at first, not even when the police were in our living room asking me questions, but when Mom left the dishes in the sink, I felt, for the first time, a penetrating tremor of fear.

I was in my bedroom, though still wide awake, when Ricky finally wandered in through the front door. Mom hadn't told me to go to bed, but I couldn't stand watching her pace back and forth across the living room, so I'd quietly put on my pyjamas and retreated to my room on my own. I had never stayed up this late before. It was as if the world had tilted to one side and everything around me was tipping over.

"What's going on?" I heard Ricky say.

"Amy, the little girl down the street, is missing," Mom said, her voice cracking. "Zoe saw her getting into a car and now —"

"Zoe saw?"

I came out of my room then. I stood at the end of the hall and looked at my brother. His hair was sticking up in places, as if he'd been running his hands through it. "She was walking in front of me," I said. "She got in a car and now they can't find her." I turned to my mom. "She's not back yet?"

Mom shook her head. "No sweetie, but everyone is looking very hard for her. It was good that you saw something. It gives them a clue, a very important clue, to work with."

I turned back to my brother. "I had to tell the police what I saw. They came in the house and asked me questions."

My brother sat down heavily. "Holy shit," he said.

I HARDLY SLEPT THAT NIGHT, but when I walked into the kitchen for breakfast my brother looked even worse than I felt. His hand was twitching beside his bowl of cereal, and when he glanced in my direction, I could see that his eyes were blood-shot, narrowed to tiny slits. Mom was there, too, standing beside the counter with a mug in her hands. She was gazing out the window above the sink, staring into the backyard.

"Oh! There you are," she said, turning in my direction. She gestured toward the table. "Have some cereal."

I wanted to ask about Amy, to find out if she had come home while we were sleeping. Each time I woke in the night, which was often, I thought about her empty bed. I pictured her pyjamas and her stuffies and her pillow — all waiting for her to come back. "Did they find Amy?" I finally managed to whisper.

Mom poured milk over my cereal. "I haven't heard anything yet," she said. "But I'm going to walk you to school today, okay? And after school, I want you to wait for me. Don't leave until I get there."

I nodded, but my throat was too twisted to swallow the cornflakes in front of me. I stirred the spoon around and around, watching my cereal grow soggy. "I wouldn't get in anyone's car," I said.

"I know," Mom said. "But still."

Ricky didn't say anything. He sat like a zombie, swallowing mouthful after mouthful of cornflakes. "Were you with Darius last night?" I asked. I wanted to know and I didn't. I had tossed the question out casually, but in the split-second before he answered, I felt the tiny fissure of suspicion in my mind widen.

"Yeah," he said, milk dripping from his spoon back into the bowl. He shovelled in another mouthful. "We went to a movie."

I kept stirring my cereal. The mushy flakes sank to the bottom of the bowl. A few drops of milk dribbled over the side and onto the table. I traced a line through them with my finger, smearing the milk into a thin white arc.

We didn't have a movie theatre in Dunford, but there was one in Leeville, which was only twenty minutes away. I wanted to believe Ricky. I had to believe Ricky. He'd gone to the movies many times on a Tuesday because it was cheap night. And yet I couldn't stop seeing Amy climb into the back seat of that blue car. Who else had been in the car? I struggled to recall specific details. Were there two shadowy figures in the front seat? And then, like a thought dropping from the sky, I remembered seeing a hat. A baseball cap. The driver was wearing a hat. I hadn't told the police that. I hadn't thought of it until now.

"The driver was wearing a hat," I said suddenly.

"What?" Mom glanced over at me, setting her mug down forcefully on the counter.

"The car Amy went in. The driver was wearing a baseball hat. I think."

"You think? Zoe, this could be important! The police said if you remembered anything else —"

"I know," I said, cutting her off. "That's why I'm telling you. I'm pretty sure he was wearing a hat."

"He? It was a man?" Mom was looking at me so intently I started to squirm.

"I — I don't know. I think so, but I don't know! I just — I just think I remember a hat. That's all."

Ricky was staring at me now, too. "So, like, every time she remembers something you have to call the police?"

Mom pulled a card off the fridge, stuck there under a magnet just above my now-forgotten paper turkey. "They left a number. We have to contact Detective Somebody. The one who talked to Zoe last night." She peered at the slip of paper in her hand. "Detective Armstrong."

I didn't look at Ricky to see his reaction. But as soon as Mom picked up the phone, he stood up and walked out of the kitchen, leaving his half-empty bowl of cereal on the table.

MOM WASN'T THE ONLY ONE escorting a child to school that morning. Standing against the chain-link fence at the edge of the playground, a group of anxious-looking women huddled together.

Mom nudged me toward the schoolyard, where the principal was wandering between groups of students. It was strange to see him outside. The teachers, too, seemed more animated, striding across the tarmac, uncommonly alert. "The police will come by sometime this morning to talk to you," Mom said. "But you don't need to say anything to anyone else. Okay?"

I nodded. As I walked toward the brick wall where my class lined up, I looked back and noticed that Mom hadn't joined the other women by the fence. She stood by herself, watching me, and as soon as I reached the wall safely, she turned away to walk home.

I hadn't been in class for more than half an hour when I was called to the office. Detective Armstrong was waiting for me and my mother was standing nervously beside him. We were ushered into the vice-principal's tiny office where the detective took out a notepad before sitting down at a low, round table designed for kids. Mom set her purse awkwardly on her lap, and I could see that her hands were trembling.

"So," Detective Armstrong began, "your mom said you remembered some more details about yesterday. Can you tell me what you remember seeing?"

I swallowed. "I think maybe the driver was wearing a hat."

"What kind of hat?"

"A baseball cap."

He wrote something down. "Do you remember anything else about the driver? Height? Build?"

"Build?" I repeated.

"Do you remember if they seemed large to you, like a football player? Or were they smaller, like —"

"Like a teenager?"

Detective Armstrong set down his pen. "Did you see the driver, Zoe? Was it a teenager? Or someone who looked young to you?"

I shook my head. "I don't even know for sure if they had a hat. But I feel like they did. I don't know anymore. I really don't know." I put my head in my hands as tears stung my eyes.

Detective Armstrong's voice was soft. "You're doing good, Zoe," he said. "You've been very helpful, but we need to know every little thing you remember. No matter how small or unimportant it may seem."

"Why would someone take her?" I blurted out. "And why don't they just bring her back now?"

No one said anything for a minute. And in that silence, I felt Amy's disappearance suck something from my bones. I wasn't sure I would be able to stand. "I want to go home," I mumbled.

"Understandably, this is going to be very hard on your daughter," Detective Armstrong said to Mom. Then to me, "If you remember anything else, don't hesitate to call. Any detail that comes to you, no matter how small or silly you might think it is."

"Okay," I said quietly. And even though I really wanted Amy

to come home, I still didn't mention how I'd thought, just for a second, that the blue car belonged to Darius. Maybe I thought she would still be okay. Maybe saying it out loud would make it too real. But even though I didn't say it, the thought snagged against my heart like a piece of barbed wire. As Mom led me out of the school, away from the playground, and back toward the safety of my bedroom, the small bead of worry that had been rolling around in my gut ever since last night made me want to throw up.

From my room, I could hear Mom talking on the phone on and off throughout the afternoon. The sound of her murmuring voice gave me no comfort. Instead, those subdued and indistinguishable conversations made me worry even more.

WHEN RICKY GOT HOME FROM school that day, all he said was, "Any news?"

"Not yet," Mom replied, casting a quick glance in my direction. "I'm bringing Janet a shepherd's pie. She'll say if they've heard anything. I can't imagine what that poor woman is going through."

Mom left to deliver her shepherd's pie and I went to the bathroom for what felt like the tenth time that day. When I came out, I could hear Ricky's muffled voice talking to someone. I crept down the hall and stood just outside the kitchen, where I could see the phone cord stretching to the landing by the back door. Ricky himself was hidden from view, but I could hear what he was saying clearly enough.

"Listen Dare, we have to tell Jeremy to say he was in Leeville with us. I already told my mom we were at a movie. So that's our story. We were in Leeville the whole time."

There was a silence in which Darius must have been saying something. Then, "No, man, nothing. Nobody knows where she is. Everyone is freaking out."

I tried to tiptoe back to my room, but my feet felt like they were tethered to bricks. I was terrified of what Ricky would do if he caught me eavesdropping. My brother, my big brother, had turned into something I didn't recognize, something I didn't have a name for at the time, and at that moment I didn't want to be anywhere near him.

Back in my bedroom, I sat on the green carpet and began digging through one of my Lego bins. As I pulled out the pieces and placed them in piles around me, I felt myself calming down. Six-by-two rectangles to the left. Four-by-twos in front. Two-by-two squares to the right. I sat on the floor in the centre of all those organized piles and concentrated on the sheer sense of them.

Mom came back and I waited for her to tell us what happened. She said nothing. It was as if she hadn't been to the Nessors' at all. She moved between the table and the microwave, heating up leftover spaghetti. We ate in complete silence. I wanted to ask if Mrs. Nessor had told her anything, but the strangeness of the afternoon, coupled with the silence at the table, made me think twice about asking any questions. As soon as we were done eating, Ricky got up to clear the table. He filled the sink with soapy water and threw a tea towel at me. "You're drying," he said.

We stood at the sink together, without saying anything. Ricky rinsed each dish carefully before passing it to me to dry. Mom sat at the table, watching us. No one spoke.

I went to bed that night confused. Ricky was still Ricky. Whatever dark secrets I was conjuring up in my crazy head, I needed to stop. I didn't live with a monster. I lived with my mom and my brother. And I loved them both. I really did.

When I woke the next morning, it was after eight o'clock. Mom usually woke me up at seven thirty on school days. I wandered into the kitchen where Ricky was eating a piece of toast, his hair still rumpled from sleep. He was wearing baggy grey track pants and a wrinkled T-shirt. Mom was sitting across from him in her housecoat. Her eyes were swollen and pink around the edges.

"How come we slept in?" I asked.

"Oh sweetie," Mom said. "They found Amy last night."

"Where?" But I knew whatever was coming next, it wasn't good. No one looked happy, or relieved. And if everything was about to return to normal, I should have been on my way to school, with a bologna sandwich and a baggie of apple slices in my lunch. My brother would be gone already too, standing with the other high school students at the corner, where some of them would be having a quick cigarette while they waited for the bus.

"They found her in the ravine. She was — Zoe — she wasn't alive anymore." Mom dissolved into tears in front of me, which was almost more frightening than the news that Amy was dead.

I looked at my brother. "What happened?" I whispered.

"Somebody killed her," he said. "So, no school for us today. Not with a killer on the loose."

I didn't know what to do. How to act. I was hungry, but it seemed wrong to have breakfast when Amy was dead. I looked back at Mom, who was drying her eyes on the sleeve of her housecoat. "Have some toast, Zoe. You should eat."

Mom stood up, then immediately sank back into her chair. She lowered her head and closed her eyes. "Whew," she said. "I got dizzy there for a second."

I sat down at the table beside my brother and tried to swallow my growing fear along with mouthfuls of toast smothered in strawberry jam. Amy would never eat toast again. Amy would never walk home from school in front of me, swinging her braids from side to side. I didn't really know Amy, but knowing she was dead cracked something inside of me.

PART
TWO

CHAPTER
ONE
·

WHILE I SIT IN MY living room, perched on the edge of my couch, waiting and watching for some piece of news about the Amy Nessor case that I can grab hold of, I feel my mind going numb. Glazing over. Just over two months ago, I went into a similar state of detachment when six days after I'd expected to get my period, it still hadn't come. I am religious about taking the pill and my cycle has always been as predictable as clockwork. Understandably, I was a little freaked out.

Feeling like an irresponsible and embarrassed teenager, I drove out of town to buy a pregnancy test at a drugstore in Leeville where no one knew me. I didn't tell Jason because I wasn't ready to consider the implications of the test being positive. I felt trapped, like I was suddenly bound to a very different future with Jason than the one I'd imagined. I waited until late Saturday night to do the test when I wouldn't have to face anyone afterwards. My hands were shaking as I set the test stick on the edge of the sink. I refused to look at it until a full two minutes had passed. During those two minutes, my mind went blank. It was as if I'd hit a switch and just turned off my brain.

Still in that strange blank state, I read the results. One pale blue line. Negative. I couldn't feel relief because at that moment I couldn't feel anything. But I knew, when I climbed under my blankets that night, that my numbness was really fear. I hugged my pillow and tried to make sense of my reaction. Would it really be so terrible to have a baby with Jason? We were both adults, for Pete's sake, in a committed and stable relationship. I already knew he was a good father so what was I so worried about? I drifted into a restless sleep, punctuated by unsettling dreams.

The next morning, when my period came, I broke into tears. All the tension from the previous week left my body in great, gulping sobs. I was almost giddy with relief. But I felt a tiny bit guilty, too, for not sharing my alarm with Jason, for not telling him about the anxiety that had been eating me up for days. It didn't matter though, because it had all been for nothing. And if I had told him, it would only have served to upset him for no good reason.

Now my mind is playing the same trick on me, trying to block out the implications of Amy's case being re-opened, but I can't escape from the pulsing fear that mom's heart might not be strong enough for what's coming. Both figuratively and literally.

A FEW WEEKS AFTER AMY'S murder, Mom was standing at the stove, stirring a pot of spaghetti sauce while I was setting the table. I don't know where Ricky was — probably out with Darius or Jeremy. What I do know is that ever since Amy's body had been found, there was a nervous tension running through our house, like the air was humming with a high, thin note of fear.

"Can you please put a hot plate on the table?" Mom asked me.

She lifted the pot of sauce from the stove, but as she turned toward the table with it, she seemed to stumble and the pot fell from her hands. She fell, too. I watched, helpless, as the boiling sauce sloshed over Mom's arm. The pot landed with a crash, sending a thick, red spray across the floor, where Mom had collapsed into a half-sitting position. She let out a startled cry of pain. I rushed over to her, side-stepping the worst of the spilled sauce.

"A dish towel, quick," she croaked, and I ran to grab one. She blew out a breath as she held the towel against her arm, gently wiping away the splashes of sauce on her skin.

I couldn't take it all in — the surprisingly loud crash of the pot hitting the floor; Mom's slow slide to the ground and her yelp of pain; the kitchen floor, the cupboards, even part of the ceiling, splattered with spaghetti sauce. I glanced around me in shocked silence, unsure what to think, what to do.

"Are you okay?" I finally managed. My question came out as a squeak and Mom must have picked up on the fear in my voice.

She scooted from the spot on the floor where she had landed until she was leaning against the cupboards. "I just ... I lost my footing for a second." She was hugging her right arm to her chest and breathing hard.

I could feel the tears, hot and insistent, that wanted to spill over, but I fought them off. "What do I do?" I whispered.

"See if Mrs. Tisdale is home."

I ran to our next-door neighbour's house, heart pounding, and stammered out what had happened. Mrs. Tisdale followed me across the front lawn and took in the scene in our kitchen. Mom was sitting at the table now, cradling her arm against her body.

"I need to get this looked at," Mom told Mr. Tisdale, indicating her arm. "Could you watch Zoe for a bit? I'm going to ask my friend Linda to take me to emerge."

I didn't want to go back with Mrs. Tisdale — she was old and her house smelled funny, like rotting flowers and strong perfume — but I wasn't given a choice in the matter. Mrs. Tisdale was a widow who had lived alone for as long I could remember; her large, empty house felt alien to me and when her pet bird squawked at me from the corner of the living room, I jumped.

"Don't mind Clover," she told me. "He's just saying hello."

I'd only glimpsed her bird before, but now that I looked at him up close I was surprised by his bright orange feathers. He cocked his head at me. I moved away, unsettled by the round, black eye he fixed on me. Mrs. Tisdale fed me a peanut butter sandwich and let me watch TV until I fell asleep on her couch, the bird thankfully hidden from sight under a blanket Mrs. Tisdale had draped over his cage to keep him quiet. When Mom came to get me, she nudged me gently and as soon as I opened my eyes, I saw that her arm was wrapped in white gauze all the way from her elbow to the tips of her fingers. When we got back to our house, Linda was on her knees in the kitchen, scrubbing our sauce-stained floor.

"Your mom had quite the scare today," Linda said, looking up as Mom guided me toward my room. "When your brother gets home, make sure you tell him to be good to her. She needs you two to be on your best behaviour."

"Linda," Mom said, in a warning voice.

Linda gave her a look, a kind of don't-blame-me look, then went back to her scrubbing. "You'll have to use some bleach on this later. But I'll get the worst of it now."

"Thank you," Mom said.

MOM SAT BOTH ME AND Ricky down a few days later. We were on the couch, facing Mom, who was sitting very straight in her reading chair. "There's something wrong with my heart," she told us. "It's nothing too serious, but I have to be careful not to get overexcited or worried because that can make it act up."

"Your heart?" Ricky said. "I thought you just burned your arm."

"Well, the reason I dropped the pot in the first place was because I got light-headed and that's been happening a lot lately. I've had a few other problems, too. Pains in my chest. The doctor wanted to run some tests. It turns out I have something called angina. It means my heart doesn't always get enough blood to do its job properly and that's what makes me dizzy."

I pictured Mom's heart, somehow broken, and my own heart squeezed with panic. I couldn't erase the image of her collapsing to the floor amidst an explosion of hot, thick sauce.

Ricky made a sound somewhere between a grunt and a huff of impatience. "Okay, so now do you, like, have to move around slowly or something?"

"No, no, not at all. But I won't be running any marathons!" Mom tried to laugh, but it came out all wrong, like a strangled cry instead of a light-hearted chuckle. "Things have just been ..." She paused. "A little stressful lately."

She meant because of what happened to Amy. I looked at Ricky, but his face didn't give anything away. And I knew in that moment that it was up to me to protect Mom so that her heart didn't break the rest of the way.

CHAPTER
TWO
.

I CAN'T SIT UP ALL night watching the news, so after another twenty or thirty minutes I drag myself to bed. Burrowing into the comforting warmth of my duvet, I do my best to ignore the seeds of anxiety drifting through my veins and rooting in my bones. My whole body aches. How I manage to fall asleep is a mystery, but eventually I do, because I am jerked awake at five thirty by the insistent beeping of my alarm clock.. I might have slept, but I didn't sleep well. Drifting in and out of consciousness, I spent a good chunk of the night rehashing all the details from the days and weeks following Amy's murder — what I knew and what I thought I knew. All night, my mind circled and circled around certain truths before finally collapsing like a tired spinning top. As soon as I lift myself to a sitting position, I feel a familiar pressure building in my sinuses and a faint pulsing above my ears.

I'm almost afraid to look at my phone, but there's nothing from Mom. Nothing from Ricky. The last person who called me was Jason and I remember ignoring my phone when it rang last night. I make myself a coffee, but when I take my first sip, it's like swallowing liquid ash. Maybe I should call in sick. Except I'm not really sick, I tell myself.

My interview is only three days away. And after that, I'm going to tell Jason that despite what I said on Sunday, I am ready for us to move in together. I cannot come undone again, not like before. I am going to pull myself together and get ready for work and act like everything is normal. I shoot Jason a quick text, promising to call him tonight. I have no idea what I'm going to say to him. I'm still trying to figure out what to tell myself.

I manage to choke down two pieces of toast and half an apple. I move through the kitchen sluggishly, washing and drying my plate, wiping the crumbs from the table, focusing on going through the familiar motions of getting ready for work. When I step outside, the grass is laced with frost and the cold air hits me like an icy slap in the face. As I drive across the bridge toward the plant, the sun is only just starting to creep above the horizon. Normally, I enjoy taking in the muted colours of the sunrise, but as the pressure behind my eyes continues to build, my attention is hijacked by the streaks of pain shooting through my head.

When I meet the junior operator assigned to the night shift for the hand-off, I take a minute to wish I could spend the entire day in the warmth and quiet of the control room. The steady hum of the computers might serve as a soothing backdrop to my roiling thoughts, although monitoring the SCADA screens requires a level of awareness I'm not sure I possess at the moment. In fact, I don't have a lot of faith in my ability to concentrate on anything other than the news about Amy Nessor's case being re-opened. After a short recap detailing the night shift's operations, which lasts less than fifteen minutes, I'm back in the bowels of the plant, where it's cold and damp and loud.

As I make my rounds, I think back to Roger's insistence when he was training me that if I didn't record every single action I took in the various log books scattered around the plant, whether it was adjusting a valve, or taking a reading, or turning a dial, it would be tantamount to committing a crime.

"If you go to the bathroom, you better write it down," he joked.

"Why is it so important to record everything?" I asked, thinking it sounded a bit ridiculous. I mean, obviously, I understood the need to record certain things, but every single miniscule adjustment made in the course of a shift?

"There are a lot of regulations around water quality," Roger explained. "If something goes wrong, they want to know exactly how and when it happened. And who's responsible. Things got a little fussy after Walkerton."

I thought being at work today would help keep my mind busy, but moving around only makes my head feel like it's doubled in size. My left eye has started to water and my aching limbs scream for a break. I push my earplugs in deeper, but the roar of equipment is only slightly muffled by the flimsy foam inserts. I fight to concentrate while I'm calculating alum levels, but my mind stubbornly returns over and over to the re-opened investigation and I can't shake the certainty that everything is about to fall apart. That my tentative hold on happiness was, once again, only an illusion.

THE NESSORS DIDN'T STAY IN Dunford after Amy's murder. Sometime after Christmas they moved to New Brunswick, where Mrs. Nessor's sister lived. I probably couldn't have pointed to New Brunswick on a map back then, but I knew enough to understand that it was far away from Dunford. It made sense to me, this running away. Every time I walked past Amy's house, I remembered her doing something outside of it: skipping on the sidewalk, having a tea party, jumping in piles of leaves. It must have been so much worse for her family, being forced to stare at her empty bedroom, her empty bed, all her empty clothes.

At school, we continued to skip and sing, turning the rope faster and faster until the jumper messed up. I chanted the words along with everyone else:

> *Blue Bells, Cockle Shells*
> *Evie, Ivy, Over*
> *I love coffee, I love tea*
> *I love the boys, and the boys love me*
> *Yes, no, maybe so*

I couldn't listen to that meaningless rhyme without thinking of Amy. Somehow the image of her skipping with the other kids at the end of our street became tied up with the line "I love the boys, and the boys love me" and I would see her skipping down the sidewalk, getting closer and closer to the blue car that was waiting to swallow her.

After her body was found, the police set up roadblocks and began searching vehicles. They went door-to-door in the neighbourhood for a second time, looking for clues. And yet, in spite of all those efforts, in spite of all the officers out there looking, there was never any trace of Amy's killer. No abandoned vehicles, no reported car thefts, nothing suspicious in any of the hundreds of blue cars that had been systematically pulled over and inspected. I was comforted by the thoroughness of the police investigation, although Mom did everything in her power to prevent me from following it too closely.

"You don't need to know all the gory details," she said. "It's just going to upset you."

I was already upset. Why hadn't I looked at the license plate? Why hadn't I stopped Amy from getting into the car in the first place? But mostly, why hadn't I told the whole truth — why had I never admitted my terrible suspicion out loud? Every time I looked at Mom's bandaged arm in those early days after the murder, I was reminded of her weak heart, about how she wasn't supposed to get worked up. Besides, what if I was wrong? It was too big a risk to voice what I had kept secret all this time. Still, the weight of that secret left me numb. I could feel myself getting thinner, becoming flat.

Ricky didn't say anything about the Nessors moving even though Mom was over there all the time helping Janet pack. When the family finally drove away in their station wagon, minus one child, Mom waved at them with this cheerfully determined smile fixed on her face. Her arm was better by then and she no longer had to keep it wrapped up, but the skin was wrinkled and discoloured from the burns.

IT MUST HAVE BEEN SOMETIME in April when Darius pulled up to our house in a pale grey Chevette. It was rusting around the wheels and a long crack ran across the bottom of the windshield, all the way from one end to the other. "How do you like my new wheels?" he asked. "Might not be pretty, but sure beats having to borrow my dad's car all the time."

I stood on the porch watching as Ricky slid into the driver's seat and ran his hands over the steering wheel. He was grinning stupidly at Darius the whole time. I had a feeling that Mom and I would be seeing a lot less of Ricky now that Darius had his own car, and we hardly ever saw him as it was.

I knew that Darius's dad's car must have been checked by the police during their road blocks, and knowing that threw my disloyal suspicions about Ricky and Darius into a river of doubt. But I couldn't drown my suspicions completely. My feelings about my brother during the months after Amy's murder were unpredictable and confusing. I still craved his attention, but I also felt as if a black hole had opened around him that I was constantly in danger of falling into. We all were. I was desperate to protect him, to protect all of us — our whole little family unit.

The hate came later.

A NEW FAMILY MOVED INTO the Nessors' house. They had twin boys, probably less than a year old, who couldn't walk yet. Mom never made much of an effort to get to know the family; I can't remember if she even brought over a welcome pan of anything: brownies or banana bread. She would have. Before.

The twins' mom was a thin woman with a poufy perm that stuck out from her head like a cloud. She looked nervous to me, scuttling from the car to the house with her head bent low, carrying first one boy in, then the other. I often wondered whether or not she knew about the Nessor family and what had happened to the little girl who lived there before. She must have. It was all over the news. How would it feel to tuck your babies into their cribs in a murdered child's bedroom?

I didn't see the dad much. As soon as he came home from work, he disappeared inside the house. Even when the weather warmed up, I didn't see him sitting outside or washing his car or playing with his boys.

One of the twins cried all the time. I could hear him whenever I played outside or walked past their house. Maybe it was both of them, and they took turns crying, but I had convinced myself that one of those boys was a quiet baby, and the other one was cranky and difficult. I felt sorry for the quiet one, the nice one, since there was nothing he could do about his brother and he was stuck listening to him shrieking for hours on end. I knew what it was like to have a brother you didn't understand, one you wished sometimes would just go away. I knew what it was like to want to be the only child. The good one. The quiet one.

"WHOSE BIKE IS THAT?" RICKY asked one morning, nodding his head in the direction of a red ten-speed that was leaning against our shed.

I was kicking my soccer ball around, and while I'd noticed the bike, I hadn't given it much thought. "Dunno," I said. "You didn't put it there?"

My brother gave me a look. "No, I didn't put it there, numbskull. I wouldn't be asking about it if I'd put it there, would I?" He opened the shed and dragged out the lawn mower.

I picked up my soccer ball and headed into the house. Now that Ricky had come outside, I wanted to be somewhere else. I was growing more and more uneasy around him, preferring my own company to my brother's confusing presence.

Mom popped her head into my room while I was building a space station out of Lego. "I'm going out for groceries. Want to come?"

I hesitated. I didn't want to be home alone with Ricky, but he was still mowing the lawn and I really wanted to keep working on the upper level of my control tower. "No, thanks," I said, ignoring the flutter of trepidation in my gut.

I didn't hear Darius pull up in his Chevette, but when the lawnmower cut out I could hear Ricky's voice, raised and angry, drifting into the house from the backyard. I tiptoed into the kitchen and peeked out the window just in time to see Ricky pick up the ten-speed and throw it at his friend.

Darius jumped back and the bike landed with a bounce by his feet.

"I don't want you bringing this shit here!" Ricky shouted. "This is not your goddamned dumping ground."

"Relax. I just needed a place to park it overnight. No one can see into your yard. It's fine."

"I'm serious, Dare. The last thing I need is the police snooping around, asking questions. Zoe's already seen the bike. My mom probably saw it, too. What if they asked my sister, huh? What if they talked to my mom?"

I ducked down from the kitchen window and crept back to my room. It seemed weird that Ricky had brought up the police. It made me think the red bike in our backyard was somehow connected to Amy. I didn't understand Ricky's anger or his fear about the police asking me questions, so his reaction became confused in my mind with Amy's disappearance and all the questions the police had asked me then. While I sat on my bedroom floor sifting through my Lego, trying to make sense of everything, my own feelings of guilt quietly solidified.

THAT'S WHEN THE NIGHTMARES STARTED. There would be a soft sound, like a light knocking, at my bedroom window and when I went over to see what it was, Amy Nessor would be standing outside, tapping her dead fingers against the glass. I knew right away she was dead because even though it looked like she was standing, her head was sagging to one side and her body was hanging in the air, limp, as if she were being held up by invisible strings.

I didn't tell anyone about the nightmares. I would wake up, heart pounding, sheets soaked with sweat, clutching my blankets to my chin. Then with my eyes wide open, I would start counting. *One, two, three,* whispering the numbers into the dark until my eyes drifted closed and my voice trailed off into meaningless mumbles. One night, I counted to over two thousand before losing track of where I was and falling into a restless sleep.

I ALSO STARTED GETTING STOMACH aches. I was in grade five by then and at first, Mom would pick me up from school and serve me ginger ale and crackers until my appetite returned, but since she worked part-time at the Dunford library, my frequent stomach complaints were becoming problematic.

"I can't keep coming to get you, Zoe," she told me one afternoon, while I lay curled up on the couch. Her voice sounded tired.

I didn't want to make things difficult for her because I was worried it would make her heart act up again, but I couldn't stop the stomach aches either. After maybe the fourth or fifth time the school called her, she took me to see Dr. Richardson. I sat on the paper-covered examination table and listened to him tell Mom there wasn't anything wrong with me. He suggested that the next time my stomach hurt I should be forced to stay at school and tough it out.

"My guess is once she realizes she doesn't get to go home, the stomach aches will go away on their own accord," he told Mom. Like I was making them up just so she would come and get me.

I wasn't making them up. They were real and I knew exactly what was causing them, but I couldn't tell anyone. We had been assigned grade one reading buddies that year, and the very first time I sat down with the pig-tailed six-year-old assigned to me, I started cramping up. Kaleigh's little voice twisted into my gut and when her wide eyes met mine I knew the nightmares were going to get worse. The stomach aches were one thing, but now Amy Nessor was showing up at my window clutching a book in her dead fingers that she wanted me to read with her.

"Please?" she begged.

I hid under my blankets, counting and counting and counting.

MOM WAS BADGERING RICKY ABOUT applying to college, but he wanted to take a year off to work instead. He wasn't ready for college, he told her. He wanted to make some money first. I remember him being irritable a lot of the time that year, his final year of high school, at loose ends with himself, with everyone.

He spent even less time at home than he had before, but he wasn't hanging out with Darius anymore. Darius had dropped out of school around the same time Ricky got a part-time job at Pizza Hut, and, when he wasn't working, Ricky was usually out with some girl or another. Sometimes they came in groups, giggling as they picked him up. Other times, he borrowed Mom's car to take one of them — Mandy or Kaitlyn or Chrissy or whoever it happened to be — to Leeville or Boelen.

The rare times he was home, he holed himself up in his room listening to Metallica and Guns N' Roses and Def Leppard. One night as I walked past his closed door, I heard the familiar pulse and echoing melancholy of "Bringin' On the Heartbreak" and I was hit with a wave of nostalgia that made my heart ache. I continued down the hall to my room, where I sat on my ugly green carpet with my bins of Lego. I kicked one of the bins, enjoying the satisfying crash of the pieces colliding against each other. Then I put my head on my knees and began counting silently, doing my best to ignore the hot tears soaking through my jeans.

Ricky became a stranger, a heavy presence in the house, a shadow. I hardly ever saw him, but I knew when he was there. Mom and I settled into a routine that didn't include him: eating dinner when he worked at Pizza Hut, watching TV together when he went out with different girls or else shut himself in his room blasting his heavy metal. My stomach aches eventually went away, but the nightmares persisted. I passed through grade five in a detached state. I worked hard at not thinking about anything, at floating through the days in a state of oblivion. It was better, I thought, than sitting on my carpet crying.

CHAPTER THREE

·

"I GOT A JOB AT the Future Shop in Leeville," Ricky announced.

Mom looked up from the pattern she was cross stitching in her reading chair and raised her eyebrows. "What about Pizza Hut?"

"I'm quitting. This is full-time."

Within a week, Ricky'd packed his things and moved into the house of a friend of a friend, some guy who worked in construction that we'd never heard of before. I don't know if what I felt after he left was relief so much as a loosening up, a spreading out. Like I was slowly expanding again.

I'd just finished grade five, and with Ricky gone, the summer seemed to stretch out before me like one long exhale. "What are you going to do with his room?" I asked Mom.

"I don't know. I thought we'd just keep it like it is for when he visits. No?"

"I guess," I said. "I wanted to move some of my stuff in there. Like my dollhouse, because it takes up so much space. Can I use his closet?"

"Sure," Mom said, but she seemed distracted. She was sorting through the mail, setting certain pieces to one side. She stopped once and put her hand at the base of her neck, a confused look crossing her face, but then she continued as if nothing had happened.

I washed our breakfast dishes and put them away, keeping a close eye on Mom. I could sense a thin bubble of anxiety around her as she opened each envelope; I knew any kind of stress wasn't good for her. Eventually, she set the mail aside and said she was going to lie down, so I snuck into Ricky's room to have a look at his closet. He'd left a bunch of stuff in it: a few dress shirts that I'd never seen him wear; a forgotten sock, balled-up in the corner; a pair of slippers Mom had given him for Christmas. He'd also left two baseball caps on the top shelf, sitting side by side. I looked long and hard at those hats.

I threw everything he'd left in his closet into a garbage bag and shoved it in a corner of the basement. If Ricky wanted any of it, he should've taken it with him. I was afraid to throw his stuff out completely in case he asked about it later and got mad, but I didn't want anything that belonged to him left in his closet or his room. Especially not the hats. They made me queasy, sitting up there, like some sort of sick joke.

After emptying his closet, I opened the bedroom window as wide as it would go and pulled the blankets and sheets off his bed. I opened every one of his dresser drawers, checking to see if he'd left any other pieces of himself behind. He hadn't. Propelled by some urge I didn't understand, I used a rag and large amounts of lemon-scented Pledge to dust his dresser, his nightstand, and even the windowsill. Finally, I lugged Mom's Hoover down the hall and vacuumed every square centimetre of his carpet. When I was done, the room smelled like lemons and sunshine, not like Ricky's old room at all.

Mom found me in there, sitting on the edge of his bare mattress. "You miss him, don't you?" she said, coming to sit beside me. I didn't know how to tell her that she couldn't have been further from the truth.

THIS WAS AROUND THE SAME time the library burned down and while a temporary new location was quickly established at City Hall, Mom had to find another job because there wasn't enough space or work for everyone to keep their old hours. It would be almost two years before the library officially re-opened in the large Edwardian mansion donated by the Gordon family and many years after that before they were able to build the collection back up.

I was thrown off by Mom's uncharacteristic tears in response to the fire. It wasn't just losing her job that she was upset about, she tried to explain to me, it was all those books. Technically, she still worked for the library, but her hours had been cut back to almost nothing and she'd started cutting coupons from the paper for everything from cereal and cheese to rubber boots.

Mom found a second job cleaning Dr. Richardson's office, but it meant she had to work in the evenings, after the office was closed. It also meant I was home all by myself for a few hours every night.

"I wish I didn't have to leave you on your own," she said. "But you don't mind, do you?"

During the summer, when it was still light out by the time she got home, I actually didn't mind. I liked being alone. But as summer faded into fall, and as the daylight hours leached away, I began dreading those hours alone in the dark. Every little sound sent my heart racing. I began turning on all the lights in the house, which drove Mom nuts, and probably made her feel guilty because she knew why I was doing it.

"Why don't you leave the TV on?" she suggested once. "For company."

I tried to play the advantage. "I'd rather get a dog."

"We're not getting a dog."

"But —"

"Zoe, we're not getting one. Period. They're too much work and too much money."

I backed down. I was always backing down, being agreeable, keeping the peace. Pretending to be such a good girl.

AS CHRISTMAS APPROACHED, MOM COULDN'T stop going on about how nice it was going to be having everyone together again. Ricky had to work on Christmas Eve, but he would be joining us on Christmas Day for our traditional turkey dinner and afterwards, he was staying overnight for the first time since he'd moved out.

Mom had been fussing all morning over the table setting and the little Christmassy touches she'd added to every room in the house. She adjusted the bowls of candy in the living room at least three times in the twenty minutes before we were expecting Ricky to arrive. I was also antsy. Partly about seeing Ricky and partly because I didn't want Mom to get all worked up and have one of her heart things.

When Ricky finally pulled up, revving the engine of the used Mustang he'd bought, I joined Mom by the front door. We stood there, both of us, waiting for him like he was a celebrity.

I expected him to head straight to his old room, to drop off his bag, but he simply dumped it in the hall and that was more disappointing to me than the way Mom kept fawning over him. I wanted him to see what I'd done to his room. How I'd taken over his space. After dinner, while I stayed in the kitchen to clean up, Ricky retreated to the living room, where he slumped on the couch to watch TV.

"Why don't you put your stuff in your room?" I called out to him.

He grunted.

"Leave him be," Mom said. "He's tired. Just let him relax."

I stared at her, incredulous. *Leave him be?* What had he ever done to deserve such special treatment? I was the one scraping plates and putting away the leftover potatoes and gravy and cranberry sauce. I was the one who got up every morning to get myself ready for school and then spent the whole day listening and trying to be good, completing my homework, making sure Mom never had to worry about anything. I was the one who stayed home alone in the dark, night after night, fighting off panic attacks because I wasn't allowed to get a dog.

Mom shook out the red and green checkered tablecloth, then folded it into a neat square, before tucking it into a drawer. She went to join Ricky in the living room while I got out the broom to sweep. When I was done sweeping, I began scraping the sides of the roasting pan that Mom had left in the sink to soak. I stayed in the kitchen nursing my resentment for as long as possible.

I could hear Mom and Ricky chatting. He was explaining the commission structure at the store and how busy it was leading up to Christmas.

"People come in sort of desperate for a last-minute gift and they just want you to tell them what to buy. It's crazy."

"And do you give them good ideas?" Mom pressed.

"I give them expensive ideas." Ricky laughed. "I have a good sense of what kinds of things people will like. Especially if it's for a kid; I know what the kids like."

Listening to him talk like that made me sick. Mom was all aglow, though, leaning toward him, soaking up every word.

WE EXCHANGED GIFTS WHILE LISTENING to Bing Crosby's *White Christmas* record. Mom put it on every year when it was time for presents. I sat on the floor, close to the glimmering artificial tree, and when I unwrapped a silver Sony Walkman, I couldn't help but think Ricky was right. He did know what people would like. I popped open the cassette player, then clicked it shut.

"Thank you!" I said, and Ricky gave a little nod. I was already planning what tapes I wanted to listen to first. I was big into New Kids on the Block and Milli Vanilli at the time.

My present for Ricky wasn't nearly as exciting as a Walkman. I'd picked out a pair of warm leather gloves from the Sears catalogue and Mom had paid for them. He tried them on and held out his hands. "Cool," he said.

Mom opened her gifts last. I was proud of what I got her. We'd gone to a craft sale at my school in November and at one of the tables I'd found a ceramic jewelry tree. The woman selling it told me you could hang necklaces, bracelets, and even rings on the many branches. "It keeps the chains from getting tangled," she said. "Plus you can see what you have which makes it easier to pick what to wear."

As Mom unwrapped the final layer of newspaper protecting the tree, I held my breath. She tilted her head to the side and slowly smiled. "Ah, lovely," she said.

"It's for your jewelry," I told her.

"Yes, thank you, Zoe."

When she opened Ricky's gift, her eyebrows shot up. "Oh, Ricky," she breathed. "It's lovely!" Carefully, as if it was a tiny newborn baby, she lifted a porcelain figurine of a woman in a blue dress from its bed of tissue paper.

I didn't see what was so special about the figurine that she had to hold it all reverently like that.

"Royal Doulton. Oh, Ricky, you shouldn't have."

Ricky shrugged. "I thought you'd like it."

"I do. I do. I love it. But, really, you didn't have to do that. Oh, isn't it gorgeous?"

Mom must have examined every single little detail on that doll while my hand-crafted tree lay forgotten on the table beside her.

WHEN RICKY PEELED HIMSELF OFF the couch and picked up his duffle bag, I followed him to his room. He kicked the door open with his foot and threw his bag on the freshly-made bed. Turning to face me, he said, "So, what's the plan tonight? Does Mom want us to watch some corny Christmas movie or something?"

"I keep a lot of my stuff in here now," I told him. "Mom said I could. Since it's not really your room anymore."

He glanced around. "Uh huh."

"It's mostly stuff I don't want anymore. Mom calls your room the dump. Like where we put things we don't want." That wasn't true at all. Mom had never even commented on me keeping stuff in here, but it sounded vaguely insulting and I wanted to see how Ricky would react.

"Well, it looks a helluva lot better than when it had all my crap in it."

I trailed him back to the living room where Mom was setting out three glasses of eggnog. She smiled when she saw us, and I felt bad for trying to incriminate her. I shouldn't have faulted her for loving us both.

CHAPTER
FOUR
·

AFTER CLOSE TO A YEAR of living without Ricky, I began to forget how uncomfortable I used to be around him. I forgot a lot of things. Little details of his personality that used to prick at my conscience evaporated from my memory. Amy stopped tapping on my window with her dead fingers. Her disappearance and the discovery of her murdered body felt far away. Almost like something I'd made up. My wavering suspicions about the afternoon she went missing faded into a hazy and unreliable non-memory. Ricky was simply my older brother, who lived and worked in Leeville, and nothing more.

"WHERE ARE YOU GOING?" I asked, thinking I hadn't heard Mom properly.

"A women's retreat in Niagara Falls. With Lorraine and Linda. It's just for three days."

"Is it a church thing?" Mom had started attending the Baptist Church just after Christmas and I knew that both Lorraine and Linda also went there.

"I guess you could call it that."

This retreat in Niagara Falls must've been a big deal for Mom because she got all excited every time she talked to Linda on the phone, hashing out details, confirming times, planning where to stop for lunch, discussing what she was packing, and on and on. I didn't begrudge her the excitement, but I wasn't too happy about the arrangements she'd made for me. Since she was leaving early on Friday and not returning until the late afternoon on Sunday, she'd decided to ship me off to stay with Ricky for the weekend.

"It'll be nice for you two to spend some time together, won't it?" Mom asked.

I shrugged. While I had originally begged to stay home by myself, the prospect of two whole nights alone kind of terrified me, so in the end I didn't put up too much of a fight. Ricky was going to pick me up after school on Friday and bring me home again on Sunday.

"I think it's the perfect way to start your March Break. You hardly see your brother anymore, so this will be a great chance for the two of you to catch up."

When Mom hugged me good-bye before school on Friday, she looked anxious. The fact that she might be worried about leaving me with Ricky made me uneasy, but I didn't want her to get stressed and not be able to go on her retreat because of me. Or worse, have her crappy heart start acting up because of me.

"Mom, I'll be fine," I said, pulling out of her too-tight embrace.

"I know. I know. Remember to brush your teeth! And don't stay up too late. I already told Ricky —"

"Mom! Stop worrying. I have to go or I'll be late for school. I'll see you Sunday, okay?" If I hadn't rushed out of the house, speed-walking down the sidewalk, I might have given in to the swirling uncertainty churning in my gut. I might have collapsed into my mom's arms, like a baby, and begged her to stay home with me.

As I marched to school, determined not to turn around and look to see if Mom was standing on the porch watching me, I remember thinking that she wasn't going to have as much fun as she hoped on her weekend away because of me. Instead of feeling guilty, I felt reassured.

RICKY WAS WAITING FOR ME in front of the house after school. He threw my stuff into the back seat of his Mustang. I watched as my pillow slid to the floor. I wanted to reach in and pick it up, but instead I climbed into the passenger seat as if my pillow being on the dirty mat in his car didn't bother me at all. I was nervous about staying with Ricky; I didn't know what to expect. Mom and I had only been to his place in Leeville once, right after he moved in, and we hadn't stayed inside for more than fifteen minutes. That time, we said hello to his roommate, glanced around quickly, then went out for dinner as a family at Swiss Chalet. After we'd dropped Ricky off again, Mom and I drove straight back to Dunford.

Ricky's Mustang was cleaner than I expected so maybe my pillow would be alright.

"How was school?" Ricky asked.

I stared straight ahead. "Boring. Our teacher gave us homework to do over the break, so that sucks."

Ricky didn't reply and we drove most of the rest of the way in silence. At one point, he informed me that I'd be sleeping on the couch. "Hope that's okay. Or, if you want, you could sleep on the floor in my room."

"Whatever," I said, but my stomach flip-flopped anxiously. I didn't want to sleep on a couch or on the floor. I wanted a bed. I wanted my own bed, in my own room. With Mom close by. I wished for probably the hundredth time that Lorraine and Linda had never invited her to that stupid retreat.

Ricky's house was different from how I remembered it. The living room was dark, even though it was still early afternoon, and as we passed through it, I could smell cigarette smoke and something rancid, like dirty socks or wet shoes. Someone had left a banana peel beside a half-eaten bowl of cereal on the coffee table. The kitchen was even worse. Unwashed dishes sat in goopy rings on the table. It stank in there, too — a mixture of stale cigarettes and sour milk. I didn't know how Ricky could stand to live like this, when our house on Lindell Drive was always so clean.

"Sorry about the mess," he said, as if reading my mind. "We're kinda slobs here."

"It's fine," I said, but some of the dismay I felt must have leaked into my voice because Ricky smiled at me apologetically.

"Not quite what you're used to, eh?"

We had Kraft Dinner and hotdogs for supper. I cleared a spot for us at the table, wiping it down the best I could with a cloth that felt greasy. Stan, Ricky's roommate, wandered in while we were eating.

"Ah, so here's the little sister," he said. "Big weekend away from Dumbford, eh?"

I nodded.

"Not everyone in Dunford is as stupid as your ex-girlfriend, Stan," Ricky said, pouring himself a second glass of milk.

"No? What about you, Zoe? Are you any smarter than this meathead of a brother of yours?"

I glanced at Ricky nervously. "I'm only in grade six —" Before I could finish, Stan started laughing.

"Oh, well, then there's time for you yet." He took a beer from the fridge and walked into the living room. My last few bites of KD stuck to the roof of my mouth like glue.

I decided that first night to sleep in Ricky's room. His bedroom wasn't as messy as the rest of the house, although he did have to kick a pile of dirty laundry out of the way to make room for my sleeping bag. Despite Mom's reminder, I didn't brush my teeth. I didn't forget, I just didn't want to touch anything in the bathroom; the spray of tiny hairs that ringed the sink made me want to gag.

Stan was getting ready to leave when Ricky and I got up for breakfast. "Where'd you sleep?" he asked me. "I was expecting to find you on the couch this morning."

I scuffed my toe against the dirty linoleum. "On the floor in Ricky's room."

"I bet that dingbat brother of yours didn't even give you an air mattress, did he?" He turned to Ricky. "What the hell is wrong with you? You make your kid sister sleep on the floor? You'd treat a dog better." He grabbed his lunch pail and banged out the back door.

Ricky had to work that morning, too, so I was left alone with instructions to "do whatever I wanted." I was used to being on my own, but it felt strange to be sitting on Ricky and Stan's sagging brown couch watching cartoons. At home, I would curl up under the afghan that was always neatly draped over the back of the sofa, but here, I didn't want my bare skin touching anything. I ended up bringing my sleeping bag out of Ricky's room and wrapping myself in it like a cocoon.

The hours dragged by. I made myself a peanut butter sandwich, adding my plate to the pile of dirty dishes on the counter. Then, because I had nothing else to do, I took out my homework. I had some math questions, which were easy, but I also had to write a fake letter to our principal expressing my opinion on our school switching to uniforms. Our teacher tried to convince us that the school was seriously considering the idea, but I knew the whole thing was made up. We all did; she did this assignment every year and word got passed on. Still, in order to make my letter convincing, I pretended to be really worked up. When I was done, I found myself staring at the walls.

Eventually, I got so bored that I cleaned the kitchen. Mom would be horrified if she saw how Ricky was living. And even though I resented having to scrub all those disgusting dishes, not to mention the counters and the table, I felt better after everything had been washed and wiped down. Like I could breathe properly again.

Ricky was genuinely impressed, I think, when he came home. "Holy shit, Zo. I should bring you here more often. You didn't have to do that, though."

I shrugged, like it was nothing. I was actually glad Ricky was home again — that's how bored I was.

"Oh, hey, I got you something." Ricky shoved a box toward me. It was an air mattress. "I got a pump, too," he told me.

When Stan walked in later and saw the kitchen, he whistled, and I flushed with embarrassed pride. We ordered a pizza and ate it in the living room. Stan and Ricky drank beer. I sipped milk from a satisfyingly clean glass.

"Why don't we watch a movie," Stan suggested, and I gladly agreed. I wasn't up to making conversation, especially not with Stan who seemed to set traps with all his questions, then laughed when I was too confused to answer.

"Leave her alone," Ricky kept saying, but even I could hear the lack of conviction in his voice. The knowledge that Ricky would be bringing me home again the next morning, before his Sunday afternoon shift, was like a life raft for my brain. I began to count down the hours until I was back on Lindell Drive.

I can't remember who chose the movie, whether it was Ricky

or Stan, but I remember sitting on that awful brown couch hoping that Ricky couldn't see how absolutely terrified I was. We were watching *Friday the 13th* and while Ricky and Stan were laughing, my breathing was becoming shallower and shallower. My hands were so clammy they left wet imprints on my pants. Several times, I thought I was going to throw up.

When the movie ended, I couldn't move.

Stan stood up from his chair and stretched. "Does your mom let you watch shit like this at home?" he asked me.

Ricky twisted around to face me. "What she doesn't know can't hurt her. Right?"

"Right," I agreed meekly. I couldn't meet his eyes — I didn't want to see the threat there that I heard in his voice; but also, I didn't want him to see the fear in mine.

At some point during that movie, I remembered exactly what kind of person my brother was. And if anyone was going to hurt our mother, it sure as hell wasn't going to be me.

CHAPTER
FIVE

•

I MOVE THROUGH THE PLANT in a distracted haze. I finish the alum calculations, then stop to blow my nose for what feels like the hundredth time. Amy's face swirls through my thoughts like a kite cut from its string. I can't concentrate on anything. The pain in my sinuses, my dripping nose, my watery eyes — it all takes a back seat to the shock of seeing Amy's innocent face again. I promised Jason I would call him tonight, but how can I explain what's going on?

I sluggishly make my way over to Section 4B where the day tanks for our polyaluminum chloride are housed. Huge metal pipes carrying treated water criss-cross the ceiling. I have to side-step a puddle from a valve that's dripping overhead. The valve is there to allow for spot checks, but I can't be bothered stopping to tighten it. I continue toward the day tanks, which are filled from much larger storage tanks outside. I record the amount of alum already in the tank before beginning the transfer process and while the chemical pours in, my mind wanders back to Jason. I imagine my future with him dissolving in a sea of useless words and hopeless explanations. How is it possible for this to be happening again?

Just a few weekends ago, I was over at his place while Parker was there and the three of us were playing Junior Monopoly on the floor in the living room. We had bowls of chips and licorice spread around us and it was so relaxing and nice and right. Suddenly, I want that. I want a future filled with cozy afternoons and a man who knows that kissing the side of my neck will almost inevitably lead to more.

I reach in my pocket for a Kleenex, but the ones I pull out are all shredded with use. I fiddle with my earplugs, but the thundering in this section of the plant closes in on me, a freight train barrelling toward my brain. My head is swimming. I need to sit down.

I flip over a plastic bucket to use as a seat a few metres away from the alum tank. I lower myself onto it gingerly, testing whether or not it will support my weight. It buckles slightly, but doesn't give. I wipe my nose on my sleeve, then shut my eyes against all the noise, against the rushing in my ears, against the panic threatening to overtake me.

Suddenly, I hear a voice shouting. I open my eyes and see Roger running toward me. No, he's running toward the storage tank, and as I awkwardly push myself to my feet, I see that the day tank is overflowing, spilling polyaluminum chloride into the containment area.

"What the hell are you doing?" Roger yells as he shuts off the transfer valve.

Shit. Shit shit shit. There's a low cement wall surrounding the tank, designed specifically to contain a spill like the one I just caused, but as I'm standing there staring at the mess, Bruce, the shift supervisor, strides toward us and I'm trying to form an explanation, but my mouth won't cooperate so I just gape at Roger and Bruce stupidly.

Bruce surveys the damage, throwing a few choice words my way, then marches off to arrange for a vacuum tanker to deal with the overflow, which he assures me, isn't how he was hoping to spend his afternoon.

"You okay?" Roger asks me.

"Yeah, I'm just —"

"Don't worry about it. It happens. Barney once miscalculated the chlorine dosage and we had to drain two entire tanks of treated water. Had to issue a statement to the whole bloody township explaining the temporary water shortage. This, this is nothing."

"Yeah, well, I doubt Bruce thinks it's nothing." I pause. "You think this'll come up in my interview?" Chemical spill due to negligence. How will that go over with the new owners?

Later, when Bruce calls me into his office to file a report, I am dizzy with fatigue and apprehension. "I don't know what happened," I start to say. "I lost track of —"

"Zoe, I'm sending you home."

My head jerks up. "What? Just because I made a mistake?"

He shakes his head. "Because you're sick. You look like hell. Get some rest and don't come back until you can function properly. I don't need any more screw-ups to report. Especially not now." He looks at me meaningfully.

I know exactly what he's trying to say. Even though he's a supervisor, Bruce has to go through the same bullshit interview process as the rest of us. This accident doesn't just reflect poorly on me, it also looks bad on him. The cost to clean it up won't go unnoticed.

"Who'll take the rest of my shift?" I ask, although at the moment, I don't really care. I just want to get out. I don't want to know what Bruce is writing in his report. I don't want to think about it. I don't want to think about anything.

"I've already called someone. Go home. I don't need you for this paperwork. If I do, I'll call you." Bruce waves me away and turns to his computer.

I stand up uncertainly and walk to the door. I make my way to my locker, where I reach with shaking hands for my bag. I glance around for Roger, but he's probably down at the alum tank, overseeing the clean-up. I've just created a shitload of extra work for everyone and I'm walking away. It feels wrong.

Everything in my whole fucking world feels wrong.

FIFTEEN MINUTES AFTER I GET home, my phone rings, and I answer without even looking at the number, thinking it's probably Bruce. It's not. It's Mom's friend Linda, and her voice is all strained and fake-chipper. "Oh, hi Zoe. I didn't think you'd pick up, but I wanted to get in touch with you to let you know your Mom's in the hospital. She had a little heart attack."

"She had a heart attack? Like an actual heart attack?" My stomach drops and my own heart begins to race dangerously. "Is she okay? What happened?"

"She's fine, Zoe," Linda insists. "She couldn't catch her breath this morning so she called me. By the time I got there she was having chest pain, worse than usual, so I called an ambulance. They've given her some medication to thin her blood and now they're monitoring her."

"Is she awake?"

"Yes, she's been talking up a storm. It was really just a minor blip. But it scared her. And me, too. I think she's worried that the next time it could be more serious."

"I'll be there right away. I'm not at work so I can come now."

"Actually, she's not supposed to have visitors. She's meant to be resting. I was just going to leave you a message so you'd know what happened."

"How long will she be there, in the hospital, I mean?"

"Oh, I don't know. Probably a few more hours. Maybe over-night. It depends on how she responds to the medication."

I sink onto my couch, slumped over with worry and an aching fatigue. I don't know what to do. I can't protect anyone. I'm almost afraid to check the news, but I need to see if there have been any new developments in the case. Is that what caused Mom to have a heart attack? Did she see something that put her over the edge?

Just typing in Amy's name on my laptop brings up a torrent of results. Every article starts with the same information: the excruciating details of her unsolved murder and how the case is being re-opened after twenty-nine years, but now there are also timelines and maps and multiple experts conjecturing about what really happened the day Amy disappeared.

On one map, Lindell Drive is highlighted in bright yellow with a large black X indicating the precise spot on the street where Amy was last seen. By me. Although I'm never named, just labelled as a young witness. The only witness. A dotted line runs from that black X to the location in the ravine where her body was found. *Parents desperate to learn the truth about daughter's tragic journey*, the caption reads.

I close my laptop abruptly. The truth is such a tricky thing.

CHAPTER
SIX
.

RIGHT AFTER AMY'S BODY WAS found, rumours swirled around my elementary school and the neighbourhood. Mom wouldn't let me watch the news for weeks and although I knew we still got the *Dunford Chronicle*, she never left it out where I could see it.

"I heard her head was cut off," Gabby Kloster confided to me by the bike racks, looking around to make sure no one else could hear her.

I didn't consider Gabby a trustworthy source. She was the kind of kid who said the teacher was dead when she was really sick with the flu. She once told me that she'd seen a house burn down with people inside it. "They were standing at the window looking at me when they caught on fire. I watched them burn up." Still, there was a ring of truth to her comment about Amy's head.

A few days earlier, I'd overheard my mom saying to someone on the phone, "One of her braids cut off, like some sort of sick souvenir." Then, noticing me in the doorway, "Oh, Zoe just came in. I'll talk to you later."

"What's a souvenir?" I asked.

"Nothing you need to worry about. How was school?"

"Fine," I mumbled. "We made paper flowers. For a remorial or something."

"A memorial," Mom said, nodding sadly and, before she could open her arms to hug me, I turned and ran to my room.

Now, leaning toward Gabby by the bike racks, I hissed back at her, "It wasn't her head, dummy. It was her hair. For a souvenir."

"A what?"

I shrugged. Gabby made a face just as the bell rang and we had to run to line up. As we were walking inside, she turned around and grabbed a piece of my hair, making a snipping motion with her fingers. I tugged my hair away and glared at her.

I dreamed that night about finding Amy's headless body in my closet, stuffed inside a plastic bag. I searched and searched for her head, growing more frantic by the minute, because I knew that if I could find it, I could put her together again and she would be fine.

We would all be fine.

I STOPPED HANGING OUT WITH Gabby. I stopped hanging out with anyone. By grade six, I had no real friends. If I had, I might have been able to stay with one of them instead of with Ricky when Mom went on her women's retreat to Niagara Falls. And then maybe I would have watched something like *The Brady Bunch* instead of *Friday the 13th* — which would have meant one less lie to tuck away in my chest, scraping, every so often, against the nervous beating of my heart.

I didn't mind my loner status at school. Solitude suited me. I didn't need any friends, or at least I didn't think I did.

On the first day of grade seven, I boarded the bus for Galtview Senior Public which was on the outskirts of town and much bigger than my elementary school.

"Good luck, honey," Mom said, patting my head. I think she

still wanted to kiss me, the way she used to when I left for school, but by then I had started flinching from her touch. Leaning away instead of toward. "Have fun today! You're going to meet a whole bunch of new people this year."

At one of the stops, a kid wearing glasses got on and sat across the aisle from me. He kept his head low and didn't talk to anyone. The bus ride was short, less than twenty minutes, and as I bounced along in my seat, I tried to ignore the butterflies flitting around my stomach. I'd been to the school for a tour at the end of grade six, but I wasn't sure I'd be able to find my homeroom. When I had my tour, all the hallways looked the same: ultra-wide and impossibly long.

I did manage to find the right classroom, but when I walked in, the only people I knew from my old school were already sitting together and there weren't any empty chairs left at their table. I recognized the kid with the glasses from my bus sitting at another table and when he acknowledged me with a slight dip of his head, I walked over.

"Is it okay if I sit here?" I asked.

He nodded, so I sat down, relieved not to be standing around looking like a loser on my first day. He told me his name was Walter and somehow or other we became friends. Never more than friends, although I'm sure lots of people assumed there was more to our friendship than there was. Like me, Walter was quiet and reserved. He came from a big family — he had four sisters, all older — where it was easy to become lost in the noise and commotion, so I think he was used to disappearing into himself, which by then was also a specialty of mine.

We spent a lot of time together, mostly hanging out at my house, because it was quieter than his, but I liked going to his chaotic house, too; I found the noise and energy refreshing. His sisters laughed a lot and they were always playing jokes on each other, and on Walter.

"Here Walter, try this! You too, Zoe. It's iced tea, but made with less sugar. It's supposed to be totally healthy."

"No thanks," Walter said, eyeing the light brown mixture suspiciously.

Not wanting to be rude, I cautiously agreed to have some. One of them poured me a glass and as soon as I took my first sip, I knew I'd been pranked. I didn't know what to do other than swallow the disgustingly salty mouthful of iced tea, but my face must have registered my shock.

His sisters roared with laughter. "We told you it had less sugar!" one of them squealed.

Walter alternated between apologizing to me and telling off his sisters. I would never admit it to him, but I liked the attention from his sisters. Their ready smiles and easy laughter made me feel light. I wanted to be one of them. I wished often in those early days that I had been born into a family like Walter's.

The eldest two, Rhonda and Rachelle, were twins and when Walter and I were in grade seven, they were already applying to universities. I assumed they would go somewhere together, so when they ended up in separate cities, it struck me as really sad. I guess I considered them to be invisibly attached, or maybe because I couldn't tell them apart, I always thought of them as a pair, rather than individuals. When I brought it up with Walter, he didn't seem to care one way or the other.

"It doesn't bother you to think of them so far apart?" I asked him once, after they'd moved out, Rhonda to Windsor and Rachelle all the way up to North Bay. His house felt strangely quiet without them.

"Not really," he'd said. "Do you wanna stay for dinner? I can ask my mom."

"Nah. My mom will have made something for me already. I should go."

Even without Rhonda and Rachelle at home, Walter's parents still had three other children to keep them company. Mom only had me.

THE SUMMER AFTER GRADE EIGHT, Walter's parents invited me to join their family on a camping trip. I looked at Walter to see his reaction, but he must have known already that they were going to invite me. He stared back at me expectantly, waiting for my answer. The two of us were sitting at the island in his kitchen, eating popcorn, and his parents were trying to figure out what was wrong with the dishwasher.

"Hand me the pliers, will you?" Walter's dad said.

Walter's mom, Sheila — although I only ever called her Mrs. Bronson — handed the pliers to Mr. Bronson, then smiled at me. "What do you think, Zoe? Do you like camping?"

What I thought was that I would die of happiness because they were treating me like a surrogate daughter. In reality, they probably felt bad about me not having a dad or essentially being an only child, but, at the time, I believed they considered me part of their family and it made me feel almost effervescent.

"DO YOU EVEN HAVE ANY camping gear?" Ricky asked, after Mom told him about the trip when he was down visiting from Leeville. We were sitting at the kitchen table, eating dinner together as if we were a normal family.

"You know I have a sleeping bag," I told him. "They have everything else. They go camping all the time."

Ricky made his face look innocent. "Yeah, but like, aren't you scared of the dark?"

"Richard!" Mom scolded, setting her fork down loudly. She gave him one of her looks.

Had she told him about that? How I used to leave all the lights on when she was cleaning Dr. Richardson's office? "I'm not a little kid anymore," I said. I pushed my plate away and stood up. "And it's not like I have to worry about Walter or one of his sisters coming after me with a knife while I'm sleeping."

"That's enough," Mom said.

Ricky nodded at me, considering. "Touché," he said.

Back in April, Ricky had woken up one night to find Darius leaning over his bed with a knife. He wanted money. When Ricky told us the story, I figured he was downplaying the actual details, giving us a watered-down version for Mom's sake, but it was still scary. Ricky had been able to talk Darius down, although he did end up giving him forty bucks. What was strange about the whole thing was that Ricky and Darius hadn't spoken in years.

"How did he know where you lived?" I'd asked.

"No idea. Someone obviously told him. Or dropped him off. I'd like to find whoever that was."

Stan was pissed when he found out. He told Ricky that if his druggy friends were going to start showing up then he'd better find a new place to live. My biggest fear upon hearing Ricky retell the story wasn't that my brother could have been hurt, or worse, but that if Stan kicked him out, he might move back to Dunford.

Darius never came back, though, so Ricky stayed in Leeville, where it was easier for me to pretend he didn't exist.

I WENT ON THE CAMPING trip with Walter's family in August. Our site bordered a small lake and the three days we spent on that little patch of wilderness were, up to that point, arguably the best three days of my life.

I envied Walter the uncomplicated relationship he had with his family. There was an easy camaraderie between all of them that was evident in the way they worked together to set up the camp-site. I fumbled around, trying to be helpful, but felt very much like I was in the way.

"Why don't you see if you can start us a fire, Zoe?" Mr. Bronson suggested.

I gathered up handfuls of small twigs and arranged them in a teepee in the fire pit. Walter's mom gave me a pile of old news-papers so I crumpled a few pieces to jam under my twigs. The first two matches I lit went out before I got them to the paper, but the third, with a weak little flame that wavered uncertainly, lasted long enough for one of my crumpled papers to catch. I lit another match and held it to the opposite side of my fledgling fire. Soon the twigs were burning and I began adding the thin slivers of kindling that Walter's dad had chopped earlier. As I watched my fire grow, I was so damn proud I could have cried.

"You're a natural," Walter's dad said.

On our second night, after a full day of canoeing and hiking, as we sat around the fire under a thick blanket of stars, I looked from Walter to his two remaining sisters to his parents and almost said the thing that I'd carried in my heart like a blade for so many years. I felt, in the warm glow of those flames, that I was with people I could trust, and there in that remote place, so far from everything I was in Dunford, I could finally unburden myself.

Remember when that little girl Amy went missing? I wanted to say. *She lived on my street. I think my brother and his friend* — what? What did I think, exactly? That they had driven off with her and killed her? I had never put my suspicions into words. I had never articulated them to myself as a complete thought. Because I didn't really believe it. I couldn't. And I certainly could never voice them to Mom.

"Is it time for s'mores?" Sheila suddenly asked, breaking the spell of silence and infinite space into which my confession might have fallen. And just kept falling.

Walter's sisters got up to grab the graham crackers and the chocolate. I stuck a marshmallow on the end of my roasting stick and concentrated on browning it evenly, being careful not to hold it too close to the flames.

CHAPTER
SEVEN

·

I HAD HIDDEN BEHIND A fog of intentional ignorance for a long time, but when I got to high school something changed.

"Zoe Emmerson? You related to Ricky?"

I turned around slowly. I didn't recognize the guy talking to me, but I answered him anyway. "He's my brother. Why?"

"What's the matter with him? Can't find a girl his own age?"

I scrunched up my face, pretending to be confused.

"Tell him the next time he crashes a party in Dunford to keep his hands off my girlfriend."

I nodded, then quickly walked away. I'd heard that Ricky was hanging around with some of the seniors at Dunford High. His name came up every so often in connection with a party or a girl or several girls, and just like that, he was back in my world. We didn't see more of him at home, but because of his weird association with the high school crowd, he clung to the periphery of my awareness.

I made it through grade nine successfully, relatively unnoticed. Then, in grade ten, our history teacher gave us an assignment that required us to search for local records on Dunford during the

Second World War — how many of its citizens had served, what the war effort looked like at home, that kind of thing — using the microfiche in the school library. When I realized I had access to all of Dunford's archived newspapers, something inside of me twigged. Instead of going back to the war years, I started scanning the newspapers from six years ago — the ones my mom had hidden from me — looking for information related to Amy's murder.

I don't know why I suddenly wanted more details. But having the history of Dunford at my fingertips — all those hundreds and hundreds of newspapers — made me think about all the information Mom had kept from me during the weeks following Amy's death. Maybe it was the awareness that Ricky had a disturbing reputation for hanging out with younger girls that was chafing at me, but I was seized with an overwhelming desire to know the specifics about what had happened without the protection of my childhood naivety. I wanted actual facts.

It was difficult to control the microfiche viewer. At first, I kept zooming across the micro pages so fast that the content was nothing more than a purple blur. Eventually, I figured out how to slow the magnifier down so I could search systematically. The first article about Amy was from the day after her disappearance, when everyone was still looking for her. When everyone was still hopeful. There were oblique references to me, the only witness, and what I had seen. My unsatisfactory and vague descriptions of a blue car were trumpeted as potentially the most useful piece of information in the search.

The best clue we have to go on, Detective Armstrong was quoted as saying.

Further down, but still on the front page of that day's edition, there was a small blurb about a fire at the Boelen mill.

Flames ravaged the abandoned mill yesterday evening as firefighters fought to control the blaze. The smoke could be seen from as far away as the water tower on the north side of town. Although slated for demolition, the mill ...

I scrolled ahead to the next day's paper. The details around the discovery of the body were grisly. It was no wonder Mom didn't want me reading about it. Amy's head hadn't been cut off, despite what Gabby Kloster might have said in grade four, but Mom had been right about her braid.

The body of Amy Nessor, the six-year-old girl who went missing from Dunford two days ago, was found less than a kilometre from her home on Lindell Drive. Her partially unclothed body was discovered in a ravine that runs perpendicular to her street. Police had searched the ravine earlier in the week and found nothing suspicious. "Her body was obviously placed there after our initial search," said a spokesperson for the police department. He went on to describe the condition of the body, saying, "Everything was intact, except one of her braids had been sheared off at the scalp."

"She was wearing Mickey Mouse hair ties," her mother Janet is quoted as telling the officers in her original description of her missing daughter. "She wanted to wear her Mickey Mouse elastics on Tuesday." The braid was not recovered with the body.

Mom's whispered conversation on the phone about sick souvenirs came back to me. My tongue was thick and dry in my mouth. I could barely swallow, but I kept reading.

Preliminary reports suggest that Amy Nessor was strangled with yellow twine. "The kind you can buy at any hardware store," said the police spokesperson. "There were fibres of it in the skin around her neck, although no twine was found with the body." Her ankles and wrists were bound with

*loosely tied lengths of rope. Her body was arranged under a spirea bush
"... as though her killer had posed her there like a doll," said the spokesperson.*

She was partially naked when they found her, wearing only her underwear, although according to the police, there was no evidence she had been interfered with sexually. Possibly the killer had taken her clothes in an effort to remove any evidence that might lead to his/her identification. I took a deep breath then, feeling something hot and angry smouldering in my chest.

But I didn't stop scrolling through the archived newspapers. The front-page spreads with their over-sized photos of a smiling and gap-toothed Amy, and then the progressively shorter and less-emotional clips did nothing to assuage my suspicions; instead they dredged up my old fears.

I sat at the microfiche machine in the library reading about Amy's braid and the Mickey Mouse hair ties and the yellow twine and an anger ballooned inside me that was so intense it made my teeth hurt. When I left the library, I walked down the locker-lined hall where Steve Marky, an entitled asshole who usually stood out by the front doors of the school smoking and whistling under his breath at all the girls, made the mistake of catching my attention. He cocked an eyebrow at me and before his mouth could form whatever insult I imagined he was about to utter, I slammed my fist into his face.

His head snapped back and hit the locker behind him with a satisfying smack. Stunned, he turned to face me and I hit him again. This time I caught him square in the nose. As the blood poured down his face, dripping onto his white T-shirt, I said, in a low growl that I hardly recognized as my own voice, "Don't fucking look at me like that."

PART
THREE

CHAPTER
ONE
.

I STARTED TO GO DOWNHILL in grade ten. Walter and I were sitting in the cafeteria one day, eating French fries out of a soggy cardboard carton, when some chick walked past our table and purposefully elbowed Walter in the back.

"What's your problem?" I called after her, getting to my feet.

She spun around slowly, an expression of mock amusement dancing across her face. Walter was trying to get me to sit down, but I knocked his hand away and approached the bitch who obviously thought she could get away with shoving people for no reason. People she probably thought were beneath her.

"You think it's funny knocking into someone like that?" I asked. "Does it make you feel like a big strong girl?"

"Cool it, loser," she said, "before you get yourself hurt."

When she turned away, with that condescending smile still lingering on her face, I grabbed her from behind and wrapped one arm around her neck, attempting to pull her to the floor. She reached up and grabbed a handful of my hair. Suddenly she pulled away from me and I stumbled backwards. A few people started laughing. As soon as I regained my footing, I lunged at her. She grabbed my arm and twisted it hard, wrenching my shoulder, then, before I had time to register what was coming, her knee connected with my stomach. She released my arm and I doubled over, wheezing. With the slightest of shoves, she knocked me to the ground. I lay there for a moment, fully aware of how ridiculous I must have looked, but in too much pain to care. My stomach and shoulder were both throbbing.

Around me, I could hear kids hooting and hollering, the excited buzz that a good fight generates. Walter reached out a hand to pull me up and I took it gratefully. "Why did you do that?" Then, in a gentler voice, "You okay?"

"I think my arm is broken."

Walter went with me to the office so I could call my mom. I needed her permission to sign out so I could get my arm looked at.

"You want to do what?" Mom asked. She was probably thinking about Ricky and how he used to skip school all the time when he was my age. "It can't wait until after school?"

"Not really. I think it might be broken, but you don't have to come get me or anything. I can walk to emerge from here."

"Zoe, what happened?"

"I'll explain later," I said. "But I need your permission to sign out."

"Fine," she said, but I could tell she was worried and I hated that I was the cause of it. I hated that I might remind her of Ricky.

THE EMERGENCY ROOM AT THE hospital wasn't busy. I only had to wait about fifteen minutes before being led into one of the examination rooms.

"You've dislocated your shoulder," the doctor informed me. He took my wrist and gently guided my arm toward him. "Sit up nice and straight," he instructed. "Can you shrug your shoulders for me?

Perfect." And with the slightest of motions he slid my shoulder back into place.

I had to wear a sling for a week and a half. The name of the girl I'd tried to fight was Jessie and the reason she'd taken me down so easily was because not only was she a wrestler, but also a known scrapper. I never got mixed up with Jessie again, but I didn't exactly stop lashing out after my shoulder healed. I just chose better targets. Only people who were jerks. I didn't want to fight everybody, just people who deserved it.

Mom couldn't understand why I was suddenly getting into so much trouble. "It's not like you at all, Zoe. Is there something else going on? You're not doing drugs, are you?" She had cornered me in the front hall and was scrutinizing my face.

"No, Mom, I'm not doing drugs. I'm defending people." Then, because I knew she wouldn't understand, I pushed past her and stormed to my room. I didn't want to talk about it. But I also didn't want her to worry and get all worked up, so I came out a short time later and helped make dinner. I apologised for being rude and reassured her again that I wasn't doing drugs.

Mom was going through her own rough patch. She'd had to quit her job cleaning for Dr. Richardson because she'd fainted there on two separate occasions and he told her that she was going to kill herself if she kept it up. By then, she was back to her regular hours at the new library so she didn't need the second job as badly, but the fact that she'd fainted twice was worrisome.

"Just so you know," I said to her as I rinsed the celery she'd handed me, "the people I get in fights with always have it coming. I'm not a monster or anything."

"Oh, Zoe, I don't doubt you think you're doing the world a favour. I just wish you'd find another way to do it. Fighting is not the answer."

"Sometimes it is," I argued.

A FEW DAYS LATER, I was called down to the guidance office. "Sit down, Zoe," Mr. Flagg said, motioning to the chair across from his desk. I was uncomfortably aware as I sat down of the black eye I'd received during my most recent altercation. "Your mom is worried about you," Mr. Flagg said. "Why do you think she's worried?"

My left foot bounced against the carpet. "Cuz I keep getting in fights?"

Mr. Flagg nodded, his eyes wide and serious. "She said you never used to be violent or aggressive and she doesn't understand what's changed." He paused. "Do you know why you keep getting in fights?"

I shrugged. Mr. Flagg kept looking at me, waiting for a better answer. "I just get mad," I finally said. I remembered, suddenly, Ricky using those exact words to explain why he'd smashed the mirror in the boys' bathroom.

"And how do you feel afterward?" Mr. Flagg asked. "Do you feel bad about hurting any of these people?"

"I don't usually care," I replied. "Like I told my mom, they had it coming, one way or another." But I did feel bad. I was turning into a horrible person. Even Walter had started to avoid me.

Mr. Flagg held my gaze. "It's not up to you to avenge all the misdeeds of the world. You're a good kid, Zoe. Your mom knows that, your teachers know that, and I think deep down you know it too. But you can't keep going around punching people every time you get mad. If you're not careful you're going to end up with something much worse than a dislocated shoulder."

I shrugged again, but I could feel his words grazing the rough edges of my heart.

"Do you know what I think? I think you need to find a healthy outlet for your anger. I'd like to meet with you again to discuss some coping strategies. Together, we can try to nip this in the bud before it gets ugly."

"Are we done, then?"

He nodded and I stood up to leave. At the door, I turned back to face him. "Thank you," I said. It was nice of him to want to help me. It wasn't his fault that he was as clueless as everyone else.

I never did go back to see Mr. Flagg to discuss coping strategies, but I told Mom that I'd met with him and that we'd had a good talk and that I was going to try really hard not to get into any more fights. And I did take his advice to heart, for the record, about finding an outlet for my anger, which is why that spring I tried out for the rugby team. As it turned out, I made a pretty good lock.

"WELL, WELL, WELL, LOOK WHO made the rugby team. I gotta tell you, I'm kinda impressed. Surprised, but also impressed. I didn't think you had it in you!" Ricky slapped me on the back and turned to Mom. "What are you feeding this girl? She's going to be taller than me soon."

"And better looking," I added.

"You'll never have my looks, sweetheart. And no matter how tall you get, you'll always be my little sister." He drilled his knuckle into the back of my head to prove his point and I swatted his hand away. I could see Mom watching me, probably worried that I'd punch him in the face if he pushed too far.

Ricky had come down from Leeville for one of his sporadic dinners with us, and Mom was cooking his favourite meal: homemade mac and cheese. She always catered to him when he dropped by, which bugged me, even though she'd been doing it for years.

"I'll try to make it to one of your games," Ricky said, and despite my best efforts, I was flattered that he'd even want to.

BEING ON THE RUGBY TEAM had its advantages. At the end of the year, I was invited to my first party — the whole team was invited, but still. It was a field party, out at Kendra Vardy's property, and I was actually looking forward to going. I knew there would be a bonfire, but other than that I wasn't really sure what to expect.

"You sure you don't want to go?" I asked Walter as we grabbed two cans of Dr. Pepper from Richter's convenience store. Now that I wasn't getting into fights all the time, we'd started hanging out regularly again. We spent a lot of time roaming around town, just walking and talking.

"I have a chemistry assignment to finish," Walter said.

"Okay, nerd." Most of the girls on the rugby team were going so I wasn't worried about not having anyone to talk to, but it would have been nice to have Walter there too. I didn't usually have much to say to the other girls on the team.

The night of the party, I was nervous as I got ready. I didn't know what to wear, then decided on jeans and a hoodie, because it was still cold at night. I spent a long time trying to decide what to do with my hair before pulling it into a ponytail since it would just get messed up anyway if I wore it down.

A few people were setting up tents in the Vardy's field when Mom dropped me off. I quickly joined a small group of girls from the team and I was standing with them trying to look cool when I noticed Ricky over by the fence, pulling a beer out of a giant blue cooler. What the hell? I didn't even know he was in town.

Suzy, one of the girls from the team, followed my gaze. "Isn't that your brother? Like how old is he anyway? Doesn't he have anything better to do?"

Ricky was twenty-three and as far as I could tell everyone else at the party was clearly still in high school. When he noticed me, Ricky held up his beer can in a greeting before being swallowed by a threesome of girls who looked like they were headed to the beach judging by their outfits. One of them, a redhead wearing a pair of exceptionally short shorts, draped her arm over Ricky's shoulder as she and her friends led him away.

Suddenly I didn't want to be at this party. But I couldn't exactly call Mom to come and get me right after she'd dropped me off, so I wandered over to the firepit and sat on one of the logs that had been arranged around it. There were a few other people sitting at the fire, but I didn't know who any of them were and no one seemed to notice me staring glumly at the flames. Eventually, someone sat down beside me. He was tall, and cute in a clean-cut kind of way. He reached his hands out toward the fire.

"It's colder than I expected," he said. "Wish I'd brought a jacket."

"It is cold," I agreed. "But I've seen people walking around in shorts and tank tops."

He laughed. "I know exactly who you're talking about. Trust me, they'll find ways to stay warm." He paused. "I'm Tommy. I've seen you on the rugby field. I play soccer, so I pass by you pretty much every day."

"My name's Zoe," I said. "Nice to meet you."

"Are you always this formal, Zoe?"

"No, I just —"

I would have kept talking, but the redhead I'd seen earlier with Ricky stumbled past the firepit and it was obvious, even in the flickering light, that she was crying. There was a commotion as her friends caught up with her and tried to put their arms around her.

"He's such an asshole!" she shrieked. Her eyes caught mine. "I know who you are," she slurred. "Tell your brother he can go to hell." Her friends pulled her away, shooting apologetic looks at me over their shoulders.

I stood up. Before I could decide what to say to Tommy, I saw

Kendra Vardy heading toward her house. "Sorry, I've gotta run." I sprinted after Kendra, and in a breathless rush asked if I could use her phone.

"I'm not supposed to let people in the house," she said. "But if you're quick, it's fine. Just don't touch anything."

"I won't," I promised. "Thanks."

I told Mom I wasn't feeling well and when she came to get me, the first thing she asked was if I'd been drinking.

"No, Mom, I wasn't drinking. I told you, it was more of a bonfire thing. Some of the older kids were drinking, but not, like, a lot." I didn't mention anything about Ricky being there. Or the scene with the crying redhead.

I SAW TOMMY AT SCHOOL after that and we said "Hi" to each other in the hallways, but that was about the extent of our interactions. There were only a few weeks left until summer break. Ricky called one night to tell us he'd been promoted at Future Shop; he was now a department manager.

"Well, we should have dinner together to celebrate!" Mom said.

Ricky came down on Sunday night and I was shocked by how much he'd changed his appearance. He'd cut his hair short and was wearing jeans that fit properly with a button-down white shirt. He looked older, more mature. Nicer. Not like the creep I'd seen at Kendra's field party.

"You have to look successful to be successful," he told me, while adjusting his collar in the hall mirror.

I nodded, but I highly doubted cutting his hair or changing his clothes meant he was any less of an asshole. I'd heard all the rumours by then, about him taking girls out to his car or to an empty bedroom at a party and then pretending he didn't recognize them the next time he saw them. There was a disturbing story about him and two sisters, but I'd only heard the tail end of it. I didn't want to know the details. I'd had more than enough of those.

"This is nice," Mom said, as she placed a pork chop on each of our plates. "Dinner with both my kids."

I eyed Ricky across the table as he served himself a heaping scoop of mashed potatoes. Why did he keep coming back to Dunford, anyway? You'd think he'd have enough of a life to keep him busy in Leeville.

Ricky passed me the serving spoon. "You still trying to beat everyone up?" he asked.

"Shut up," I mumbled.

"Sorry? I didn't catch that. What'd you say?"

Mom cleared her throat. She turned to Ricky. "So, when do we get to meet Sophie?"

Almost as soon as he'd walked in the door, Ricky made sure to mention that he was sorry he was late, but he'd had to drop Sophie off first.

"Who's Sophie?" Mom had immediately asked.

"My girlfriend. You'll like her."

"Is she from Dunford?" I'd asked, picturing the redhead, wondering what on earth would possess her to actually date my brother.

"No, she's a Leeville girl."

I hoped that meant Ricky might stop spending all his free time in Dunford, although I couldn't help but wonder how long they'd been dating or if she'd already been in the picture when he disappeared with that redhead at the party.

"You could invite her to dinner sometime," Mom suggested.

"I'll ask her," Ricky said, biting into a roll, chewing with his mouth open just wide enough for me to want to smack it shut.

SOPHIE WASN'T IN THE PICTURE long enough for Ricky to invite her to dinner. He didn't give any explanation, other than shrugging and saying, "Sophie? She's long gone" when Mom brought up her name.

"What happened?" Mom pressed.

"Heather," Ricky said, laughing.

Whoever Heather was, we never met her, either.

CHAPTER
TWO
·

AFTER LINDA'S PHONE CALL ABOUT Mom's heart attack, I don't know what to do with myself. I wonder, after the fact, if Linda called Ricky, too. I can imagine Mom telling her not to bother him, downplaying the whole incident for everyone's sake, including her own. I would normally text him in a situation like this, to see whether or not he'd heard, but with everything else going on, I don't want to touch base with him. I'm afraid to start a conversation.

If I wasn't so sick, I'd ignore Linda's advice and stop in to visit Mom. But then, seeing me might just make things worse. It might get her all worked up. Besides, Linda said she wasn't technically supposed to have visitors, so it's probably better if I leave her to recover in peace. I'll check in on her in a few hours, after I've had a nap. I'm too tired to come up with a better plan.

It's hard to find a comfortable position given how congested my sinuses are. I can't lie flat without my face throbbing, so I end up on the couch with my head tipped back against the armrest, which seems to alleviate some of the pressure in my face. As soon as I close my eyes, I hear Roger's voice yelling about the overflowing alum tank. I've never done anything so careless at work before, not even when I'd just started and didn't know what polyaluminum chloride was.

After about thirty minutes or maybe longer of trying and failing to fall asleep, I drag my sorry self to the kitchen. I don't know what I'm looking for, but when I open the cupboard and see a packet of Mr. Noodles, it seems like the perfect antidote to my shitty day. I fill the kettle and while I'm waiting for it to boil, I wallow, just for a minute or two, in self-pity.

I carry my steaming mug of noodles to the living room and switch on the TV. I may as well know what's coming. If there are any new updates on the case, I don't want to be the last one to know. The news segments revolve through a seemingly endless loop of world politics, weather systems, sports, and entertainment before finally landing on the investigation into Amy Nessor's murder. My heart ratchets into overdrive. Amy's elementary school picture appears in the top left-hand corner of the screen while the news anchor, in his sombre grey suit, gravely reveals the latest development: the source of the information that led to the case being re-opened is an as-of-yet-unidentified inmate of Collins Bay Institution.

I should have known.

MY GRADE ELEVEN YEAR HAD some promising moments. I signed up for Mr. Hart's photography class and discovered a new world involving f-stops, ISO values, contact sheets, and darkroom etiquette. It was the first class I truly enjoyed in high school. In addition to that, I ended up dating Tommy that year. He asked me out just as I was about to get on the bus at the end of the day so I barely had time to answer him before stepping through the doors. Then, when I was sitting down, I looked out the window and saw him standing beside the bus, smiling. He broke up with me a few

months later for Ingrid, the captain of the girls' soccer team, and
we didn't talk much after that. I pined after him for a few days, and
my heart did this weird twisty thing whenever I saw him holding
hands with her, but it wasn't as if I was heartbroken. She probably
made a way better girlfriend than I did.

Then, sometime after Christmas, when each fresh dumping of
snow stopped being festive, Mom practically accosted me one day
at the front door the minute I got home from school.

"I just found out from Lorraine that Darius is in jail!" she said.
"Did you know anything about that?"

I was trying to take off my boots without getting slush on the
hardwood. "Why would I know anything?" I said. "It was Ricky
who was friends with him. Not me." My hands had started to shake,
making it difficult to untie my laces, but I had to know. "What'd he
do?" I asked, trying to sound casual.

Mom looked around, as if someone might be lurking in a corner
of the house, eavesdropping on our conversation. "I don't know
exactly, something to do with drugs. Remember when he threat-
ened Ricky with a knife that time? I'm glad he's behind bars.
Something wasn't right with him."

I let out a shaky breath. Knowing that Darius was in jail gave
me both a jolt of satisfaction and a creeping sense of dread. I
avoided Mom's eyes as I moved past her into the kitchen. "What's
for dinner?" I asked, opening the fridge, doing my best to appear
unconcerned.

"Leftovers. Pulled pork."

Over the course of the next few days I waited nervously for
something to happen. Darius going to jail felt like the beginning
of the end to me and I kept expecting our house of cards to come
crashing down at any minute. Each day, when I came home, I met
Mom with my breath half-held, assessing her face for signs of shock

or distress or just plain, blank disappointment. But everything went on the same as before.

After a month, I relaxed a little. Ricky came over sometime around Valentine's Day with chocolates and roses for Mom. He knew about Darius, but the fact that his former best friend was in jail didn't seem to bother him in the least.

"I'm certainly glad you stopped hanging around him when you did," Mom said. "I heard he was into drug trafficking! You know what goes along with that. He was a bad egg from the beginning, wasn't he?"

"He was a loser," Ricky said. "Dunford breeds losers."

He was looking right at me when he said this, but I ignored him. I really didn't care what Ricky thought anymore.

"You seem to like hanging out with enough of them," I said eventually, not looking up from my plate of pasta.

"Only the pretty ones," Ricky replied.

I SET DOWN MY MUG of Mr. Noodles. I can't not talk to Ricky now, not after hearing about the source being an inmate, so I send him a text. Maybe he's already been arrested. There was nothing mentioned in the news about suspects or arrests, though. Why on earth would Darius speak up now? He's been in and out of jail so many times, you'd think he'd know better than to open his mouth and admit to one more thing. The last I heard he was serving time for stealing a car, which brings to mind the red ten-speed he'd stashed in our yard so many years ago.

Where are you? I text Ricky. *Mom's in hospital. She had a heart attack.*

I would put money on it that right now Ricky's only thinking about himself. I want him to know exactly what else is at stake. For someone who checks his phone compulsively, it takes Ricky an awfully long time to respond. With every minute that passes, my panic inflates. Finally, he writes back.

Spoke to her earlier. She seems fine.

SHE HAD A HEART ATTACK! I want to scream, but the best I can do is put my message in all caps.

I know. So don't give her anything else to stress about, Ricky replies.

Is he kidding right now? If I wasn't practically on my deathbed I would drive to Toronto and string my brother up by his testicles.

Then again, who knows what Darius actually admitted to? I wouldn't put it past him to lie to save himself. I wish I knew more about what was happening, about what new information the police have. I think back to the camping trip when I almost came clean to Walter and his family and I am filled with the same nagging doubts that dogged me as a child.

What did I really see that Tuesday afternoon?

CHAPTER
THREE

·

I STOPPED GETTING IN FIGHTS during my senior years of high school, but the anger I'd inhaled when I researched the details about Amy Nessor's murder continued to smoulder under my ribcage. Walter and I were still friends, although by then things were starting to get weird between us. We were joking around one day in his basement about how so many people assumed we were dating when there was this awkward pause in our conversation. Walter was looking at me funny and my heart started to race.

"I mean, have you ever thought about —" He glanced past me, at the wall. "Like maybe there's something there?"

No, I wanted to say. But instead I put my hand on his knee — to get his attention and bring him back to reality — which was the wrong thing to do because he looked surprised, but then quickly placed his own hand over mine and we were sitting there on his couch almost holding hands and it felt so, so wrong.

"I think we're too good of friends for that," I finally said. "Plus, I'd make a crappy girlfriend."

He looked at me a moment longer, then pulled his hand back. "Yeah, and it'd be too much like a brother sister thing."

I'D NEVER CONSIDERED MYSELF ONE of the pretty girls — I would have placed myself squarely in the unremarkable category — but by grade twelve more and more guys started paying attention to me. Walter attributed it to my legs.

"Guys always stare at you when you wear those short shorts. You have nice legs. Guys like long legs."

Tommy broke up with Ingrid, and the two of us briefly got back together, but it didn't last long, which was too bad because Mom really liked Tommy. I did, too, but Mom thought he was just the sweetest thing. She never gave me a hard time about Walter, or questioned our friendship, but she poked and poked about Tommy.

Walter and I continued to hang out, even when I was dating Tommy, but after our awkward hand-holding experiment in his basement, things never quite went back to normal. I still pretended, every once in a while, that I was part of his family — even going so far as to refer to his parents as my adoptive parents — but after his remaining two sisters moved out, his house became as empty and as quiet as mine.

Near the end of grade twelve, when Walter was applying to universities, I started looking for a job. My plan was to work over the summer, then do a victory lap at Dunford High in an attempt to raise my average. By staying an extra year, I would also be able to play one more season of rugby, although by that point I had pretty much completely stopped lashing out at the world in the off-season. My outrage, all that boiling fury in my veins, had leached away over the last year.

By the time prom rolled around, neither of us had a date so Walter and I ended up sitting on his front porch in our jeans drinking Coke. Walter had just accepted an offer to the University of Waterloo for their math program and his approaching absence was gnawing at me. We watched as a limo pulled up across the street to collect a group of six people decked out in gowns and tuxes. The couples posed on the lawn in front of a flower garden while someone's mom, or maybe it was an older sister, took pictures. There was a lot of giddy laughter.

"Do you think we should've gone?" Walter asked.

"No."

"I don't mean together. But I bet there were lots of guys who would've gone with you."

"I didn't want to go. Did you? You could have gone! Why didn't you ask someone?" I had never considered the fact that Walter might've actually wanted to go to prom. I knew his parents had wanted him to go — all four of his sisters had gone — because to them it was like a right of passage, but Walter had seemed just as scornful of the whole thing as I was. I had nothing against prom itself, but given the fact that I was single, it was easier to scoff at the event than to admit it sucked to be on the outside looking in.

"Nah. There's no one I wanted to ask. Except maybe Lisa, but she would never have agreed." Walter scrunched up his face and laughed. Then he kicked at the ground on the porch and dumped the rest of his Coke over the railing and onto one of his mom's rose bushes.

Lisa had been Walter's long-standing crush since grade nine. Once, when I was dating Tommy, Walter and Lisa came on a double date with us. We went out for pizza and then to see a movie in Leeville. Walter was so nervous that he barely spoke to Lisa. At one point, when Lisa and I were in the bathroom at the theatre, she admitted to me that she thought Walter was boring. He must have known the whole thing was doomed because he never asked her out again, although by the end of grade twelve they were friends.

"I don't know," I said to him, attempting to be loyal. "I think she might have said yes. It seems like she likes you."

"Yeah, but not like that." He put his empty pop can on the ground and crushed it with his foot. "You wanna go inside? Play some foosball?"

"Yeah," I said, draining the rest of my Coke. "Screw Lisa. You're leaving soon anyway."

THAT SUMMER, I GOT A job with the Township, working in the Parks division, mowing the lawns of the municipal buildings and driving around in a golf cart to empty the garbage bins along the path that bordered the Still River. Walter was working at the Pioneer gas station, saving up for his tuition, one foot already out the door.

"I've decided to get my Operator-in-Training Licence so I can switch divisions and work at the Water Treatment Plant in the fall," I told Walter one night while we were wandering through town on one of our walks. "Steve said they're looking to hire more people because of the rubber factory or whatever it is that's opening. The factory will be using raw water and that means the water plant has to add a night shift."

"So, you're not going back to school then?"

"I'm going to take these courses instead," I said. "Steve says he can pretty much guarantee me a job at the plant if I get my OIT licence."

We were heading toward Ice Cream Island, mainly out of boredom. It was one of those hot, still evenings, where the sky remains strangely lit with pale summer sunlight long after the street lights have come on. Walter and I crossed the short, wooden bridge that led to the ice cream hut and stood in line behind a group of girls who kept changing their order and laughing as if not knowing what kind of ice cream they wanted was the funniest thing in the world. We took our cones to one of the benches at the edge of the island and sat down. The water reflected the murky, pinkish-grey light from the sky and lapped against the shore. Neither of us said much. Three seagulls hopped around our bench, looking for scraps. Walter kicked his foot out at them angrily and they flapped away, squalling.

I knew, as I sat on that bench beside Walter, that this moment was the beginning of the end for us. In less than two weeks, he would move to Waterloo where he would make new friends — friends who were more like him than I ever had been. The days, the weeks, even the years loomed ahead of me. I swear, sitting on that bench, I could already smell the loneliness that awaited me.

WE WERE IN HIS BASEMENT playing foosball when Walter brought up the school thing again. It was a Sunday afternoon and my brother was in town with some new girl. I had promised Mom I'd be home in time for dinner, but was otherwise avoiding the house while Ricky and his girlfriend were visiting. He and Sabrina or Serena or whatever-her-name-was would be driving back to Leeville after dinner and knowing he was leaving that quickly was a relief. Mom was so excited he'd brought a girl with him, likely reading all kinds of hopes and dreams into it, that she was kowtowing to him like he was royalty.

Walter scored the game-winning goal and as we were resetting our points he said, "So, I guess you've completely given up on the whole college or university thing, then? You're just going to stay in Dunford forever?"

"I'm not giving up on anything," I said. "There's no guarantee I'd get into college anyway. Not everyone is as smart as you."

"Don't be an idiot," Walter said. "You had a plan. And you're not stupid so don't pretend like getting out of here and doing something with yourself is out of your reach." He walked away from the foosball table, toward the stairs.

I followed him. "How is getting my OIT not doing something

with myself?" My fists were clenched at my sides and I could feel the blood in my veins surging.

"You always hate being compared to your brother," Walter said, turning to look right at me. "But if you ask me, you're acting an awful lot like him."

I stepped forward and shoved Walter. He stumbled backwards. "This has nothing to do with Ricky!" I shouted. I drew back my fist and smashed it into the drywall inches from Walter's flinching face. Then, I pushed past Walter and fled up the basement stairs.

Sitting behind the wheel of my mom's car, I examined the scraped knuckles on my hand and fought back angry tears. I didn't want to drive away, but I also didn't want Walter, or his parents, to see me in front of their house, choking back sobs like a child.

IT OCCURRED TO ME THEN that choosing to stay in Dunford did have something to do with Ricky. But Walter had the reasons all wrong. It had nothing to do with giving up. What I was choosing wasn't just about staying; it was about not leaving. About not running away. About not being like my brother. Which made the unfairness of Walter's comparison sting all the more.

CHAPTER
FOUR
·

MY MUG OF MR. NOODLES has gone cold and tastes like paper. I dump the contents into the garbage and set the mug in the sink. Clearly, I can't drive to Toronto to string Ricky up the way I want, and, even if Darius did come completely clean, which I doubt, that doesn't mean my story has to change. No one knows about my suspicions except for me. I never breathed a word to anyone. But if I'm questioned again, will I be able to lie? Will I be able to pretend I didn't know all along who was in that car? *But you didn't*, I remind myself. *Back then, you really didn't.*

Mom won't survive learning that both her children are implicated. She just had a heart attack, and that was before this whole thing was ready to blow up. What would it to do to her to discover that her precious son is a monster? And that her sweet little girl kept that small fact a secret?

I'm going to lose my mind if I stand around waiting for my world to cave in. Despite my throbbing head and aching limbs, despite the panic coursing just beneath my skin, I flee to my darkroom.

I can forget myself here. And if I force myself to focus on the next print I need to develop for Parker's birthday collection, maybe

I can trick myself into believing that everything will be fine. Everything will be just fine.

One of the places Parker has always loved in Dunford is the duck pond behind the old train station. It's really a stormwater management pond, but to him, and likely almost everyone else in Dunford, it's the duck pond. I took a series of shots at the pond last spring, before I even had the idea to do a photo montage for Parker, and I'm hoping that once I develop them, I'll have a shot that's good enough to include in the collection.

The low red lighting and soothing warmth in the darkroom calm my nerves. I can feel my muscles relax as I measure out my baths of developer, stopper, and fixer. When I breathe in the scent of the chemicals, I wonder, briefly, if they might help clear my sinuses. I start by making a contact sheet of all the duck pond negatives. Once I have miniatures of each shot, I choose which one looks most promising. Sliding that negative under the lens of the enlarger, I reflect the image onto a sheet of photo paper, making test strips at various exposure times so I can get the tone I'm looking for in the final print. I'll develop several of the shots, but my instincts tell me this is the best one.

Back when I was taking these photos, a swan came in for a landing directly in front of me and I clicked my shutter just in time to capture him in the split-second before he touched down, enormous wings fanned out and feet hovering inches above the water. Mirrored in the shot is the swan's reflection, an upside-down wavering image that gives the photo a dream-like quality.

Even after years of developing black and white prints in my darkroom, I am still struck by the magic of dropping a piece of photo paper into the developer bath and watching the image slowly appear.

Using a pair of tongs, I transfer the print of the swan to the stop bath, before dipping it in the final tray to fix it. After I've rinsed it off, I hang the sample print on my drying line, admiring the breath-taking power and grace in the swan's wingspan. It's a great shot.

I go through the same process with a few of the other shots, but none of them come close to the dramatic intensity of the swan caught mid-landing. As I'm considering how to crop the image so that it works as a square ten-by-ten, I realize there's a duck on the far edge of the picture, completely unconcerned with the swan's imminent arrival. I don't want to crop out the duck, but I do want to zoom in a bit closer on the swan. If I keep the duck, I risk sacrificing detail on the swan, which is the focal point. The duck, however, adds a tiny bit of character.

Who am I kidding? It doesn't matter. None of these shots really matter. I sag against my work table and draw a shuddering breath.

Normally, I am very particular about cleaning up my darkroom, but I do a rushed job, leaving the trays of chemicals where they are. I can deal with them later. Right now, I feel like I could collapse at any second. Back in my too-bright kitchen, I make myself a cup of chamomile tea; just holding the hot mug calms me. I sit at my table sipping it slowly, staring straight ahead. At nothing. I don't look at my phone and I don't turn on the TV. When I finish my tea, I go to my room and lay on top of my neatly made bed. I close my eyes.

I wake up almost an hour and a half later, strangely calm. When I check my phone, I see that Jason has called again. Shit. I can't ignore him forever.

"Hey," I say when he picks up after only one ring. "Sorry I didn't call sooner. It's been a crazy day." Is it possible that I sound completely normal?

"You sound stuffed up," he says.

"Yeah, I've got a bit of a head cold. Maybe a sinus infection." *Have you seen the news?* I want to ask. *Have you been following the case about the missing girl?*

"I was calling to see if you wanted to watch *Survivor* tonight. We haven't seen last week's episode yet."

As much as I would love to snuggle up on the couch with drinks and popcorn to watch a show with Jason, tonight I am definitely not up for it. Just hearing Jason's unsuspecting voice makes me feel as though the floor is about to fall out from under me. "You don't want to be around me," I say. "I'd probably get you sick."

"Do you mind if I watch it without you? Otherwise it's going to lock." His voice has an edge to it.

"No, go ahead. I'm probably just going to bed anyway. I feel like crap."

"I'm sorry you're sick," he says, and he genuinely sounds apologetic. I decide to forgive him for his unsympathetic tone a minute ago. "I hope you're feeling better in time for your interview."

"Me too," I say. I don't mention the alum spill or the fact that I was sent home early or that my mom had a heart attack. I don't mention anything that matters, except for this one fact that I am suddenly desperate to cling to: "I love you," I say.

There's a strange pause before he replies. "Love you, too."

His words sound mechanical. And that hesitation, that brief scrap of silence before he answers, drops into my stomach like a hot stone.

LATER, AS I'M LYING IN bed staring at the ceiling, when nothing has happened, when no one has shown up at my door to take me away, or to question me, I convince myself that there's still a chance my life isn't about to disintegrate before my eyes. Jason's hollow words echo in my mind, along with the empty space before he uttered them. Words trying to sound like truth.

But we do love each other. We have to.

I made a mistake with Amir. I told myself I did it to protect him, because he deserved more, but doesn't Jason deserve just as much? Doesn't Parker? Because if the reason I let Amir go was to save him from me and all of my miserable failings, then shouldn't I do the same for Jason? Jason, after all, is the one who made my life worth living again when I'd pretty much given up on the whole happiness thing. Doesn't he deserve at least as much as Amir?

What I should be doing right now is confronting Ricky to find out exactly what's going on. I can't just blunder blindly into making life-altering decisions without knowing the facts. So why haven't I called him instead of exchanging cryptic texts where I pretend nothing else is happening other than the fact that our mother had a mild heart attack? But I know why. I know exactly why. Because I don't really want to hear the truth. I will cling to my flimsy shards of doubt until they are ripped, piece by piece, from my bleeding hands.

CHAPTER
FIVE
·

I WENT TO SEE WALTER the night before he left for Waterloo.
Neither one of us ever mentioned the incident in his basement
where I almost punched him in the face, except for the one feeble
suggestion I made about paying to fix the wall. Walter had waved
away my offer and I didn't pursue it. That last night, even though we
did the same things we always did, the entire evening felt contrived.
Even our normally competitive foosball matches lacked conviction
and I got the impression that Walter was letting me win.

"You nervous?" I asked him.

"A little. Liz had a terrible roommate her first year and it got so
bad she had to move. I just hope I get someone who's okay."

Liz was the youngest of his four sisters. I'd never heard Walter
mention anything before about her having problems at university.
It seemed to me that his sisters had fluttered away to different
schools, and when they came back to visit, they all chirped happily
about their lives: activities and people and places impossibly removed
from tiny Dunford.

"It's going to be weird, not having you around," I said. And even though Walter was standing a few feet away from me, it felt like he was already gone.

THAT SEPTEMBER, I DID GET my Operator-in-Training license and, true to his word, Steve got me a job at the Water Treatment Plant. I was the only female. As the newest employee, not to mention the youngest, I was given all the crap jobs, like cleaning out the bottoms of the clarifier tanks, which are twenty feet deep.

"Here," Roger said, handing me a harness the first time I prepared to scale to the bottom of an empty tank. "You ever gone rock climbing? Same idea."

I rappelled myself down the still-wet wall until I landed on the bottom of the cement basin, shivering in the damp air. Roger yelled out instructions from the catwalk. The whole time I was blasting the layers of sediment and sludge with a heavy hose, I was imagining Walter shaking his head at me in disappointment. *Is this really what you want?* his imaginary eyes asked.

During those first weeks at the plant, I thought a lot about my summer job with the Parks Division, when I'd spent my days outside in the sun, puttering alongside the Still River in a golf cart. It had been a good gig, but it was a kid's job. And seasonal. Working at the plant was a real job, full-time, and while I might have originally considered it to be temporary, I could see myself settling in, falling into a rhythm of days that were reassuring in their predictability.

Walter came home that first Thanksgiving full of stories. He said his roommate was cool, the campus was huge, but most of his classes were only a twelve-minute walk from his residence, and then he went on and on about Wednesday nights at the Bomber — the on-campus pub — which was so popular you could wait in line for over an hour just to get in. I don't think he was trying to rub it in, how much fun he was having, but hearing him describe his new life and his new friends made me jealous. I started to second-guess my plan not to return to school, glimpsing an alternate future for myself in Walter's detailed descriptions of a life outside of Dunford.

Walter asked me about the plant, too, and he pretended to be interested while I explained what I did there, but it was obvious, at least to me, that already we had almost nothing left in common.

AFTER HEARING ABOUT WALTER'S LIFE in Waterloo, I began to crave the kind of independence he so clearly enjoyed. I considered the very real possibility of moving out of my childhood bedroom. I looked at a few different rental units around town and after more than a year of hemming and hawing, I bought the small bungalow on Pine Street where I still live.

Ricky was already living in Toronto by then — he'd quit his job at Future Shop to go into real estate — and had started using his full name, Richard, which he'd had embossed on fancy business cards. He'd also met a woman named Lauren that he seemed semi-serious about.

When I told Ricky about my bungalow on Pine Street, I thought he might be impressed that I'd purchased my first house before I was even twenty-one. "I bet you don't get too many clients my age," I said.

"Houses are dirt cheap in Dunford. You want to make an investment? Buy something in Toronto."

Mom was more supportive, but she couldn't understand why I needed my own place when she was happy to have me live at home for as long as I wanted. And by that, I think she meant until I met my Prince Charming and went to live with him in his castle. Still, she never tried to stop me. She just made sure I knew I was more than welcome to stay with her on Lindell Drive instead of spending all my money on a down payment for a run-down little property on Pine Street.

Walter was in his second year at UW by then, living in a house off-campus. Even he seemed unenthusiastic about my purchase, still voicing his hope that I would one day see what else there was outside of Dunford.

"You could still apply to college," he told me, while he was down visiting for Christmas. We were sitting in his basement since I didn't have any furniture in my new house yet, other than a kitchen table and a bed.

I made some sort of noncommittal motion with my head, as if I was still open to entertaining the idea. It was hard to know what to talk about with Walter anymore. I'd gone up to visit him in September, in the house he shared with a group of friends, but the whole weekend had been one long stretch of awkward interactions. His roommates were nice enough and they tried to include me in their conversations, but eventually someone would start talking about a theory or math problem or professor and I would be stuck silently listening to their academic jargon, wondering what on earth Walter and I used to talk about before our lives veered in opposite directions.

It was better when he came to Dunford. Right now, three of his sisters were also home for the holidays and his house had regained much of the noisy energy I had coveted when we were younger.

"Yeah, I could," I finally said in reply to his comment about college, hoping to stave off any more discussion around my decision to stay at the plant, and to put down roots in Dunford by buying a house. "You guys doing anything for New Years? Your family, I mean."

"My parents are hosting a dinner party. They want us to help out. You?"

"Dunno yet. Roger, a guy from work, is having some people over. Should be half decent."

"Yeah," Walter said. "Beats hanging out with your mom, I guess."

I HAD JUST PICKED OUT some furniture in Leeville and was walking back to my car when a skinny puppy limped toward me in the Leon's parking lot. I glanced around for its owner before crouching down to hold out my hand. That sad-looking little pup didn't even hesitate to walk right up to my empty hand, staring up at me with unabashed hope.

The dog had obviously been abandoned. It had no collar, and was dirty, hurt, and hungry. I reached over to scratch the pup's ears and instead of flinching, it just leaned right into me, lifting those hope-filled eyes to mine. I could see it was a boy, and already names were running through my mind. Champ, I decided. And in that moment, I knew I was going to bring him home.

After a quick stop at the nearby pet store, I had everything I thought I'd need: puppy chow, food and water bowls, a chew toy, a collar, and a leash. Then, with Champ scrabbling around on the front seat beside me, I drove back to Dunford, my heart twisting with something like love for my new, pitiful companion.

Champ followed me around my empty house, wagging his tail like a metronome. I fed him a small portion of kibble, mixed with some water, just like the pet store clerk suggested, and watched as Champ gobbled up the entire amount. When had the poor little guy last eaten? Within minutes of emptying the bowl, he threw up.

As I cleaned up the mushy, still-warm pile of undigested kibble, Champ hovered beside me, and he looked so small and forlorn that I pulled him onto my lap. "It's okay," I told him. "I'm going to take care of you."

He licked my chin and I sat on the kitchen floor, rocking him in my lap, wondering what kind of person would abandon a helpless puppy. Immediately, an almost-forgotten image of my brother and Darius surfaced: the two of them hunched over a sparrow in our backyard. Darius was poking the bird with a stick, and before he noticed me come around the corner, Ricky was just standing there, watching as the tiny bird struggled to flap its one good wing.

"I'm not like him," I whispered.

Champ wagged his tail, then peed in my lap.

MOM CAME BY A FEW days later to see my new furniture, and of course, my new puppy. The furniture had just been delivered that morning and I wasn't sure I liked it as much in my house as I had in the store. I heard Mom's car door as I was mopping up Champ's latest accident. He'd stopped throwing up every time he ate, but he still peed regularly in the house. I couldn't be angry with him, though; he didn't know any better and I hadn't exactly been doing much to train him. I knew he would have to relieve himself inside when I was at work, but I sort of hoped he would gravitate to the newspapers I laid out for him.

Champ followed me to the front door; he liked to stay within a few feet of me at all times. "Hi," I said, holding out my hands for the lasagna Mom had told me she was bringing. "Come on in."

"So here's the little guy I've been hearing all about!" She reached down to scratch Champ on the head and he wagged his tail happily. "What do you do with him while you're at work?"

"I slide a board across the entrance to the kitchen so he can't get out and he hangs out in there."

I set the lasagna on the stove and began putting together a Caesar salad. The table was already set so Mom sat down and watched me. "Have you talked to Richard lately?" she asked.

"Not recently." Mom loved talking about Ricky and his new girlfriend Lauren and how happy it made her that he seemed to be in a serious relationship. I think she must have been more worried than she let on about how he would turn out. She was always saying how she thanked her lucky stars that he hadn't kept up ties with Darius, who, after serving his sentence for drug trafficking, had wasted no time landing himself back in jail for something else.

Mom heard all the gossip about Darius and the rest of his family from her friend Lorraine, who lived just down the street from them. Darius's older sister, Michelle, we had learned, was also in and out of trouble with the law, and her two young kids had both been put into foster care.

"Drugs," Lorraine said, shaking her head. "If Michelle wasn't already living at home, her parents maybe could have taken the kids, but they have their hands full enough as it is."

The fact that Richard had an expensive condo and a pretty girlfriend in Toronto made him rank pretty high in Mom's books. As far as she was concerned, he was a world removed from the likes of Darius and that must mean she'd done something right.

After our dinner, I made a pot of tea to go with the store-bought cookies I'd put on a plate for dessert. We took our tea and cookies to the living room and sat across from each other, my mom on the new couch and me on the matching plaid armchair.

"It's nice," my mom said, running her hand over the plaid pattern on the couch. "I like the colours."

The material was a mix of blues and greys, with a thin line of green shot through some of the squares. "It was on sale," I said.

"It's perfect," she said. "Fits the space nicely. Oh! Is the dog —"

I turned around to see Champ peeing on a pair of my work boots at the front door. I jumped up. "No, Champ! Don't — ugh." He wagged his tail, staring at me as I rushed over. "Sorry," I muttered to my mom. "He's still being trained."

Mom merely raised her eyebrows, but that tiny flicker of judgement stung the same as if she'd slapped me.

CHAPTER
SIX
·

I HATED MY NEW FURNITURE. The material scratched against my skin and the foam inside the cushions was so firm I may as well have been trying to plop onto a sheet of plywood every time I sat down. I covered the couch with an old throw my mom had given me, which helped with the scratchiness, but did nothing for the overall hardness. The only one who seemed to like the furniture was Champ. I often found him curled up on the chair or the couch with his chin propped on the armrest. He would fall asleep like that, with his little head tipped upward. I didn't stop him from jumping onto the furniture; no one else was using it, so I didn't see why he shouldn't at least enjoy it.

I no longer barricaded him in the kitchen when I was at work since he was soon big enough to jump over the piece of wood I'd been using to block the entrance. He had full access to the house while I was gone and even though I put newspapers out for him in every room, he still peed wherever he felt like it. I got used to checking for puddles when I got home, but I still stepped in one every so often. Mostly he peed under the kitchen table, so that was considerate. My plan was to put in a doggy door, but if

I didn't install one soon, it would be too late to train Champ to use it so he could pee outside. His one saving grace in the toileting department was that he waited for me to take him outside before doing a number two. Although, if I'd been stepping in dog shit every day, I might have been a little quicker with the whole doggy door thing.

"Why don't you put him in the spare bedroom while you're at work?" Mom suggested. "You're not using it for anything else. Then at least he won't be making messes all over the house."

"I don't want to lock him in a little room. Besides, he likes sleeping on the couch. And maybe looking out the window."

My spare bedroom was completely empty. I didn't have any furniture for it, and I didn't really see the need. If I'd had extra stuff lying around, or junk I didn't know what to do with, I guess I would have put it in there, but I didn't hang on to things for no reason. My whole house was a bit spartan that way.

Did I ever imagine the rooms in my house filling up with stuff? With other people's things? Not then. Even when things got serious with Amir, and we were planning a future together, I had no plans for that spare bedroom. Although it became clear soon enough that he did.

It's only been over the last few months that I've imagined any-one in that room, when Jason and I first started talking about moving in together. I have, a few times now, pictured what it would look like as Parker's bedroom — his books scattered on the floor, his stuffed animals lined up on the bed. But back then, when Mom suggested I keep Champ locked up in that room, I'd never given any thought to it one day becoming a child's bedroom.

IT WAS A SUNNY MARCH day after most of the snow in the backyard had melted and when spring felt tantalizingly close that I decided it was finally time to install Champ's doggy door. I didn't know the first thing about how to do it, but I figured it couldn't be all that hard. I knew I had to cut out part of my back door, insert the frame of the doggy door into the opening, then screw the frame into place. All in all, it seemed rather straightforward. Roger lent me his skill saw, which he promised would cut through the wood like a hot knife through butter. After measuring and marking out where I wanted the opening to go, I took my back door off its hinges and laid it on the floor of my garage. When I tried to cut along the straight lines I'd so carefully traced, the saw seemed to follow its own wobbly route and I ended up with far less than perfect cuts. It's too bad I hadn't met Amir before then, because he could have installed that door in five seconds flat and it would have looked a hell of a lot better.

Even though I had measured exactly, the stupid frame for the doggy door wouldn't slide into my cut-out. I tried to bang it in with a hammer, but it wouldn't go. I needed to make the opening bigger, but just by a hair. I didn't like my chances of attempting precision adjustments with the skill saw, but I didn't exactly have any other options so I started cutting slowly, aiming to shave off just a sliver around my jagged opening, perhaps smoothing it out a bit in the process. When I was done, though, the left side veered off at an obvious angle.

I sat back and studied my lopsided cut-out. Something about it brought me back to the afternoon Ricky found me crying in our backyard because I couldn't get the training wheels off my bike. "You're not going to cry about this," I muttered, although the same feeling of ineptness was clawing at me, making my throat thick.

The frame sure slid in now. With room to spare. I marched into town with Champ trotting happily beside me, tied his leash to a tree in front of Canadian Tire, and went inside to buy a tube of caulking. At the end of the day, with a thick line of caulking around the frame of the doggy door, you could hardly see what a hack job I'd done. Besides, it was the back door, which nobody, other than me or my mom, would likely ever see. It's not like I was entertaining hordes of guests on the weekends.

All that was left was to train Champ how to use his new door. First, I had to teach him that he could push through the flap. He wasn't too keen to try it. I stood outside with his bag of treats and called him over and over, but he remained on the other side of the door and barked. I ended up pinning the rubber flap open so that all he had to do was climb through the wide-open hole. I figured that would at least be a start.

Very gingerly, eyeing me with suspicion the whole time, he stepped through the hole. I rewarded him with several treats and an overly enthusiastic rub-down. Then we switched places and I encouraged him to come back through, this time into the house. We repeated this charade again and again. Him walking through the hole, me acting delirious with joy and giving him treats.

Once he'd stopped hesitating and was stepping confidently through the hole, I unpinned the flap and we started all over again. He nosed past the rubber material, pushing his face through the opening, but he wouldn't step all the way through.

"No Champ, your whole body has to come through!" I said, backing farther away from the door, shaking his bag of treats.

Finally, he climbed through and the flap slapped into place behind him. I was so excited that he'd actually done it, I nearly cried. Instead, I went back inside, insisting Champ use his new doggy door to follow me, and I celebrated our success by having a very full glass of white wine.

Life was good. If Champ would just use the doggy door to go outside when he had to pee, we'd be set. Even though we practised using the doggy door every day, I still came home from work to puddles of pee under the table.

"He doesn't know he's not supposed to pee inside," Mom said on one of her visits. "You let him do it for so long."

"He'll learn," I said, and the hope in my voice sounded, at least to me, just like conviction.

"OH, COME ON, CHAMP!" I did my best to sound angry. When he looked up at me hopefully, I dragged him over to where he'd piddled in the back hall, and in the harshest voice I could muster called him a bad dog. Roger had suggested I stick Champ's nose in the pee, but since I figured I was just as much to blame as poor Champ, I didn't have the heart to be that cruel.

"Bad dog!" I repeated, before dragging him by his collar to the doggy door and shoving him through. I made him stay outside, alone, for almost an hour, which I figured was punishment enough to both of us.

Eventually, I think he got the message. There were fewer accidents. And some days, when I came home, Champ would come bursting through his doggy door to meet me, suggesting that he was starting to spend more and more time outside on his own.

I settled into a comfortable routine, working at the plant, then returning to my bungalow where Champ would greet me happily, trailing my feet as I puttered around the kitchen making myself a simple dinner. Walter called one night near the end of April to tell me he was staying in Waterloo for the summer, and I knew, as I listened to him, that we'd never hang out again. He said he planned on coming down to Dunford at least a few times over the course of the summer, and we both pretended like that meant we'd stay friends or stay in touch. I didn't offer to visit him in Waterloo, and he didn't suggest it, either.

This was around the same time that Richard proposed to Lauren, and I remember my brother telling me that he'd known right after meeting her that he was going to marry her.

"Really?" I asked. "How did you know she was the one?"

"I just did," he said. "But I needed to wait for a bit to make double sure. You know, in case something better came along!" He laughed then, and I probably smiled, even though his words didn't strike me as particularly funny. But I said nothing.

A FEW WEEKS LATER, RICKY came down to Dunford and took me out for lunch. It was weird, him inviting me out like that. He didn't want Mom to come, just me, so I had my hackles up as we slid into a booth. I couldn't figure out what he wanted with me. After we'd ordered, and our drinks had been delivered, he lifted his beer to toast my glass.

"Here's to getting married," he said. "The reason I wanted to talk to you is because Lauren and I aren't going all traditional with the wedding. Well, mostly we are, but she wants her brother to stand up with her. Like, she's not having any bridesmaids. Just her brother."

I knew where he was going with this and suddenly it made sense, him asking me to have lunch with him, making nice.

"I know we're not, like, real close, but I wanted to ask if you'd stand up for me. On my side."

"You want me to be your bridesmaid?"

"We're not calling it that. We're not having bridesmaids and groomsmen and all that, just you and her brother, as our — I don't know — as our people."

I wasn't sure what to feel. I mean, I was surprised, and even touched, but part of me wanted nothing to do with standing up beside my brother, championing him in any way. At the same time, this was his wedding and I was his sister. I couldn't exactly refuse.

He must have sensed my hesitation, because he quickly added, "Think how happy it would make Mom. Well, me too, but Mom would really love it."

"Of course," I said. "What do you need me to do?"

"Show up." He laughed.

I'M SURE RICKY BELIEVED HE was truly in love when he got married that first time. The wedding was actually nice. Ricky — Richard — was making good money and his whole lifestyle had shifted into new territory. I was surprised at his success. I sort of assumed other people could see through him the way I could, but people seemed to trust him and he was never short on clients.

When he met Lauren, he was still hosting his own open houses — now he pawns them off on rookie agents, because he has better things to do with his weekends, like sneak around with women named Dee Dee — and Lauren happened to stop by, alone, to see the house he was showing. I don't know exactly how things went from there, but somehow or other Richard ended up with her number and they met for drinks.

Lauren was, and still is, a graphic designer. She was smart, pretty, and single enough for my brother. I'm pretty sure she had a boyfriend at the time, but it wasn't serious or it wasn't going well or something that made it easy enough for Richard to step in, probably looking like a hero in the process. There are multiple versions of how they hooked up, so I'm hazy on the particulars. On the day of their wedding, though, even I was convinced that Richard had done it: gone and found true love.

"I'll have to sell at least three houses, just to pay for your drinks," Ricky told me, clinking his whiskey against my glass of wine. It wasn't the first time he'd mentioned the cost of people's drinks or how many houses he'd need to sell to cover the open bar. I think he wanted everyone to know he was the one paying for it.

"It's not me you should be worried about," I told him. "Your friends are the ones pounding back the hard liquor." I gestured around the reception hall.

Ricky laughed. "Take it easy. I was only joking. Trust me, I can afford this."

Mom was sipping white wine, making polite conversation with Lauren's parents, who were both downing gin and tonics like they might never see another one. I wonder if they already had a foreboding sense that Ricky wasn't going to be the best thing that happened to their daughter. I'll confess that I didn't. And if anyone should have guessed, it was me.

That night, watching Ricky and Lauren holding hands and laughing while they made the rounds of the banquet hall, I truly wished them well. I believed, in spite of everything, that Ricky had finally found a path to happiness. Which meant that it might also be possible for me.

CHAPTER SEVEN

·

AT SOME POINT IN THE night, I get up to take a Sudafed, desperate for some relief from the pain in my sinuses, but also because I've been lying in bed for what feels like hours and I can't sleep. Is Mom lying awake right now too, in the hospital, all alone? I should have gone to see her. Linda said she was talking up a storm, so at the very least I could have spoken to her on the phone. Unless, that is, she didn't want to talk to me. That possibility slices through my heart as I swallow what turns out to be my last Sudafed.

I wish Jason was here right now. Anybody. Someone to tell me everything's going to be okay. But after Jason's strange pause at the end of our phone conversation, I feel like things are weird, even with him. And I don't have anyone else to talk to, anyone else I can lean on.

Pulling my coat on over my pyjamas, I slip out the front door to breathe in the cold night air. Right away, I'm shivering, but I don't go back in. Instead, I shuffle to the sidewalk, where I must look like a lunatic, standing alone on the dark street with my pyjama bottoms flapping around my legs. I wrap my arms around myself, briefly relishing the discomfort of being outside in the frigid air.

It's almost enough to knock the creeping uncertainty and dread from my brain.

The moon, pendulous and full, briefly disappears behind a scrim of clouds. The stars, too, blink out as if they have been erased by a veil of gauze. This hazy sky and the full moon would make for a great photo, if I had the energy to set up my tripod, toy with lighting levels, and wait for just the right diffusion of clouds to scud past the luminescent orb. But I don't. As I stare up at the shifting sky, the night suddenly feels unbearably vast and lonely. Part of me wants to sag onto the wet grass, just let myself fall. I turn around to head back inside. I'm sick. I need to stay warm and get some rest so I can figure out what to do about Mom, and Ricky, and the fact that my life is quite literally falling apart.

I have stood outside in the cold like this before, overwhelmed then, too, with a despair not all that different from what I'm feeling now. How is it that my life keeps cycling back to these kinds of moments? I plod up the path to my front door, trembling with cold or fatigue or emotional weariness, and make my way back to the comforting warmth of my bed.

EVEN AFTER I MOVED INTO my bungalow on Pine Street, I still spent a lot of time on Lindell Drive. I continued helping Mom with some of the bigger chores around her house since she wasn't supposed to do anything too strenuous. Sometimes, in the winter, I'd go to her house twice a day to keep the sidewalk clear. Every so often, while I was shovelling snow, or raking leaves, or mowing the lawn, I would see the family with the twins that had moved into the Nessors' house. The boys were practically teenagers, all gangly arms and legs, while the mom looked the same to me under her cloud of poufy hair. Other than those brief sightings, though, the street was lifeless and quiet.

I took Champ with me whenever I went to Lindell Drive. He was still technically a puppy, but had grown into his full size and his head reached almost to my waist. He was a big dog. While I worked outside, he would bound around me in circles, leaping playfully across the front lawn. Often, he would go racing down the sidewalk before looping back again, barking with reckless abandon.

"I don't know if you should let him run loose like that," Mom said. "Shouldn't he be on a leash?"

"He needs to run around," I replied. "He won't do anything to anyone."

"Well, they don't know that."

Had it always been so easy for her to find fault with me? "He's fine," I said firmly.

WALTER CAME BACK TO DUNFORD a few more times, but we never hung out in his basement the way we used to. His parents got rid of the foosball table, he said, as if that was reason enough to avoid spending too much time together. He could have come to my place, but that seemed weird too. Almost formal. We tried, I think, to recapture something of our one-time friendship, but our conversations seemed to require too much effort and even going to Ice Cream Island together felt forced. Eventually, he stopped calling and I heard from his dad that he had a girlfriend in Waterloo. I was kind of surprised Walter hadn't told me that himself. I figured either he wasn't all that serious about this girl, or I had officially been reduced to a person not worth telling.

I had new friends, anyway. Not friends so much as people I spent time with. Guys from work. They'd started inviting me out for lunch at Mackie's or a group of us would go out after work for beers. At first, they treated me differently, because I was the token girl in the group, but after a while I think they started to view me as one of them rather than potential dating material. On top of that, Roger and his wife invited me over for dinner at least once a month. It didn't occur to me to think it was strange that I didn't have any close girlfriends; I was comfortable being one of the guys, where everything stayed at a surface level.

When I wasn't working, I mostly hung out at home, with Champ. I didn't — at least, not at the time — consider myself lonely. In addition to my dog and the guys from work, I had Mom, so my life felt full enough. And as far as a welcoming committee went, Champ was one of the best. As soon as I opened the front door, he would bark out a joyful greeting and come skidding across the hardwood to meet me.

Then one Friday, I came home from work to an ominously empty house. I knew Champ spent a lot of time outside, but even when he was in the backyard, he always heard my car and would come crashing through his doggy door before I'd finished opening the front door. But that Friday, after I'd shut the door behind me, the house remained silent.

I opened the back door and called his name. Nothing. The yard was clearly empty. Heart thumping, I walked to the side of the house, to see if the gate was open. It wasn't. I jogged back into the house and checked the bedrooms and even the bathroom, thinking he might be sleeping or sick, but every room I looked in was empty.

"Champ!" I called over and over, as if he might spontaneously appear out of thin air.

Mom was on her way over for dinner and when her car pulled up to the curb, before she'd even climbed out, I ran to meet her. "What's the matter?" she asked, alarm flitting across her face.

"I can't find Champ," I said. "He wasn't here when I came home."

Mom looked around helplessly. "Did he run away?"

"I don't know," I said. "The gate was closed. Maybe someone took him. Who would steal a dog?" And as soon as I said the words, something about my voice, and the panic spreading through my chest, reminded me of Mrs. Nessor on that awful day when I told her that I'd seen her little girl get into a car. I remembered her eyes and the way her hands fluttered at her sides.

"I'm sure no one took him," Mom said. "He probably got out of the yard somehow and is off exploring. Where would he go if he got out?"

"I don't know!" I cried. "He could be anywhere! Champ! Champ! Come here, boy." I was standing on the road beside Mom's car, scanning the street for any sign of my dog: an excited bark in the distance, a glimpse of his tan-coloured fur streaking toward me. But there was nothing. Just me and my mom, standing beside her open car door, staring around in disbelief.

After too long a pause, Mom reached into her car for the Crock-Pot of chili she had prepared. "Here, plug this in," she instructed me. "Then we'll go for a walk and look for Champ. He'll likely make his own way home as soon as he realizes he's hungry. I bet he'll be waiting at the house for us by the time we get back."

Mom's practicality made me relax slightly. She was probably right. Then again, Mrs. Nessor had also been soothed by my mother's calm assurances and that situation hadn't turned out fine at all. If Champ was hurt, or worse, dead, I would never forgive the person who did it. I would never forgive myself.

We walked down to the park by the river, where I thought Champ would most likely head given the choice, since that's where we usually went for our walks. It was cool out and Mom wasn't dressed for being outside. She was wearing a thin coat and I could tell from the way she was hugging herself that she was cold. The ground was littered with leaves and I thought about how just the other day Champ had dug his face into them, snapping his teeth with joy.

"Why don't you head back?" I suggested. "I want to check a few more places."

I went everywhere I could think of, calling Champ's name until I was almost hoarse. All the while, I was harbouring the hope that he was already at home, waiting with Mom for me to return. I trudged up my front walk, listening for his telltale bark, but was met with the same empty silence as before.

"No luck?" Mom said, as I kicked off my shoes.

I shook my head. It was stupid, to be this upset over a dog. I wasn't thinking clearly. I hadn't even called the humane society. If anyone had found him out wandering, they probably would have brought him there. "I'm going to call the pound," I said. "Maybe they have him."

They didn't. But after taking his description, they promised to call me if anyone brought him in. I went back to the yard and in the growing dark checked all around the fence. Sure enough, there was a hole near the side of the house. How had I never noticed it before? He must have been digging it for a while.

"I know how he got out," I told Mom as she filled a bowl for me with chili. "He dug a hole under the fence."

"Well, that's better than thinking someone stole him," she replied. And again, I thought about Amy's mom spending that first night without her daughter, knowing that little Amy hadn't simply wandered off, but had been taken.

I ate Mom's chili standing up at the counter, restless, anxious to be back outside looking for Champ. I'd put a bowl of his food on the front porch, hoping for what? That he'd be hungry enough to smell it and return to me? If he'd been able to come home, he would be here already. I had no doubt about that.

Mom stayed a bit longer while I went out searching again. As the remaining light faded from the sky, my mood became blacker and blacker. I didn't see how I would be able to sleep knowing Champ was out there in the dark. I couldn't look at his mat beside my bed. After Mom went home, I stayed out on the front porch, sitting beside Champ's untouched bowl of food.

Eventually, I went inside. I left the gate to the backyard propped open so that if Champ returned, he could find his way in. I opened my bedroom window, despite how cold it had become, and fell asleep straining for sounds from the street. I woke often. And just as I had when I was younger, I left the lamp beside my bed turned on. I dozed on and off throughout the long, slow night of shifting shadows.

As I lay in the half-dark, wavering fitfully between sleep and wakefulness, I hated my brother with a new ferocity. I could feel my hatred for him burning at the base of my skull, and for the first time in a long time, I wanted to punch somebody. Not just somebody. Ricky. Richard. I wanted to punch my brother until his face turned to pulp. I wanted to rip his limbs, one by one, from his body and listen to him scream.

And I wanted Mom to know why I was doing it.

CHAPTER
EIGHT
·

THE SATURDAY MORNING AFTER CHAMP went missing, I called
Mom. "What did you do with all of Ricky's stuff?" I asked. No pre-
amble, no explanation as to where this was coming from.

"What stuff?" Mom replied. She'd already asked if Champ had
come back in the night and I'd been terse when I said no. Now I
was interrogating her.

"When he moved out. When he went to Leeville. Didn't he leave
any boxes or anything in the basement?"

"If he did, I'm sure he has them now. I don't have anything of his
anymore. Why?"

"I was just curious. He used to have a bunch of my Barbies and I
wondered what happened to them, that's all."

There was a slight pause. "Why would Ricky have your
Barbies?"

"I don't know. He took them. I saw them in his room once when
we were kids. Don't worry about it. It's not important."

But it was. I wanted to know where those Barbies were.

AFTER TALKING TO MOM, I headed outside, re-tracing my steps from the previous night. I walked beside the muddy Still River, calling Champ's name over and over, all the while fighting to ignore the despair that was ballooning in my chest. I checked back at the house, in case he was there, then headed out again, this time in my car. I drove all the way to Leeville and then in the opposite direction to Boelen. I'd already walked the entire length of Old Canal Road, but I returned in the car and bumped slowly along the rutted route, thinking about the dog that Ricky and Darius hit when they were teenagers. Did they have any clue what they'd taken away from that dog's owner?

Champ's not dead, I told myself. *This isn't the same.*

I spent a good chunk of the afternoon moping around my house, hoping that Champ would miraculously re-appear. I forced myself to eat a peanut butter sandwich for dinner, but I wasn't hungry and each bite was difficult to swallow. Then, exhausted, both mentally and physically, I went to bed praying for my dog to come home.

I woke to a sound outside the window I'd once again left open. I knew that sound, and my heart pounded with excitement and relief. I got up slowly; my limbs were oddly sluggish, and as much as I wanted to race to the front door, it was as if I was wading through water. When I finally pulled open the door, I knew without looking that he was already gone. I had taken too long. Something moved in the darkness in front of me and I could just make out a shape on the bottom step of my porch. I squinted into the gloom, then stifled a scream. Standing there, staring up at me solemnly, was a little girl holding something in her outstretched arm. It was Amy Nessor, offering me her severed braid.

I woke for real in a cold sweat. I sat up, grateful for the light beside my bed, and listened to the noises from the street for a few minutes, until my heart resumed its normal beating.

"Champ?" I whispered into the still, night air. Foolishly, I refused to go near my open window, although I was desperate to shut it. "Champ, where are you, boy?"

SUNDAY WAS MUCH OF THE same. I drove for hours searching along the rural roads outside of Dunford. I went all the way to Leeville, back to the parking lot at Leon's where I'd first found Champ. I sat in my car and cursed myself for not posting pictures around town the minute I noticed he was missing. When I got back to my house, all I wanted to do was curl into a ball and hide from the rage and hopelessness that were washing over me in waves.

I had thrown myself face-down on my bed when the phone rang. I assumed it was my mom again, calling to see if there was any news, and I moved reluctantly to answer it.

"Hi, is this Zoe? It's the Dunford Humane Society calling. We just had a dog brought in that matches the description you gave us."

I didn't let myself believe it could really be Champ, but when I was shown to the kennels, sure enough, there he was, staring at me, wagging his tail like a maniac.

"A woman found him on her back deck. You're lucky she brought him here," the staff member who'd escorted me to the kennels said. "She lives halfway to Port Sitsworth and could just as easily have brought him there."

As soon as the kennel door was opened, Champ bounded over to me. "Where have you been, you crazy mutt?" I asked him, kneeling down so he could lick my face. "I was so worried about you!"

The staff member — Katie, according to her nametag — stood to the side while Champ and I had our little reunion. "I think he's just as happy to see you as you are to see him," she commented while I clipped on his leash and led him back to the reception area.

No one knew where Champ had spent the two nights that passed before he showed up on that woman's deck, or how or what he ate, but he didn't seem too much the worse for wear. His fur was caked with dirt — that was all. No broken bones, no cuts, no scratches even.

I paid the recovery fee, thanking Katie profusely, as if she was single-handedly responsible for reuniting me with my dog, then took Champ home. My heart felt bloated, it was so swollen with relief. I called Mom right away.

"Have you fixed the hole under your fence?" she asked.

"Not yet. I thought maybe he'd try to sneak in the same way he left." But now that he was back, I needed to fix it, and soon. I also needed to find a way to keep Champ from digging any new holes. I wasn't sure I could survive losing him again.

I came up with a plan to create an underground barrier that I hoped would prevent Champ from ever escaping again. I reinforced the entire perimeter of my backyard with chicken wire that extended from the bottom of my fence two feet into the ground. It was a long, slow project that took me an entire week, in the fading light after work, to complete. During that week, I sealed Champ's doggy door and asked Mom to come over in the afternoons while I was at work to let him outside, supervised. Amazingly, during the time that he was trapped in the house, he didn't have a single accident. Not one. But as soon as the backyard project was done, and he was expected to use his doggy door to get outside on his own, he peed on the floor right in front of the back door.

I loved that dog, but damn he could be annoying.

WHENEVER MOM TALKED ABOUT US, her kids, to other people, she would go on and on about Richard's success in real estate and his life in Toronto. Her big-city son. I wanted to remind her that when Ricky was my age, he was working at the Future Shop in Leeville, renting a room in a disgusting house, but I guess my accomplishments paled in comparison to her shiny firstborn with his embossed business cards and expensive suits. Plus, he had Lauren.

Even Walter's girlfriend turned out to be more than a fleeting interest. He brought her to Dunford to meet his parents, which suggested a seriousness I hadn't anticipated when his dad first mentioned the fact of her existence. Walter actually stopped by to introduce her to me, which completely shocked me given how little we talked anymore. Maybe he wanted to flaunt her in my face, but I couldn't see why there'd be any point to that, so I invited them in and we sat in my living room awkwardly trying to come up with things to say.

"I won't be in Dunford over the Christmas break this year," Walter told me. "I'm going to Vancouver with Jiwan."

"Oh? Wow. So, obviously that's where you're from," I said, turning to face Jiwan.

She nodded. My impression was that she was shy and sweet. I could see why Walter was drawn to her. Like him, she was studying math, so in addition to being very quiet, they probably had a lot in common. I imagined the two of them bending their heads together to solve complex equations as a way of getting turned on. It was uncharitable of me, to think of my former best friend and his girlfriend as such ridiculous stereotypes, but, with Jiwan in the picture, Walter really had no use left for me. After that visit, we fell out of touch completely. If he did come back to Dunford to see his parents, he never bothered telling me.

His parents built a house out on Lake Erie and, once they left town, any news of him I might have gathered vanished. I figured he'd graduated, but for all I knew, he had up and married Jiwan and was living in British Columbia. Or, they'd broken up, and he was living in his parents' basement out at the lake. We had become less than strangers; we no longer existed for each other at all.

Yet there I was, still in Dunford, still working at the plant, and still single. Bobby, one of the guys I worked with, cornered me at the coffee machine one day. "Hey Zoe, would you ever consider going on a date with my nephew? He's a nice guy and I think you'd get along real good."

"Uh ..."

"His name's Jonathan. He lives out in Boelen. Works as a bartender right now, but wants to open a hockey camp for kids one day."

I didn't know how to say no to Bobby without seeming rude, so I agreed to meet Jonathan for coffee at the Dunford Donut Diner.

"You're perfect for each other," Bobby said. "You're down to earth and not all prissy like the girls he usually dates. I swear, they may be pretty, but not much between the ears, if you know what I mean."

I wasn't sure how to take that, but I was interested in the idea of meeting someone new. I was beginning to worry about my single status. Tommy was the only person I'd ever dated, and we'd never done more than grope each other with our clothes on. In the last six years, I hadn't met anyone worth dating in Dunford, and I didn't have the energy, or the desire, to start going to bars in Leeville or anywhere else so random strangers could hit on me. At the same time, I didn't exactly want to turn into an old maid who'd never had sex either.

I got to the Donut Diner ahead of schedule and then wasn't sure what to do. Should I get a table? Would it look strange if I was sitting at a table without having ordered anything? But if I ordered before he arrived, that would be rude, wouldn't it? I was sort of hovering by the doors, trying to make up my mind about what to do, when a cute guy in a navy sport coat glanced in my direction.

"Jonathan?" I asked, although I knew from the picture Bobby had shown me that it had to be him.

"That's me. You must be Zoe." He laughed. "Nice to meet you." He stuck out his hand and I shook it awkwardly before we stepped into line to order. "Uncle Bob kept telling me there was someone at work he wanted me to meet and at first I thought he was kidding around, but here we are!"

At first glance, I was glad I'd agreed to meet Jonathan. He had an athletic build and a sweet smile. I could immediately see why women would be attracted to him. My worry was that if he usually dated girly girls, like Bob had hinted at, he would quickly be disappointed by me.

While we were sitting across from each other in one of the booths, with our Donut Diner mugs positioned in front of us like chess pieces, I wondered if Jonathan was as nervous as I was. Most of my conversations, outside of work, were with Champ or my mother. I didn't exactly have a rip-roaring social life.

More quickly than I expected, I relaxed enough to enjoy myself. Jonathan was easy to talk to and I kept looking at his arms wondering what it would feel like to have them wrapped protectively around me. Or to snuggle up against his broad chest. When we agreed to exchange numbers, my hand was shaking as I wrote on the napkin, and for a minute, I almost forgot my phone number. Quite apart from the sexual attraction I felt, I was aware of a tiny thrill at the prospect of telling Mom I had met someone.

We slept together on our third date. I expected it to be more momentous — not as rushed and clumsy as it turned out to be. Jonathan didn't know how inexperienced I was and I didn't feel the need to volunteer the fact that I had been, up until that point, a virgin.

I did wish, after that night, that I had someone to talk to about sex. It's not like I could call up Walter and ask him anything, despite the easy understanding we used to share — all those conversations on his front porch or in the basement with the foosball table as a convenient and constant diversion. I needed advice, or reassurance, but had no one to turn to, and I sure as hell wasn't going to ask my mom for pointers.

Eventually, I began to feel more natural about the physical aspects of our relationship although I think Jonathan would argue that he did most of the initiating. It was a good period of my life. I had a job, a house, a dog, and a boyfriend. I felt almost normal.

"DID YOU KNOW RICHARD MOVED OUT?" Mom practically shouted at me. "Lauren just told me."

I moved the phone away from my ear. Ricky and Lauren were one week away from their fourth wedding anniversary. Mom was practically in hysterics.

"She doesn't even know where he's staying! I just can't understand it."

I could. Ricky had already told me all about Erika and how he was in love with her. Since meeting her, he said, his life with Lauren had begun to feel like a lie. I wasn't surprised to hear he'd finally left Lauren, and I could guess exactly where he was staying. What I didn't anticipate was how upset Mom would be about the whole thing. For what seemed like the first time in a long time, I felt the weight of her affections shift, and I became the golden child. The favoured one.

The only problem was that things were fizzling between me and Jonathan, too. We'd been dating for a few months, but lately we'd seen less and less of each other. It was hard for me to spend any amount of extended time at his place in Boelen because of Champ, but he didn't exactly like staying at my place either.

"Ugh. Your dog peed in the kitchen again!" he would call out, making no effort to hide his disgust.

When he stayed over, Champ was ejected from my room and it was hard to concentrate on Jonathan with the dog whining outside the door. It wasn't just the peeing in the house that bugged Jonathan, he complained about the dog hair and the smell, too.

Given how much he didn't like being at my house, I was surprised when Jonathan invited himself over one afternoon. Thinking he must have missed me because we hadn't seen each other in a few days, I was preparing to tease him, but when I opened the door, he greeted me with a half-hearted smile that already felt like an apology.

"This is a surprise," I said. "You want a drink?" I was unnerved by his sad smile.

"Maybe just water."

I sent Champ outside, blocking off his doggy door so he couldn't get back in, and grabbed two waters. When I carried the drinks to the living room, Jonathan was perched stiffly on the edge of my plaid couch.

"Here you go," I said, setting his glass on the coffee table. I briefly considered sitting next to him, but then opted for the armchair, a safe distance away.

Jonathan took a long sip of water. "Zoe," he finally said, "I don't think this is working."

I could hear Champ barking at the back door. Even though it was a beautiful day, he didn't want to be outside. He wanted to be near me. I fought the urge to get up and let him in. "Okay," I said slowly. "You mean us, obviously. Are you breaking up with me?"

"It's just — we don't —"

"You don't need to explain." I shook my head and stared at the glass in my hands. Was I upset? I couldn't tell. The thought that I would miss sleeping with Jonathan briefly flashed through my mind.

"But I want to explain. Zoe, I like you, I really do, but it's more like we're good friends than two people who are in love with each other."

In love. Wow. Had he been waiting for me to tell him that I loved him? We'd only been dating a few months for Pete's sake. Maybe that was the problem. Maybe after a few months most people knew whether or not they were in love.

"So you think something's missing." I was a bit surprised, to be honest, that Jonathan had summoned up the nerve to drive all the way to Dunford just to break up with me. This was a guy who talked all the time about creating some sort of camp for kids who couldn't afford to play hockey, but had never taken any steps to making that plan a reality. He struck me as someone who wanted more, but who didn't have the wherewithal to go out and do anything about it. I must have sucked as a girlfriend more than I realized.

"I can't even tell if you want to see me half the time. It's like you agree out of politeness. Even now. Do you care that I'm breaking up with you? Are you even going to try to talk me out of it?"

"What do you want me to do, Jonathan? Beg? If it's not working, it's not working. I mean, I am sorry you want to end things, but I agree things haven't been great lately."

Jonathan nodded, then stood up. "So that's it, then?"

I stood too. "I guess so."

He carried his glass back to the kitchen and dumped the water into the sink. He paused there for an extra second and I wanted to tiptoe up behind him, to wrap my arms around his thick torso one last time. He turned around and walked past me to the front door. I did go to him, then. He took my head in both hands and kissed me softly on the lips. It was such a sad, gentle kiss that I felt my indifference waver. But before I could say anything or really react, he had let go of me and was reaching for the door.

I watched him walk to his car. He gave me a little wave before climbing in and driving away. I walked back through my house, wondering how disappointed Mom would be when she found out I'd been dumped. I opened the back door to let Champ in. He had given up barking and was lying in the sun. As soon as he saw me, he leaped up and rushed over. He sniffed my hand which was hanging at my side and stared up at me with absolute understanding.

I wasn't really sad. Just sort of let down. Like after you see a movie that didn't quite live up to your expectations. Champ followed me inside and lay down at my feet, while I sat in the armchair and finished my water, the golden child no more.

CHAPTER
NINE
·

WHEN I CRAWL BACK INTO my bed after my stupid stint on the sidewalk where I likely made myself even sicker standing out in the cold staring at the moon, I still can't sleep. It seems impossible that just two nights ago I thought Jason was going to propose. And to be honest, following our dinner at The Crow's Nest, the thought did cross my mind that if Mom found out about Ricky and Dee Dee, then found out that Jason and I were getting engaged, I would slip right back into the better offspring slot. But after the news about the Amy Nessor case, not to mention Mom's heart attack, such petty thoughts have all but been erased. I am more concerned with survival — not just for Mom, for all of us.

In the past, Mom has always been quick to forgive Ricky. After his marriage to Lauren ended — which definitely upset Mom — it didn't take her long to warm to Erika, and soon it was as if Ricky had never done any wrong. She didn't even fault him when he chose to marry Erika at a private beach ceremony in Mexico — no family, just the two of them.

"Isn't this nice?" she asked me, after they'd come back and we were driving to Toronto to see the pictures. "Erika said she made a slideshow."

When we got to their house, Mom cozied up on the couch with Erika and her laptop while I stood off to the side, faking half-hearted interest. Ricky was tanned and smug. He'd seen the pictures enough times, he said, so he didn't need to look at them again.

Erika was a good-looking woman; I had to give my brother that. And she seemed genuinely nice, not at all stuck-up or full of herself. I liked Erika, but I still felt bad for Lauren because I liked her, too. I could see why my brother had fallen for Erika, though. Not only was she gorgeous, she was smart, friendly, and apparently a kick-ass volleyball player. I didn't want to like her, out of loyalty to Lauren, but just as she instantly had my mom under her spell, I couldn't seem to fight her pull either. In a sense, I guess I was pretty quick to forgive my brother, too.

"If you ever decide to tie the knot," Ricky said to me while Mom was oohing and aahing over the photos, "I totally recommend a destination wedding. Take out all the people and other crap and getting married's not so bad!"

Judging by my failed romance with Jonathan, and my barren dating history both before and after, I didn't think it likely that I would ever get married, destination wedding or otherwise.

"You're giving out marriage advice now?" I asked.

Mom looked up at me. "When Zoe gets married, she'd better do it where I can see it! Pictures are all fine and good, but I'd rather be there for the real thing."

I took her comment to mean she wouldn't really believe it had happened unless she personally witnessed it. Apparently, the idea of me getting married must have seemed rather fantastical to her, too.

"Don't worry, Mom. I'll make sure you have a front-row seat," I assured her.

My brother raised his eyebrows. "Ah, is there something we should know? Or rather someone we should know about?"

Everyone was looking at me now. "No," I said quickly. "Unless there's someone I don't know about yet."

Ricky laughed loudly and slapped me on the shoulder. "You need to get out of Dunford," he said. "Who are you ever going to meet there?"

Indeed.

"WHY DO YOU HAVE TO work Christmas Day?" Mom asked, when she found out I wouldn't be able to join her for our traditional turkey dinner. "You worked on Thanksgiving, too! Someone else should take a turn. It's not fair that you get stuck working all the holidays."

"I volunteered," I said. "Other people have kids and stuff. It doesn't make any difference to me, so I might as well help them out."

"You have a mother!" she admonished. "You have family too, you know."

"I get paid time and half on the holidays. We can eat our turkey any other day."

"It's not the same," she sniffed. "It means I have to sit around all by myself on Christmas now. My son too far away to make the effort, my daughter too selfish!"

"Selfish? How is me offering to work on Christmas selfish? I'm doing it so other people can actually spend Christmas with their kids and their wives."

"Well, maybe I'd like to spend Christmas with one of my kids!"

"I'm not a kid anymore. It's different and you know it."

It wasn't as if I liked the idea of having nothing better to do on the holidays. Besides, Mom wasn't going to sit around by herself like she claimed. She had plenty of friends who, when they heard she had no one to spend the day with, would promptly invite her to join them. I wasn't so lucky.

I showed up for my shift on Christmas Day wearing a green sweater, which was my way of being festive. There were only four of us working and no one was particularly happy about being there — including me. To top it off, the weather was crappy: windy, cold, and wet.

Instead of sitting in front of a fireplace drinking eggnog, I was stuck in a building where the cold cement walls only mirrored the dreary atmosphere outside. Grey. Damp. Heavy. Even the stupid bits of tinsel strung up in the lunchroom looked pathetic. George O'Brien, the Super assigned to the Christmas shift was nursing a hangover. He disappeared into his office and we didn't see him until after lunch when he emerged onto the floor bleary-eyed and rumpled.

"All rested up?" David asked him. "Do we get to take turns having naps today?"

"We can take turns getting fired," O'Brien said. "Or we can all shut up and get the hell to work."

David raised his eyebrows at me, but I kept my mouth shut. That was the one thing I was good at: keeping silent.

JANUARY BROUGHT WITH IT MUCH colder temperatures, and every time it snowed, the same people who had been praying for snow in December began complaining. My mother prime among them.

"You can't keep coming here in the morning to shovel me out," she said. "I'm going to hire someone. Besides, as soon as you're gone, the sidewalk just gets covered again. I've never seen so much snow!"

"It's like this every year. And you say the same thing every year."

"I do not! And there is more snow this year. I heard them talking about it on the radio. We've had a record snowfall for January."

I didn't mind the record snowfall. There was something immensely satisfying to me about shovelling out a driveway and sidewalk in neat, precise rows. My mind would numb as I lifted shovelful after shovelful of heavy snow, muscles burning in the cold. Often, I kept going, shovelling out the houses on either side of me. Then I'd get in the truck with Champ and head over to do Mom's.

When I got home from work, depending on how much it had snowed during the day, I would head outside and do it all over again. My one neighbour, an older man who had recently had knee surgery, gave me a bottle of Baileys as a thank you. On many nights, I poured myself a healthy portion, over ice, to enjoy with whatever I'd thrown together for dinner. Usually I took my food to the living room and watched TV while I ate. Mom never let us eat in front of the TV growing up and I still felt a flicker of defiance every time I balanced my plate on my lap and turned my body to face the screen.

When I was done eating, like a good girl, I dutifully carried my dishes to the kitchen and washed them. At the very least, Mom could not find fault with me there. My kitchen was spotless. Then, knowing that I would likely be up early to start shovelling, I made sure not to stay up too late.

Sometimes I went to bed just to escape my own company.

WHEN RICKY ANNOUNCED TO ME that he was going to be a father, I felt nauseous. But since I genuinely liked Erika, for her sake, I tried to be happy. It's actually strange when you think about it: I've liked all of my brother's wives. At any rate, when Leah was born, like any good sister, I went with Mom to meet the baby. I congratulated my brother with an awkward half-hug and followed him to the living room where his jaundiced daughter was lying in a bassinet by the window. Her yellow skin was dry and wrinkled.

"Isn't she beautiful?" Ricky asked.

I nodded, all the while wondering how he felt about his baby being a girl. Did seeing her cause regret to pool around his heart, giving him the sensation of slowly drowning? Even though I'd tried for years to disconnect any memories of Amy Nessor from my brother, the idea of him having his own little girl seemed wrong to me. I didn't want to think about it, but I couldn't ignore the unease that crawled up my spine after seeing Leah for the first time. Ricky looked happy enough, though. Erika, less so. She looked exhausted. Defeated.

Erika started to stand as soon as she saw us, but my mom stopped her with a hand. "No, no. Don't get up. You just sit tight and relax. Goodness knows you need it."

"Do you want to hold her?" Ricky asked Mom.

"Oh, can I?"

I excused myself to use the bathroom, then stood in front of the mirror trying to even out my breathing. When I returned to the living room, Mom was sitting beside Erika, with Leah bundled in her arms. She looked so happy, gazing down at her grand-daughter, and I couldn't help but contrast the expression on her face with the one on Erika's.

The thought struck me then and there that it wouldn't be long before Ricky started screwing around again. If he hadn't already. And yet all Mom saw was the miracle of Ricky's little girl and how much joy that tiny wrapped up bundle of pink was going to bring her.

I was twenty-seven when Ricky became a dad, and a little worried about my own prospects regarding having a family. And here was Ricky, my jerk of a brother, on his second wife, and now with a baby to boot. I felt sorry for Erika. Partly because she looked so awful and partly because now she was irrevocably tied to my brother, no matter how things turned out for the two of them. Even if she wanted to, she would never be truly free of Ricky.

Mom was all smiles. She was so proud of her son, you could tell. On that day, everything was forgiven. The past, the heartaches, every single little disappointment.

Which is why I believe she might also finally forgive me for the way things ended with Amir if I actually end up marrying Jason. Amir and I were never married — unlike Ricky and Lauren and Erika and now Brenda — but that small fact makes no difference to Mom. "You were engaged," she says. "That's as good as married in my books."

But when Leah was born, I was still disappointingly single, and had been for a long time. I was years away from even meeting Amir, and all of Mom's energy was focused on Ricky and Erika and the new life they had brought into being. You would think they were the first humans to procreate, the way she went on.

I had a very different reaction. Whenever I looked at Leah, my heart thudded with guilt. And fear.

PART
FOUR

CHAPTER
ONE
·

ON WEDNESDAY MORNING, AFTER MY horrible sleepless night, even though I know I'm not expected to be at work, I get up early. I check with Bruce to make sure he found someone to cover for me, then warn him that he should probably find someone for tomorrow, too.

"My interview is on Friday," I say. "So, I guess I have to be better by then."

He doesn't say it, but I can imagine what he's thinking: I'm not doing myself any favours as far as Crystal Clear Solutions is concerned.

"Yeah, get on that, would ya?" he jokes.

He makes no mention of rescheduling the interview. I don't ask about the possibility either because, quite frankly, Friday feels so far away. Anything could happen between now and then. By Friday, my tidy little life could be blown completely to bits.

I don't want to leave the house, but I need more Sudafed. And maybe some NeoCitran. My goal is to stock up on enough cold and sinus medication to be able to sink into drug-induced oblivion. Later, when I've had some much-needed rest, I'll talk to

Ricky properly. And Mom. And Jason. I have to talk to Jason. To warn him.

Stofer's Pharmacy isn't far from my house, but I don't have the energy to walk. I park right out front and just as I'm stepping around the hood of my car, I hear my name.

"Zoe?"

I look up and for a second I think I must be hallucinating. Amir is standing outside the door of the pharmacy. At first, I am too stunned to speak. Finally, I say, "Amir. I — I didn't know you were here. In town, I mean. Hi. Wow." We're standing next to each other now and he's looking at me with a quizzical expression that could just be surprise, but I also think he's expecting me to say something else and I'm just staring back at him, my arms hanging uselessly at my sides. "I'd shake your hand or hug you or whatever, but I'm sick," I say. "Sorry. Wow. I don't really know what to say. I —"

"I thought I might run into you, but I didn't think you'd be one of the first people I saw," Amir says. "I just got in last night. I'm here for a bit to help out my aunt."

"Right. I heard ... about your aunt. Mom mentioned it. How is she? How are *you*?" My legs are trembling and I can feel my nose about to drip, but perversely I make no move to end the conversation.

Amir looks at me steadily for a minute. "I'm good." He lifts the paper bag in his hand as if just remembering he's holding it and adds, "I should run, though. Aunt Maureen's waiting for this."

"Of course," I say. I motion to the pharmacy door. "I need to get in there myself."

He nods. "It was nice seeing you, Zoe. And I mean that." Then he is walking away from me and I enter the pharmacy completely disoriented.

MOM CALLS JUST BEFORE TEN. I don't hear her message until much later though, because I am asleep when she leaves it. As I listen to her breathless recording, my heart starts racing.

"Hi Zoe. They sent me home a few hours ago and you'll never believe what I just found out. Call me as soon as you can, okay?" Her voice sounds urgent, but not panicked. She does not sound like a woman who just had a heart attack, which should be reassuring, and if her message has anything to do with Amy Nessor, she shouldn't sound so excited. She must have seen the news about Darius, though. I'm still half-convinced that's what caused her to have a heart attack in the first place. But then why hasn't she mentioned the case to me yet? You'd think from the first moment the news aired she'd be calling to ask if I'd seen it. Unless, like me, she's biting her tongue, just waiting for the hammer to drop. But then, if that were true, she wouldn't be calling now, with this voice, this breathless excitement.

I'm relieved she's home from the hospital. Even though she sounds fine, I can still taste the panic from Linda telling me about her heart attack. How did she get home? Did she ask Linda to come and get her? Why in god's name wouldn't she have called me? It's almost like she's avoiding me as much as I'm avoiding ... well, everyone. After hearing her message, I decide to ignore it for just a bit longer. I'm not ready to talk.

It's been a few hours since my last Sudafed so I head into the kitchen to get another one. My head feels groggy from all the medication I'm taking, but it beats the otherwise constant pressure behind my face. As I struggle to remove one of the capsules from its foil packaging, I relive my surreal encounter with Amir. I may be getting good at ignoring a lot of things right now, but I'm sure as hell not doing a very good job suppressing the flurry of feelings stirred up by his unexpected appearance.

He looks almost the same as I remember, except his hair is a bit longer, and there are hints of grey at the temples. His face still has that openness, those kind eyes that radiate warmth. Where has he been living? How long is he planning on staying? I should have asked more questions, but I was caught off-guard by the sight of him and the moment was so rushed. He was in such a hurry to get away from me, or was I the one in a hurry?

I look down at the track pants I'm wearing and wonder what kind of impression I made. Did he notice my bedraggled appearance? When I was with him, I made more of an effort. He always looked so put together, so effortlessly fashionable, that I started paying more attention to my wardrobe. He was good at picking out things that would look good on me, too. I remember asking his opinion about what kind of shoes to wear with what pants, what top to wear. Did I mention to him this morning that I was sick? I'd hate for him to think I'm always such a mess now. He probably figured it out, seeing as I was heading into the pharmacy. I bet his first thought was how terrible I looked. This bugs me more than it should.

I swallow the Sudafed and head back to my uncomfortable couch. It's times like this that I miss having a dog. If Champ were still alive, he'd be keeping me company right now. He'd rest his head on my knee and let me know, with his big, trusting eyes, that he understood. He was the only one who ever completely did.

THE FIRST TIME CHAMP HAD a seizure, I was sitting on the back deck with him, drinking a cooler, enjoying the feel of the warm sun on my skin, when his legs jerked out from under him and he started convulsing. The seizure only lasted a few seconds, but it scared the crap out of me. After he'd stopped shaking, he just lay there on the deck, panting, staring up at me.

I scooped his large body into my arms and carried him through the gate to the front lawn. I set him down and ran back to the house for my keys, tripping over my own feet. It wasn't far to the vet's office, but every time I had to slow down to make a turn or stop at an intersection, it felt like a hand was closing around my throat.

I explained to Dr. Ruigrok what had happened.

"How old is he?"

"Ten."

Dr. Ruigrok nodded and after a physical examination and six hundred dollars' worth of tests she informed me that Champ was suffering from kidney failure.

"Without an MRI or CT, I can't be certain that the kidney failure is what caused his seizure, but ultimately his prognosis is very poor. I can refer you to a specialist for further investigation or we can try outpatient care with specialized food and medication which may not help, but may buy him some time." Dr. Ruigrok waited for a moment, then left me alone with Champ to consider what she'd just said.

I stood beside the metal examination table scratching Champ's head, murmuring over and over to him what a good dog he was. Eventually, I lifted him down and set him gently on the ground. He wagged his tail and followed me to the reception desk where I told the woman sitting there that I wanted the special food and medication Dr. Ruigrok had recommended.

Dr. Ruigrok appeared behind her. "You understand that this is a palliative measure," she said. "It won't fix or reverse his condition."

"I know," I said. "I still want it."

On the short ride home, Champ seemed unusually subdued, as if he understood everything Dr. Ruigrok had said about him and his chances. I called Mom to tell her what had happened, looking for some reassurance, or maybe some sympathy.

"You should put him down," she said, and before she could say anything else, I hung up. She never really loved Champ. Like Jonathan, she was put off by the fact that he sometimes still peed inside the house and she thought he was clingy.

"He never leaves you alone!" she complained at Thanksgiving, when Champ was following me from the living room to the kitchen and back again. That particular Thanksgiving wasn't a very happy one. Ricky and Erika were in the midst of divorcing and Mom couldn't wrap her head around what had gone wrong this time. Leah was three at the time, and at least Mom's concern for her granddaughter outranked her irritation with my dog.

"I just don't understand!" she said for the hundredth time as we sat down to eat. I'd made us a turkey roll instead of an entire turkey and I'm sure that was a disappointment as well. "Why are they doing this?"

"Because Ricky was cheating on Erika," I told her. "Just like he cheated on Lauren."

Mom was silent, but only for a moment. "Why?" she said. "Why does he do that?"

I shrugged, feigning indifference. But my skin prickled with loathing for my older brother and the casual way he ruined lives.

I SLEPT ON THE FLOOR with Champ that first night after his seizure. He whimpered a lot in his sleep and I wondered if Mom was right, if I should put him down so he wouldn't have to suffer. But I couldn't bring myself to do that. So, I fed him his special food and gave him daily pills and slept on the floor beside him night after night until one morning I awoke to his unmoving body lying cold and heavy beside me. He had died in his sleep. My only consolation was that at least he had died with the only person who ever really loved him on the floor next to him.

Regular life continued — I went to work, I put my cheques in the bank, I shopped at Foodland — but I felt as though I were moving under water and whenever I returned to my empty house, I was hit anew with the loss of Champ. I contemplated getting another dog, even another rescue dog, but I didn't want just any dog — I wanted Champ.

The stupid doggy door reminded me every time I saw it that he was gone. I even missed stumbling across his puddles of pee. Mom tried to cheer me up, but I hadn't forgiven her for her callous suggestion to put Champ down at the first hint that he was sick. It didn't matter that she was probably right; I wanted to play the injured party for once and wallow in my self-righteous pity.

IT WAS AROUND THIS TIME, when I was wading through the long, humid days of August, circling aimlessly around a gulf of sadness, that I saw a man at the bank with honey-toned skin and closely cropped brown hair. As I stood in line, waiting to deposit my cheque, I couldn't help but stare at him. He was strikingly handsome and it had been so long that I'd been interested in anything, I found my curiosity about this stranger behind the counter almost startling. Before I could get a closer look, Mrs. Collins, who had worked at the bank for as long as I could remember, waved me over.

I made my way to the counter, mildly distracted by the good-looking man in a suit. Mrs. Collins took my cheque and my bank book, asking if I wanted any of my pay in cash, oblivious to my racing pulse. *Who was that guy?*

I pretended to be thinking about Mrs. Collins' question so I could stand there a few seconds longer, trying to catch another glimpse of the stranger. I think now that what drew me to him so strongly were his eyes. Something about his face emanated kindness, and I believe it was quite simply the warmth in those eyes.

I figured if anyone knew anything about him, it would be Mom. She had a finger on the pulse of the comings and goings in town and loved gossiping about everybody's business, repeatedly mistaking my quiet indifference for interest. I waited until Sunday to call her so I wouldn't appear over-eager, then casually mentioned that I'd seen someone new at the Royal Bank.

"The mortgage person? That's Maureen Dawson's nephew. You remember Maureen? Her nephew transferred from some other bank about two weeks ago. He's staying over at the Willow Flats." There was a brief pause, then, "You should introduce yourself. Offer to show him around. I don't think he knows anyone else here."

"He doesn't know me either! I didn't even talk to him. I just saw him and wondered who he was. That's all."

"You could use somebody your own age to hang around with for a change."

Point taken. "What's his name?"

"Ahmad, I think. No wait, that's not it. Do you want me to ask Maureen —"

"No, Mom. I don't want you to do anything. I was just curious about who he was."

If my mom was disappointed by how our conversation ended, she had plenty of cause for excitement later, when Amir and I did meet, quite by accident, and ended up hitting it off. I had stopped at the park near the river, where I still liked to walk along the path that Champ and I had frequented so many times. I was on the swings, lazily rocking back and forth, when Amir came strolling down the path. As he approached the park, he gave a friendly little wave. I hesitated, unsure whether I should wave back and keep swinging or actually introduce myself as per Mom's suggestion.

"Hi," I said, hopping off the swing to join him on the path. "You're Maureen's nephew, right?"

"Wow, word sure gets around, doesn't it?" He laughed. "Amir," he offered, holding out his hand.

I had no choice but to take it. "Zoe," I said. "I saw you at the bank last week."

He raised his eyebrows. "I see I have no secrets from you." Before I could think of something to say to that, he added. "So, Zoe, please tell me: what do people do around here for fun?"

I looked around helplessly. "For fun?" I echoed. "Um, mostly people go to Leeville or Port Sitsworth or Boelen to do stuff. There's not a lot to do here. In Dunford, I mean."

"So I've noticed. What about for drinks? Is there a good place to get a drink? In Dunford."

My hands were sweating. "There's Red Whiskers. It's a decent bar, but the music can be really loud." I sounded like an idiot. As if I was too old for loud music and dancing.

"That's the only place to get a drink?" he asked, his brown eyes sparkling with mock incredulity.

"No. There's also the King's Tavern, but it's usually an older crowd. It has kind of a depressing atmosphere. I wouldn't recommend it."

"Okay," he said, laughing, "Then tell me, where do you go?"

I had two places I liked to frequent, neither of which I'd mentioned because I didn't think they were the kinds of places he had in mind when he asked about drinks. The first was Mackie's, the greasy bar and grill where I hung out with the guys from the plant. It was not somewhere I'd otherwise hang out; in fact, I'd never even gone there with Jonathan. The second was Dunford Lanes, the bowling alley, which even I recognized as a corny place to go for a drink, but I liked sitting at the tiny bar in the lounge, watching the bowlers, lost in the commotion around me, with no pressure to engage in conversation with anybody. Silas, the bartender — who also happened to be the shoe rental clerk — knew me well enough to understand that I wasn't there to socialize. He just served me my cheap wine and went about his business.

Amir was staring at me, waiting for an answer.

"Uh, sometimes I go to the bowling alley actually," I admitted. "It sounds dumb, but they have a decent little bar there."

Amir cocked his head and appraised me for a moment. "Maybe you could show it to me some time."

I'm not sure what came over me. "Sure. You free this Thursday?"

A group of kids were running toward the playground, shrieking about the last one there being a rotten egg. Without saying a word, Amir and I began walking down the path, away from the shouting kids, to the other end of the park where the river neared the dam.

"Thursday is great. How does around seven sound? I could pick you up or just meet you there."

"Why don't I pick you up?" I asked.

"I'm in Willow Flats. Number nineteen. You know where that is?"

"I grew up here," I said. "I know where everything is."

We walked along the river together and I pointed out some things I thought he might find interesting like Ice Cream Island, and across from it, Dunford's most famous residence.

"See that massive house over there? It's called Copperly Mansion and the building behind it used to be a carriage house. It was used in a movie once."

I slowed down to give Amir a chance to take in the mansion's grandeur: the immaculate flower beds that skirted the wrap-around porch with its fluted columns, the tower-like turrets, the multi-gabled roof, and the four brick chimneys jutting like sentinels into the sky. Apparently, the house had eight fireplaces inside, each one a work of art in and of itself.

Amir nodded appreciatively. "What was the movie?"

"I don't remember. Something with a plane. I think George Clooney was in it. It was someone famous, because I remember Mrs. Copperly was worried that people were going to trample her gardens trying to get a picture of him."

"Did they?"

"No. The film crew closed the street. He was only here for like half a day."

I ended up walking Amir back to Willow Flats where he waved to me before calling out, "See you Thursday!"

It was only when I was walking alone again, heading back to my house on Pine Street, that I realized I'd never asked what brought him to Dunford. I mean, other than the job at the bank. At least we'd have something to talk about on Thursday. And while I still missed Champ's eager footsteps greeting me at the door, I didn't feel quite as desolate as I had in the previous weeks.

CHAPTER
TWO
·

I DROVE TO WILLOW FLATS just before seven, my palms leaving wet fingerprints on the steering wheel. Amir was already standing outside, wearing jeans and a casual button-down shirt that made him look super sexy. He climbed into the passenger seat and smiled at me.

"Thanks for picking me up. The service around here is amazing." Even though he was mocking me, his teasing voice and gentle smile helped loosen the knot of grief in my chest that had been ever-present since Champ's death.

I was worried about choosing Dunford Lanes. It seemed like such a weird place to take someone for drinks that I almost changed my mind. Maybe I could casually suggest one of the other bars in town, one of the ones I had already dismissed just days earlier. In the end, I decided to stick with the original plan because there would be less explaining that way.

The lounge of Dunford Lanes consisted of four round wooden tables, in addition to a few stools at the bar. From those tables, you could watch the bowlers, or, if you were facing the window, look out into the parking lot and the woods behind it. I liked it here because my mind could wander. But now, with Amir sitting across from me, my attention was fixed on him. In the background, over the tinny speakers in the bar, "You Found Me" by The Fray was playing and I couldn't help thinking it was the perfect song for this moment with Amir.

"We should bowl," Amir announced. "Don't you ever actually bowl when you're here?"

"Not usually," I admitted.

"So why do you come here if you don't like bowling?" He was already getting to his feet and I realized he was serious. Then, reaching for my hand, he pulled me out of my chair and toward the shoe rentals. Silas winked at me as he moved from behind the bar to take our sizes.

It became a passtime of ours. We'd go bowling once a week, sometimes just the two of us, sometimes with friends. I had more friends when I was with Amir. He had the kind of personality that attracts others, and when I was dating him, I found myself, more often than not, thrown into the company of other people. For a while, I had an actual social life outside of work.

On that first date, I learned a lot about Amir. He'd grown up in St. Catharine's and gone to university at Laurier, where he studied business. He got a job as a mortgage broker for a small firm in Waterloo, then moved to a bank where he felt like he was only ever given menial tasks and was more of an assistant than anything else, so when the job for a Mortgage Specialist opened at the Royal Bank in Dunford, he applied.

"My aunt Maureen was really excited about me moving here. Ever since her husband died, she's been starved for family. Now she figures my parents will come to visit me and we'll have all these cozy family gatherings in Dunford."

"And will your parents come?"

"Oh sure. But more likely, I'll visit them in St. Catharine's. I'll take Aunt Maureen with me, though, so she'll still get her reunions. And you, you've lived in Dunford your whole life?"

"Born and bred," I said stupidly.

"Tell me about your job. It sounds interesting. I don't know the first thing about what has to happen for my tap water to come out clean enough to drink."

"Not many people do. It's not that interesting, though. I kind of fell into it after high school. I was supposed to go to college, or maybe even university, but then I started working and I guess I just got comfortable. Plus, my mom's here, and she's had a bad heart since I was a kid so being close lets me keep an eye on her."

Amir's foot knocked against my leg as he leaned toward me. My pulse quickened even though the contact was probably accidental. I didn't want to talk about me; I wanted to know more about him.

"You said something about working in theatre. Are you an actor?" I kept my foot firmly rooted to the floor, but I wanted to stretch my leg out, closer to him, so that his foot might bump against it again.

"No, no. I did set building. Just for small theatre groups. All behind-the-scenes stuff. But I like building things. I probably should have gone into something more hands-on, like you did, but I figured I'd better put my business degree to good use or I'd have wasted four years of my life. You know what I mean?"

I did know, but I didn't want to think about what it meant to have wasted years of my life. Years I could never get back.

"ZOE, THIS IS YOLANDA."

I reached out to shake Yolanda's hand, after surreptitiously wiping my palm on my jeans. My hands were wet from filling water balloons in the basement kitchen of the Baptist Church. A bucket of filled balloons sat by my feet. "Nice to meet you," I said.

"Yolanda is Gary's wife," Amir explained.

Gary was one of Amir's friends from baseball, and also a cop. I'd felt a twinge of unease when I first found that out, but it was nice that he and Amir seemed to get along so well. Gary was also new to town, so they had that in common.

"Thanks for coming today," I said to Yolanda. "When my mom roped Amir into helping at this picnic, I didn't know he was going to turn around and recruit his friends as well."

Mom's church was hosting a strawberry social and while I generally didn't participate in the Baptist Church's events, Amir thought it sounded like fun and eagerly volunteered both of us to help. He then convinced Gary to join us, and I guess Yolanda, as well.

I picked up the bucket of balloons to carry outside, while Amir gave Gary and Yolanda instructions on where to find the hotdog buns. Mom was standing behind a long table on the church lawn ladling strawberries onto dozens of plates of shortbread. She gave me a happy little wave.

I didn't know it then, but Yolanda and Gary would become regular fixtures in our life. It wasn't long after that picnic that the two of them started joining our bowling nights. Officer Anderson, as Amir liked to call Gary, turned out to be a surprisingly talented bowler. He showed all of us up week after week.

"Is there such a thing as a bowling shark?" I asked. "How do you keep throwing strikes?"

"I'm just naturally athletic," Gary replied. "Gifted at so many things."

Yolanda snorted. "He used to play in a league."

I made a bowling shirt for Gary with his name embroidered on the left pocket over a logo of a shark. He wore it every time the four of us went bowling and when I pictured Gary in uniform, that was the shirt I imagined him wearing, instead of the one that was part of his police outfit.

"YOLANDA AND I ARE GOING to a yoga class together," I said to Amir, kissing him lightly on the cheek one day.

"I'm glad you two get along. It'll be good for you to have a girl-friend to talk to."

"Why do I need a girlfriend to talk to when I have you?"

"So you can talk about girl stuff."

I didn't want to talk about girl stuff. I never had. To her credit, Yolanda wasn't a fan of sharing deep secrets or bonding over gos-sip, either. There was an immediate comfortable understanding between us that reminded me of my friendship with Walter before he left for university. Before we became two different people.

It was nice to have Yolanda as a friend. Someone close to my age who didn't work at the plant and who wasn't male. Thanks to Amir, instead of sitting alone at the bar in Dunford Lanes, watch-ing other people live, I became part of a laughing group in rented shoes, who could tease an off-duty police officer after he bowled his fourth strike in a row.

I didn't do much bowling after Amir left town. I tried a few times to get together with some of the friends we'd made, mostly at their insistence, but eventually the invitations dwindled and I gradually reverted to my isolated and solitary ways. Without Amir, there was no one to draw me from my shell.

Even Yolanda and I drifted apart. I'm sure I was difficult to hang out with after everything fell apart. We still exchange pleasantries when we run into each other in town, but it's not like we call each other up to do yoga. Gary, I think, hates me. He tried to talk to me once about what happened, before Amir left Dunford for good. I think he must have hoped that as long as Amir was still in town, there was a chance the two of us could work things out.

He was waiting for me one day in the parking lot at the plant when I finished my shift. At first, when I saw him standing beside my car, I had a horrible thought that Amir had done something, hurt himself or worse, but that would have been giving myself too much credit.

"Zoe," Gary said, looking at me sadly. "What the hell are you doing?"

"Trust me," I said. "I have my reasons, but I don't want to talk about it."

"What does that mean? 'You have your reasons?' Zoe, just tell me what's going on. This can't be what you want."

I looked Gary square in the eye. "It is," I said. "It is what I want." I got into my car and slammed the door. When I drove away, Gary was still standing there, watching me.

But that was after. Long before that day in the parking lot with Gary, I was happier than I'd ever imagined being. And Amir was at the centre of it all.

CHAPTER
THREE

·

"YOUR JOB IS TO ENTERTAIN the guests," Amir told me. "And to make sure you're having fun."

"What about you? Are you going to have any fun stuck behind the barbeque all night?"

"I like grilling meat," Amir replied. I stood on my tippy toes and kissed him. We were standing in my kitchen waiting for our Labour Day party to begin, which Amir had pretty much single-handedly organized.

Even though this was Amir's brain-child, I found myself caught up in the excitement. It had turned into a gorgeous day, sunny, but not too hot, with just enough of a breeze to keep the air from becoming heavy. It had been cloudy and spitting rain when I first woke up, and I couldn't imagine all the people Amir had invited fitting inside my bungalow, so I was glad when the sky cleared up and the sun came out. Also, Amir's enthusiasm was infectious. As we bustled around my kitchen, putting last-minutes touches on the food we'd prepared together, I was reminded of the way I used to feel right before my birthday parties, staring out the window, waiting and waiting for that first person to show up with a present in their hands.

Those parties all took place before Amy Nessor's murder. Before I stopped inviting kids to our house. Before I stopped having friends to invite in the first place.

"Here, this can go outside," Amir said, handing me a bowl of beer nuts. We'd made way too much food: a multi-layered taco dip, bacon-wrapped water chestnuts, vegetarian chili, a fruit salad. This was in addition to the bowls of chips and nuts we'd already carried outside.

Gary and Yolanda were the first to arrive. I offered Yolanda some wine, pouring myself a full glass, and soon the backyard was dotted with small groups of people.

"Those sausages are about done, eh?" I said to Amir, peering over his shoulder at the barbeque.

"Are you questioning my cooking skills?"

"Well, if they're anything like your bowling skills ..."

I STOOD ON THE DECK, doing my best to make small talk with people, and looked around at the clusters of guests milling around the yard. Amir had put up a badminton net; there were lawn chairs strewn across the grass; everywhere I looked, people were smiling and laughing. Hell, even I was smiling and laughing.

Amir abandoned his post at the barbeque and came to stand beside me. I put my arm around his waist and pulled him close. Leaning into his shoulder, I whispered, "I am so glad I met you."

He dipped his face toward mine and kissed me on the lips. "Ditto," he said.

Mom was sitting not too far away, under the shade of the patio umbrella. She'd seen our quick embrace and was smiling at me.

Later, when I was re-filling her water glass, Mom put her hand on my arm and said, "Zoe, you deserve this. You deserve to be happy."

"Thanks," I said, wondering why she felt compelled to tell me that, as if I might think I didn't deserve to be happy.

It bothered me, her saying that.

I WAS HAPPY WHEN I was with Amir, and if my life felt unfamiliar to me, it was unfamiliar in a good way. Finally, for the first time maybe, I was actually living. When Amir left, my newly acquired *joie de vivre* went with him. Or maybe it was never mine; it had always been his, and for a while, I had just been lucky enough to be pulled into its orbit. Regardless, without him, my life quickly deflated. Returned to its regular proportions.

"YOU TOOK A PHOTOGRAPHY CLASS in high school, right?" Amir asked. We were walking along the path beside the Still River and his hand was warm in mine.

"Yeah ..." My voice came out sounding defensive. I had my camera with me — I almost always had it when we were out walking — and I wasn't sure what he was getting at. Was he suggesting I should be taking better pictures, given that I'd once studied photography in high school?

"I saw a thing at Gulman's Studio. They have a professional photographer coming in to teach a class and it made me think of you."

"You think I need to take a class?"

"I thought you'd like to take it. You're always taking pictures, and you're good, your pictures are good, but this would be a chance to develop your skills even more." He squeezed my hand. "It was just a thought."

I DID SIGN UP FOR the photography course and when I arrived for my first class in Gulman's Studio — which used to be Gulman's Textiles — I was surprised by how many different kinds of art classes were offered in the refurbished factory: painting, wood-working, glass-blowing, quilting, and pottery. Gulman's Textiles had been one of Dunford's original industries and even though I was a child when it closed in 1982 after over sixty years of pro-ducing woolen socks and flannel, I remember Mom shaking her head sadly the day they boarded it up. Now that it was home to so many different studios, I figured she must be happy that the building had been given a new life.

I was intrigued by the pottery classes and imagined enrolling with Amir. When I broached the subject, he was more receptive than I'd expected.

"You know the scene in *Ghost*, with the pottery wheel?" I asked him one night while we were trying to decide what to do.

"Yeah, what about it?"

"Gulman's Studio has a pottery class on Tuesday nights and I thought it'd be a fun thing to do together."

"You want me to take a pottery class with you?" Amir looked at me quizzically, probably trying to gauge whether or not I was serious. "Hmmm, I do like the idea of playing Patrick Swayze to your Demi Moore."

I swatted his arm playfully.

After only a few pottery classes, however, any thoughts of recreating the iconic scene from *Ghost* likely disappeared from Amir's mind. There was nothing sexy about using a pottery wheel. It was messy and frustrating and way harder than it looked. I much preferred my photography class, where I was experiencing a growing competency in my skills.

"Are you enjoying this?" I asked Amir one night, as he struggled to throw a simple bowl.

"Not really," he admitted.

Our projects were on the pathetic side: I made two lopsided vases, and Amir created something that looked like a mini milk pitcher with a squished handle. But the photography class turned out to be a winner; I was excited to show Amir a print of mine that had been chosen by my instructor to showcase in the lobby.

"That's incredible!" Amir gushed, examining my study of shadow. "I think photography is your hidden calling."

The picture wasn't really worthy of that much praise, but I liked that Amir was so enthusiastic. So supportive. I'd taken the shot in one of the building's old stairwells, where the shadows from a barred window fell across the steps. The lines of the bars were distorted by the stairs, creating a disrupted pattern of shadow and light.

"With black and white photos, it's all about contrasting tones," I told him. "We were experimenting with depth and shadow and tonality. But my favourite part was developing the print. I love playing with the image after it's been taken, in the darkroom."

"I could build you one," Amir said.

My head jerked up. "What?"

"If you wanted your own darkroom, like in your basement, I could make one for you. Zoe, this is your passion. You should pursue it."

"I'd have to get all kinds of equipment. An enlarger, safelights, trays."

Amir didn't say anything else, so I dropped it. I figured it had been a fleeting idea, and sensing my resistance, he'd immediately thought better of it.

So I was surprised when a few days later he told me he'd made a list of everything I would need for a darkroom and had sourced out some prices. "You can get an enlarger for about four hundred dollars. The rest of the stuff isn't that expensive and some of it you can improvise. Come downstairs, I'll show you where I was thinking."

One thing led to another and Amir built me my darkroom. He also bought me a used Canon 35mm film camera that he found online. I don't know about photography being my calling, but it's certainly turned into my passion, and it's one of the few remnants of my life with Amir that stuck.

CHAPTER
FOUR
·

WHILE I WAS DATING Amir, I was lulled, or maybe thrust, into the hope that my life was going in a new and much better direction. I even had a few normal conversations with Ricky, which, given how infrequently we spoke to each other, seemed significant to me.

"I ordered Mom a planter for her birthday," Ricky told me over the phone. "Can you drop it off and help her set it up?"

"Are you going to see her soon? She wants to know how Leah's doing."

"Leah's good. We're all good. Although I've been thinking about getting out of the city for a bit, just a few days, to unwind. Doesn't Amir's dad have a property or something up north?"

I hesitated. "It's his dad's friend's and it's a fishing lodge, but the place is falling apart. The last time Amir and I were there a section of the dock was under an inch of water and most of the cabins were empty. I think the owner, Lance, is slowly shutting the place down."

"Maybe we could go before he does," Ricky said. "It would be nice to just hang out, relax. Spend some time together like we used to."

When had Ricky and I ever spent time together? "You would hate it, Ricky. It's really rustic and completely rundown."

"I'm okay with rustic. In fact, I think that's what I'm looking for. I just need a change. Some fresh air. Besides, doing a little fishing together wouldn't be so bad, would it?"

Part of me was repulsed at the idea of spending a weekend with my brother, stuck for hours in an aluminum boat out in the middle of Georgian Bay, but the little sister buried deep inside of me was excited that he wanted to spend time with me. His divorce from Erika must have been taking more of a toll on him than I expected.

"Are you serious about this?"

It was already September, so if Ricky really wanted to visit Windy Pines, we'd have to go soon. I expected him to laugh at the suggestion of making real plans, but he surprised me.

"When are you off next?" he asked. "I'm pretty flexible."

When I broached the subject with Amir, he was overly enthusiastic. "Oh, Zoe! I think that's great. Lance would love to have you. I'd try and go too, but there's no way I can get the time off right now."

"Would that be weird, me going up there without you?"

"What's weird is that you and your brother hardly ever see each other. Maybe this will be a bonding experience for the two of you."

That's exactly what I was afraid of. I wasn't sure I wanted to do any bonding with my brother. But at the same time, I was strangely buoyed by the thought of Ricky choosing me. And if I thought Amir was excited about our impending Brother/Sister Weekend, I wasn't prepared at all for Mom's reaction. As soon as I mentioned it to her, she started to cry.

"That just makes me so happy!" she said, pretending that she didn't have tears running down her face.

The only person who had any reservations about the whole thing, it seemed, was me. Because hovering right next to my cautious enthusiasm was the memory of the horrible weekend I had spent with my brother in Leeville, when he thought it would be a good idea for his little sister to watch *Friday the 13th*.

WE WEREN'T KIDS ANYMORE, THOUGH. I was thirty-one that fall, and Ricky was almost forty. We met up at a carpool lot on the side of Highway 400, just north of Toronto, and Ricky threw his duffel bag into the back of my car which was loaded with supplies that Amir had helped me pack.

"So," Ricky said as he settled into his seat, "you know how to get there?"

"Are you sure you're ready for this?" I asked. "You know the cabin's not in great shape. And you have to boil the water before you can drink it. Oh, and there's no cell service. Well, in some places out on the water you can get a signal, but not from the cabin."

"Zoe, relax. You've mentioned all that already. I won't need my phone, anyway. I'm taking the weekend completely off. Did you know I've never done that? Not even on my honeymoons. Both times, I was checking messages, doing business, sealing deals."

I wasn't sure if he was trying to say he was long overdue for a vacation, or if he was suggesting that this weekend with me was somehow more important than his first days as a newlywed.

"Yeah, and look how those turned out for you," I joked.

"No kidding," he replied, as if his doomed marriages could be blamed on his addiction to work or his phone, rather than the women he'd slept with on the side.

We spent a good chunk of the five-hour drive listening to the radio, hardly talking. Ricky checked his phone compulsively and I assumed he was trying to make the most of it while he still had a signal. When we stopped to eat in Parry Sound, I called Amir to update him on our progress.

"Are you having fun?" he asked.

"We're still getting used to each other," I replied.

As we pulled into the gravel driveway of Windy Pines, Ricky said, "You weren't kidding about this place, eh? Is he hoping to sell it or what?"

"I think he's just sort of gradually retiring so he's not keeping it up like he used to. But he lives here, and as far as I know, he has no plans to move. Please don't talk to him about real estate, Ricky. You're taking a break, remember?"

"I'm just saying, he'll have a hard time selling it in this condition."

Lance must have heard my car pull in because he came ambling over to greet us. "When you've unloaded," he said, "come on back to the house for a drink and I'll go over what you need to know."

The main house was cozy, dominated by a giant stone fireplace in the living room. The first time I'd come here with Amir, I'd been freaked out by the bear skin rug in the middle of the room, with its stuffed head that sat like a bowling ball on the floor. When I mentioned to Amir how creepy I found it, he'd laughed.

"When I was little, and I came here with my dad, I used to sit on that rug and pet the bear's head. I read stories to him."

"Okay," I'd said, backing away from him in mock horror. "That's more than creepy."

Ricky raised an eyebrow when he saw the bear skin, but he didn't say anything.

Lance offered us each a beer and motioned for us to sit at the scarred wooden table in the kitchen. He pushed a map of the bay toward us and pointed out the marked hazards. "The water's low this time of year so most of these aren't hidden anymore, but some are still covered, so keep an eye out for markers. And since the water's so low, you'll have to watch for shoals, too."

I got the sense he missed this — sitting down with guests to talk about the water, offer advice, and pass on a small bit of the knowledge he had acquired through a lifetime of experience.

"You should go out tonight for an evening fish," Lance continued. "Get used to the boat, pick some spots for tomorrow."

Later, when Ricky and I were in our own cabin, heating up the lasagna I had made at home, he said he didn't feel like going out that evening. "It's Friday night," he reasoned. "We still have all day Saturday and most of Sunday to be on the water."

I didn't argue. The lasagna was filling the cabin with a mouth-watering aroma and staying in to eat and relax didn't seem like a bad idea. I thought about all those nights I'd watched my brother across the kitchen table, praying he'd stay home long enough to play a game with me, or watch TV, anything that indicated he was at least aware of my presence.

Apart from a tiny bathroom and two bedrooms, the cabin consisted of only one other room: a combined kitchen and sitting area. Most of the space was taken up by a round wooden table with five mismatched chairs, along with an ugly couch jammed against the wall.

I set out the lasagna and a Caesar salad while Ricky grabbed himself a beer from the fridge. "So, I take it you're a good cook then?" he said, eyeing the food. "Cuz if you're not good in the kitchen, then you'd better be good in the bedroom, eh?" He laughed at his own unfunny joke.

I GOT UP EARLY AND brewed a pot of coffee using bottled water. The tap water was safe to drink after boiling, but it had a strong smell. Besides, I was sensitive about water quality after working for so many years at the plant where water was disinfected and deodorized and treated within an inch of its life.

I stepped outside onto the weather-beaten deck and sipped my coffee as the sun slowly spread in a pink band across the water. The morning air was pierced by the sudden haunting wail of a loon. I breathed it all in: the sights, the sounds, the smells. Amir was convinced this trip would do both me and Ricky a world of good, and I hoped he was right, but he didn't know the lurking truth behind our seeming estrangement. I wasn't sure that even nature would be enough of a balm to combat the tension I felt around my brother.

When Ricky stumbled out of his room at ten a.m., he plonked himself at the table. I cooked us scrambled eggs and thick slabs of back bacon. Ricky disappeared into his room again as soon as we were done eating, so I cleaned up and did the dishes alone. The sink was streaked with a large, rust-coloured stain from all the iron in the tap water.

Lance was waiting for us at the dock with the tackle and rods he was lending us for the day. He wanted to see us off and to wish us luck. Did it bother him, I wondered, that we hadn't gone out last night, after all his careful explanations and suggestions?

I had my camera slung around my neck. I planned to fish, but I also planned on getting some good shots while we were out on the water.

"Have fun out there," Lance said, after helping us to load our gear into a beaten-up aluminum boat. The vinyl seat covers were cracked and peeling and the wooden floorboards looked like they were rotting. I eyed the tiller apprehensively, wondering when this boat had last been used.

"You know how to drive this thing?" Ricky asked.

"Yeah, Amir taught me. He made me get my boater's licence the first time we came up."

To my relief, the motor caught on the first pull. I waved at Lance as I guided the boat into the channel and toward the little island he'd pointed out yesterday.

"Is there a bailing bucket in this thing?" Ricky asked. "I can't believe he doesn't have anything better for us to use than this piece of crap."

"I think people usually bring their own boats. Besides, he's not charging us to rent it."

We trolled around the island for a while, neither of us catching anything, or saying much. The sun bore down on us, and at one point, Ricky took off his watch.

"I don't want a weird tan line," he explained, as he dropped his Rolex into one of the plastic compartments in the tackle box. "I bought that watch after my first quarter million in commissions," he added, seeing me eyeing the glinting silver. "A little thank you to myself."

"It's nice," I murmured. My real focus, though, was on the scenery. I couldn't take any good pictures while I was driving, so my camera sat unused by my feet. At some point, I knew I had to capture the wind-swept white pines along the rocky shoreline. It was like a painting by Tom Thompson. The landscape around us had a fierceness to it, all jagged edges and raw surfaces. As I took it in, I wished I had been born with that same kind of rugged resilience, able to withstand life's harshness.

Ricky was unmoved by the craggy rocks and the wind-swept pines. When I pointed them out, commenting on their beauty, he looked at me like I was nuts. He was irritated by our lack of success on the water; he wanted to try something new.

"You have to be patient," I explained.

"Let's be patient somewhere else. I'm sick of circling this island."

I steered us through a narrow pass and into a larger channel. At some point, I realized, Ricky and I were going to have to strike up an actual conversation; our seemingly companionable silence was beginning to wear thin.

"How's your new place?" I asked. After his split from Erika, Ricky had moved into an apartment temporarily, but he'd just recently bought another condo.

"Expensive," he said. "But its value will only go up. In ten years, what I paid for it will seem like peanuts. And Leah has a bedroom now. She was sleeping in the living room in the apartment."

"She must like it then," I said, although I doubted that, as a four-year-old, Leah really cared about having her own room.

"Erika likes it. She hated the idea of her precious little angel sleeping on a mattress on the floor."

The bitterness in Ricky's voice surprised me. And the way his lips curled when he referred to Leah as Erika's "precious little angel" made my skin crawl. "At least you gave her a mattress," I said. "Remember when you made me sleep on the floor in your room?"

"I gave you a mattress too! That was one night, by the way."

I turned away from him to adjust my lure and as I untangled the line from where it had snagged on one of the hooks, the barbed edge of the hook caught in my thumb. When I yanked it out, my thumb started to bleed. "Is there a first aid kit in here?" I asked.

Ricky reeled in his line and began digging through the tackle box. I pressed my thumb, which was now throbbing, against my leg. I kept my other hand on the tiller as I watched the blood from my thumb spread in a slow circle.

Suddenly, the boat shuddered violently and a horrendous scraping sound penetrated the air. After a series of sickening thumps, we jerked to a standstill, perched awkwardly on a submerged rock shelf.

"What the fuck?" Ricky yelled.

I pulled the motor up and when I saw the mangled blades, it crossed my mind that we might not be able to make it back to the lodge. My thumb was still bleeding, leaving trails of blood all over the back of the boat and on my torn seat cushion.

"Here," Ricky said, throwing me a roll of black electrical tape. "Wrap up your thumb."

"Are there scissors or something?"

Ricky sawed off a piece of tape with a rusty Swiss army knife. Then, using an oar, he pushed us off the rock. The motor started again, but when I tried to accelerate, nothing much happened. The prop blades were too damaged to garner any traction in the water. It was going to be a long, slow ride back to the lodge.

"How pissed do you think Lance is going to be?" Ricky asked. "He'd better not ask us to pay for this."

"Ricky, we just wrecked his boat!"

"Yeah, but he's going out of business anyway. Besides, this boat was already falling apart before we hit the rock."

"You're supposed to warn me about shit like that. You didn't see the giant rock?"

"I was trying to find you a Band-Aid!"

"Try to keep an eye out now," I muttered.

LANCE ACTED LIKE THE WHOLE thing was no big deal. He had other motors in storage, he said. He would just switch it out. He waved off my attempts to offer some kind of financial compensation, promising to have us back in a working boat after lunch. I was embarrassed, but Ricky looked completely unconcerned, like a cat licking his paws in the sun.

After lunch, Ricky announced that he was having a nap. He retreated to his room and I was left alone in the main room where I could feel the familiar twinges of rage stirring in my ribcage, that old desire to lash out and hit something. To distract myself, I wandered outside with my camera. I followed a trail to a derelict cabin at the top of a steep hill where Amir told me he used to play when he was little.

"Lance only rented it out to people who came alone and didn't want to interact with anybody, so it was usually empty when we were here."

People like me, I remember thinking. It struck me as a sad place for a little boy to play. Especially someone as friendly and sociable as Amir. Which begged the question: what was a fun-loving, open-hearted guy like him doing with an emotionally-stunted loser like me?

Lance was down at the dock, attaching a different motor to our boat.

"She's all ready for you," he said as I approached. The motor we'd wrecked was sitting beside him.

"Thanks," I said. "Again, I'm so sorry about this."

Lance waved his hands. "Don't even mention it. But catch some fish this afternoon, eh? It will make my efforts worthwhile. I can't very well send you back empty-handed. Amir will never let you hear the end of it."

"I doubt he'll let me hear the end of crashing into a rock shelf either."

"Only if you choose to mention it. There's nothing saying you have to tell him." Lance hefted the broken motor into his arms and turned toward the boathouse.

"I can't not tell him," I said to his back. "I'm no good with secrets." Which was about as far from the truth as I could get. But it sounded nice, the idea that I didn't have any secrets.

CHAPTER
FIVE

·

RICKY DIDN'T WANT TO GO out fishing again. After his nap, he sat on the couch eating Doritos and playing on his phone. Even without a signal, he couldn't stop doing stuff on it. Since Lance had gone to all the trouble of replacing the motor, I thought we should take the newly repaired boat out, but when I said as much to Ricky he just shrugged.

"You worry too much," he said, reaching for another handful of Doritos. "We'll go tonight. Evening fishing is supposed to be better anyway."

"I'm going this afternoon."

It was peaceful on the water. I stayed close to the lodge at first, skirting around the island we'd circled earlier, casting along the shoals. The sun warmed my skin and my heartbeat settled into an easy rhythm. Without Ricky in the boat, I felt calm for the first time since we'd arrived. And I could stop to take as many pictures as I wanted.

Eventually, lured by the increasingly rugged shoreline, I ventured farther and farther from the lodge. I was enjoying being by myself, but at some point, conflicting emotions began to skitter across my thoughts like spiders. I was both mad at Ricky for wanting to stay in the cabin and grateful to have a few hours away from him. His comment earlier about Leah kept playing in my mind. His tone when he referred to her as Erika's precious little angel bothered me, but at the same time the casual way he brought up her having her own room was comforting. I couldn't nail down the way I wanted to feel, and as I angled the boat back toward Windy Pines, my frustration and anger intensified.

"Why do you have to be such a confusing bastard?" I mumbled, my question swallowed by the sound of the water slapping against the boat and the steady drone of the motor.

Intending to delay my return, I cut the engine and let the boat drift. When I opened the tackle box to replace the lure I'd been using, Ricky's Rolex blinked up at me from one of the plastic slots. I couldn't believe he'd left it there. As I drifted through the bay, eyeing Ricky's expensive watch, my mouth hardened into a tight line. It didn't look all that special, yet I knew his watch probably cost more than my car. And he'd just left it in the tackle box, like a discarded toy.

I picked up his Rolex and hurled it into the air. It flew in a long arc over the water before hitting the surface with a soft splash and sinking out of sight. Taking a deep, satisfied breath, I restarted the motor and turned the boat toward the lodge.

Ricky was sitting on the deck, drinking a Corona with four empty bottles lined up beside him. I wondered how long it would take before he remembered his watch and went looking for it.

"You know," he said, "if Lance took care of this property, it could generate some good revenue. The location is prime. I mean, can't you see the potential of this place?" He tipped his head back and drained his beer.

"I'm pretty sure Lance knows how to run a lodge. From what

I've heard, he used to be really busy. He's just done with the business now. I told you, he's semi-retired."

"Then why doesn't he sell it?"

"I don't know. Maybe he doesn't want to. Why do you care, anyway?"

Ricky got up and grabbed another beer from the cooler. He tossed me one. "It's stupid, what he's doing. If he wanted to quit the business, he should have sold this place while it still had a customer base. Before letting the whole property go to shit."

I didn't answer. There was no point arguing with Ricky about real estate. I lifted the lid on the barbeque and scrubbed at the grill with a dirty brush. "Why don't you grab the burgers?" I suggested. "Make yourself useful." I took a long swallow of beer. I didn't usually drink Corona, but it was Ricky's favourite and he'd brought a lot of it.

We ate inside because there wasn't a table on the deck. Amir had packed us a tub of potato salad, as well as an onion, a tomato, and several cheese slices to go with our burgers. Amir had been so enthusiastic about this trip and I knew he was looking forward to hearing how my special bonding weekend had gone. How could I explain to him the constant unease I felt around my brother? Or that I'd thrown Ricky's Rolex into the lake? Why had I done that? I'd have been better off tossing Ricky into the water.

It started to rain as we were washing the dishes. First just a spattering, a few gentle drops, but then it came down in sheets. "Oh, great," Ricky said. "I hope our crappy cabin doesn't leak."

"Are you done complaining?" I asked. "Because I told you this place was rustic and you said it was fine. You said that's what you wanted. Then you bitched and moaned about the boat, which we wrecked, by the way, and now you're complaining about the weather. Are you always this hard to please?"

Ricky opened his mouth, but I wasn't done yet.

"You know what I think? Lauren and Erika were probably glad when they found out you'd been screwing around because it gave them just the excuse they needed to kick your sorry ass to the curb!" I wanted to tell Ricky about his precious Rolex and the sound it made hitting the water, but I bit my tongue.

"That was a pretty shitty thing to say. About Lauren and Erika."

I ignored him.

Ricky studied me for a minute. "We'll go out for a final fish tomorrow and we'll catch something just before we leave, and then we'll both have fond memories of the wonderful trip we took to Windy Pines Lodge before it was sold and bull-dozed."

"You're such an asshole," I muttered, but my words sounded conciliatory instead of accusatory, and Ricky only smiled before slapping me good-naturedly on the shoulder with his sudsy hand.

IN THE MORNING, THE RAIN was still pouring so we both agreed to cut our losses and head home. I was relieved, to be honest. I kept waiting for Ricky to mention his watch, but it never came up.

We had a quick breakfast — just bagels, no eggs or bacon this time. It was as if once we'd decided to leave, we couldn't get away fast enough. When I went to get my car, to bring it closer to the cabin, I stopped at the main house to tell Lance we were leaving and to thank him for everything, but he didn't answer my timid knock and I didn't want to wake him up if he was still sleeping. I decided to leave a note in our cabin instead.

It didn't take us long to load my car. Ricky sat on the couch, messing with his phone, while I gave the sink in the bathroom a quick scrub to remove the tooth paste spit Ricky couldn't be bothered to rinse away, then wiped down the counters and the table in the kitchen one last time.

"You almost done there, Mr. Clean?" Ricky asked.

I glanced around. "Yup. Thanks for all your help."

After we'd been driving for fifteen minutes on the rutted road that led out to the main highway, I realized I'd forgotten to leave Lance a note. Given the weather, I doubted he would be surprised that we'd decided to leave early, but it still seemed rude not to have thanked him for everything.

Ricky was quiet on the ride home, and as soon as his phone picked up a signal, I lost him completely. Apparently, he had a million messages that needed his immediate attention. I sent Amir a quick text when we stopped for gas to let him know I'd be home earlier than expected. I didn't call him because I didn't want to talk about the weekend in front of Ricky.

As we pulled back onto the highway, I turned to my brother. "I'm sorry your weekend get-away sucked." Now that it was over, I did feel kind of bad about how disappointing the trip must have been for him.

"Yeah, well, next time we'll go someplace better," he said. "No offence to Amir or his dad or anything."

I nodded, but if I was sure of anything, it was that there wouldn't be a next time. When I dropped Ricky off at the carpool lot, my whole body sagged with the release of tension and I was hit with a sudden and urgent need to use the bathroom. I called Amir five minutes later from the parking lot of a Burger King.

"I miss you," he said. "I was happy when I got your text about leaving early. I can't wait to hear all about your adventure."

"That's one way to describe it," I said. "I missed you, too."

But as I continued driving toward Dunford, and toward Amir, it occurred to me that what I'd been looking forward to, ever since letting Ricky out of my car, was being alone. I didn't want to think about, much less talk about, my weekend with him and the frustrating haze of impotence that dogged me in his presence. How when I wanted to yell and scream and kick and hit, instead all I could do was mumble and apologize. The truth was, even more than I hated my brother, I hated the version of myself I became around him.

CHAPTER
SIX
.

AS I'M LYING ON MY couch, doped up on cold medicine, my head feels as if it's floating. I am disjointed. None of my limbs feels securely attached to my body and my thoughts are just as discombobulated. Mom's message plays in my mind, her voice lilting in an eerie sing-song: *You'll never guess what I just found out!* Then, suddenly Amir materializes in front of me, holding out Amy's braid, swinging it back and forth like a pendulum.

I jolt upright. I must have cried out in my sleep because it's the sound of my own voice I hear echoing in my ears as I sit up, my heart thumping erratically. Amir is back, I think to myself, and for a moment my accelerated heart rate has nothing to do with the dream that startled me awake. Then I know. That's what Mom's message was about, her breathless excitement: Amir. Surely Mom doesn't think...? I don't let myself finish the thought. Going down that road, even glancing in its direction, feels disloyal to Jason. And Mom knows I am committed to Jason and to Parker. She doesn't know we've talked casually about marriage or about moving in together — true — but I'm pretty sure she would never suggest I toss Jason aside just because Amir has suddenly reappeared. That would be more Ricky's style.

Still. What did Amir say this morning? It was good to see me. And he meant it, too, if I can still read him. Those simple words were underscored by a gleam of sincerity in his eyes that I remember all too well from the years we were together.

Yet, in my dream his eyes had been narrowed in accusation as he swung Amy's braid back and forth in front of my face. The re-opened investigation comes rushing back at me and I am reminded again that my safe little universe is about to implode. At least — and this is a selfish and stupid thought — at least then Amir will know. He might finally understand why things turned out the way they did. And at the thought, I feel the tiniest spark of vindication.

I should have called Mom back right away. I want to know how she's doing, but now I'm also curious about how she'll bring up Amir being in town. Not to mention the investigation, given that the case was so pertinent to our lives — a drama that fully engulfed our family. At the same time, I'm almost afraid to mention the case because I'm worried Mom will pick up right away on my panic, so instead of calling her, I slink down to my darkroom and stare at the trays I left out last night, still full of chemicals. I dump the trays and rinse them out properly. Usually, I'm good at leaving the rest of the world behind when I'm in the darkroom, but as I clean up the mess I left, my mind is spinning. Everything I'm working on in here, the prints for Parker, it all seems so futile. My future, suddenly, feels as flimsy as paper.

There is so much I should do. Obviously, I need to talk to Jason. I can't keep putting him off forever. Perversely, I keep replaying Amir's startled greeting from this morning. And then, too sick and too tired to keep thinking, let alone standing around in the dark, I wander back upstairs and burrow under the heavy duvet on my bed, trying to hide from the confusion and worry battering my brain.

This time, I don't dream.

WHEN I WAKE UP, I am still thinking about Amir. The fact hits me, plain and irrefutable, that around Amir I was a better person. I have spent years hating my brother, and hating myself, but now I can't help but wonder what would have happened if Amir and I had stayed together. What kind of transformation would my life have gone through if we had both made different choices? For example, right now, with the news of Amy's case being re-opened, would I be surrounded by the rallying support of friends, leaning on Amir's calm and capable shoulders, instead of burrowing away in an empty house with my worst fears pressing in on me?

One thing I do know is this: I wouldn't have been able to shut Amir out the way I am shutting out Jason, but then, Jason and I don't live together so it's easier to create space, to give myself some breathing room. Once Amir moved in with me, I had nowhere to hide.

AMIR PROPOSED TO ME IN the park where we first met. He had packed a picnic, complete with white wine and expensive choco-lates, and under the setting sun on the bank of the Still River he asked me if I would marry him.

I threw my arms around him, knocking him over, laughing as I lay sprawled on top of him, saying, "Yes! Yes! Yes!" over and over again. Someone's wine spilled and the sleeve of my shirt was cold and wet against my skin, but in that moment, all I felt was pure happiness bubbling up from my soul.

It was late September and since I had my heart set on a fall wedding, we started making plans for the following October. Amir dove into the planning with me, offering his opinion on invitations, flowers, and menu options. We confirmed the date. From then on, October fourteenth was mentioned in every conversation and as we moved through the days, the weeks, the months, our lives twined ever closer, like a rope, the separate strands so tightly woven together they were effectively one.

Amir's enthusiasm dulled some of the doubts I had about whether or not I was worth marrying. In all the hubbub, I had begun to question if I was really the right person for him. If I could ever love him with the same kind of steadiness and unreserved tenderness with which he loved me. A shadow of self-doubt trailed me on my worst days. We were happy, both of us, but we also had some not-so-great moments. We argued. Amir was always kind, but even that kindness sometimes grated on me. Especially when I found myself incapable of returning it.

In the spring, he moved in with me because his lease was up and we were about to get married and it made sense. My house quickly filled with his mismatched furniture and his books and his shoes. He once referred to the spare bedroom as the future nursery and as soon as he said it, my heart jerked painfully. I became aware, again, of the shadow that haunted my heart and I wrestled with the idea that agreeing to marry Amir was unfair to him.

IN SPITE OF ALL MY misgivings, I don't think I could have predicted how things ended up turning out for the two of us. Just like I could never have anticipated the mess I'm in now. The case re-opening. Amir back in Dunford. There is so much being thrown at me that even without this sinus cold clouding my thoughts and making my limbs heavy, I doubt I can safely navigate to the other side of it all.

I feel like I'm underwater. I'm not kicking for the surface though — I'm not kicking for anything. Just sinking. Slowly and deliberately.

I think back to my most recent phone call with Jason and the way he paused before saying he loved me. How is it that the space of a second can swallow so much certainty?

CHAPTER
SEVEN

·

"RICHARD WENT ALL OUT FOR this party," Mom was saying. "He told me he rented one of those jumpy castles and I think he said he hired a clown!"

"Well, it's not every day your little girl turns six," Amir said, from behind the wheel. I was sitting in the back seat of my own car, so Mom could have the front. Amir often drove my car, because I preferred to be a passenger.

It was August, only two months before our wedding, and we were headed to Toronto for Leah's birthday party. Everyone was in a good mood, except for me. But since Mom and Amir were so busy chatting with each other, my sullen mood went unnoticed.

Something about Leah turning six was wreaking havoc with my emotions. Okay, not just something — it was the fact that Amy Nessor was six years old the last time I saw her. I knew it was a stupid thing to get stuck on, but I couldn't shake my feelings of unease. Plus, all the extravagance Mom was describing seemed so unnecessary. A jumpy castle and a clown? Come on.

At the actual party, I sat in the backyard, which was overflowing with streamers and balloons, and watched Leah run around excitedly while my brother smiled and made small-talk with all the guests. The clown Mom had been so excited about was creepy. He had a giant painted-on smile and was walking around making balloon animals for everyone whether they wanted one or not. Leah skipped past me toward the inflated jumpy castle, her pigtails swinging, and my breath caught. She could just as easily have been Amy Nessor in that instant. The vision was so real that my heart stammered in panic and my hands turned cold and clammy. Leah's laughter, as she disappeared inside the castle, echoed around me while the backyard seemed to tilt, first one way, then the other.

I turned my head and saw Amir talking to my brother, laughing at something he was saying. The clown stepped in front of me.

"And what would you like, ma'am? A poodle? Maybe a hat?"

I waved him away distractedly. Amir put his hand on Ricky's shoulder and leaned toward him to say something. The sounds of the party receded until all I could hear was a loud humming that grew louder and louder and I had to close my eyes to keep my head from exploding. Amir wanted us to have a baby. Probably more than one. I forced my eyes open and accepted the reality that I'd been ignoring for years. I stood up unsteadily and made my way inside where I threw up repeatedly in the upstairs bathroom.

The humming in my ears subsided and sounds drifted up to me from the backyard. Children's laughter. A little girl's voice, sweet and clear, chanting the same skipping rhyme from my childhood about bluebells and cockle shells. It must have been Leah or one of her friends. It didn't matter. That little sing-song voice drilled into my skull. I leaned my head against the edge of the toilet, defeated.

Eventually Amir came looking for me. I heard footsteps on the stairs and his concerned voice, calling out gently. "Zoe? Are you up here, Zoe?"

"In here," I called back weakly.

"Are you okay?"

"I'm not feeling well," I said. "I'll be fine in a minute." But I wasn't fine. My imagined future was imploding with every shaking breath I took. I couldn't keep anybody safe. I didn't even know if Leah was safe. I wanted to grab Erika — who hadn't been invited to the party on account of Brenda — by the shoulders and scream in her face, "Don't let him see her!" But of course, Erika had no reason to think that her six-year-old daughter might not be safe with her own father. I had no reason to think that. I was losing my mind. Leah was fine. Richard obviously doted on her — just look at this party.

I got up from the bathroom floor and wiped my face. I found a tube of toothpaste in the drawer and used my finger to smear a dab of it over my teeth before rinsing out my mouth. I made my way back downstairs and joined the others outside, mouthing the words to "Happy Birthday" as everybody sang and Leah's cake was presented. I clapped along with everyone else when she blew out the candles, but through the whole charade, I was an empty shell standing in the sun just waiting to shatter.

I BROKE OFF OUR ENGAGEMENT two days later.

At first, Amir refused to accept what I was saying. He suggested I was having cold feet, asked if I wanted to postpone the wedding to a later date, pleaded with me not to be irrational. I didn't offer much by way of explanation. After three days of awkward silences and gentle entreaties to please tell him what was going on, Amir told me he was moving out to give me space. I didn't argue. I didn't ask him to stay. I don't know where he went during that last week, but at the end of it, when I hadn't changed my mind, he left town. He transferred to a different bank and his aunt wouldn't tell me where.

Mom was furious with me, and when I refused to elaborate on what had happened between us, she began to suspect Amir, throwing out one wild accusation after another. Finally, in a fit of anger, I came as close to telling the truth as I could.

"It had nothing to do with Amir!" I screamed. "It was me. I changed my mind, okay? Would you rather I'd gone through with it and then done to him what Ricky does to all the people he marries? I couldn't drag him into my sorry mess of a life. You don't need to understand, but for god's sake will you let it go?"

"Zoe," she said in her maddeningly calm way. "You are nothing like Ricky. Is that what this is all about?"

I didn't answer. It was too complicated for me to figure out. At Leah's birthday party, something in me broke. I couldn't keep trying to outrun my past, and if it was going to devour me, I didn't want it taking down Amir, too. Amir and his kind soul. Amir and his laughing eyes. Amir and his big, open heart. He deserved so much more than me and all my demons. Ricky being prime among them.

And if Amir still hates me for letting him go, he's in good company. Although, this morning, Amir did not strike me as someone consumed by hatred.

With Jason, everything is different. We didn't go into things with any kind of wide-eyed innocence or reckless enthusiasm. Also, and I think this is important, Jason doesn't necessarily want more children. That alone makes things so much safer. With Jason, I thought I had left my demons behind. Until I turned on the news and discovered they'd caught up with me after all.

I finally cave in and call Ricky because I can't handle not knowing what's going on, but since he doesn't pick up, I end up leaving a distracted message on his voicemail. Then I burrow into my bed again, hoping that sleep will stop me from thinking. I don't want to think any more tonight. About anything. What I crave right now is oblivion. Maybe it's what I've always craved.

CHAPTER
EIGHT
·

I TRIED TO FIND AMIR once. It was a month after we'd broken up and I filled my car with gas and drove to St. Catharine's. I had no plan. When I pulled up in front of his parents' house, the air was still, as if it, too, was holding its breath, waiting to see what would happen. I stared at the house, blood roaring in my ears. I wanted to scream Amir's name, but instead I released a pitiful, strangled, choked-out sound that was more whimper than shout. I sat there for five minutes, maybe less, waiting for something to happen. Then, I swung my car around and drove back to Dunford.

This is the kind of inaction and indecision that has defined my life. I see myself floundering about, unable to love fully, unable to hold onto anybody or anything, but am seized with helplessness even in the face of that knowledge. That night, after my road trip, I dreamed about Amy Nessor again. She was standing in front of me, holding her detached braid out to me, pleading with her dead eyes for me to help her, and when I tried to speak, my lips wouldn't open, and I could only mumble incoherent nonsense that even she turned from in disgust.

The next morning, I was filled with relief that the worst I had done was park in front of Amir's parents' house. What would I have said if his parents or even Amir had seen me and come outside? What could I say? That I'd made a mistake and wanted everything to go back to the way it was before? Because that wasn't quite true, was it? And I knew at that moment, with a cool certainty, that the only fair thing to Amir was to leave him alone for good. I couldn't keep chasing ghosts.

ON WHAT SHOULD HAVE BEEN my wedding day, Mom dropped by. I had just finished breakfast and was pouring myself a second coffee when she rapped on the front door, with her peculiar staccato knock. I didn't want to see her. I didn't want to see anyone.

"Hey Zoe," she said, when I reluctantly opened the front door. "I thought you might like some company this morning. A bit of an off day, no?"

"I'm trying not to dwell on it," I said.

"I thought maybe we could do something. Or go somewhere."

"I'm fine," I said. "I don't really feel like going anywhere or doing anything. I was just going to take it easy and relax at home."

"Well, I'll just stay for a coffee and then I'll leave you alone," Mom said, sitting down in my kitchen.

We sat there together, not saying much, both probably imagining how different this morning was supposed to be. Right now, in some other kitchen, Amir was likely doing the same thing — thinking about the tux he should have been getting ready to put on and the ceremony that wouldn't take place despite months and months of anticipation.

I still didn't know where he was, but I assumed that if he wanted me to know, he would have made sure I found out. His silence told me more than enough.

Mom tried to make small talk, but eventually, possibly sensing my exasperation, she stood up to leave.

I thanked her for coming and walked her to the door.

"Take care of yourself, Zoe," she said. I realized then that she had walked from her house, and for some reason I was touched by that small detail. It seemed more thoughtful, somehow, to have purposefully hiked across town to get to my house than simply getting in her car and driving over.

"I will," I promised. I returned to the kitchen where I sank onto a chair and dropped my head into my hands. A gesture that was already becoming overly familiar.

RICKY CALLED LATER THE SAME day. Mom probably set him up to it. I doubt he would have thought of something like that himself. I didn't answer his call that day, or the next. He was the last person I wanted any sympathy from, assuming that's why he was even calling.

I honestly don't remember what else I did to pass the hours or what I thought about as the clock ticked closer and closer to three o'clock, the exact moment I should have been making my slow and steady way up the aisle to Amir's side. At some point, I started drinking. Gary and Yolanda had given us a bottle of scotch before everything went to shit, and I do remember cracking that bottle open to pour myself a healthy measure. Then another. And another.

After that, I tried to be strict with myself about not wallowing in the past. I went on, as I had before, working as much as possible to avoid being alone in my empty house with my empty thoughts. I tried to pretend that everyone was better off — Amir primarily, but also me.

IN DECEMBER, BRUCE CALLED ME into his office to offer me a promotion of sorts, naming me one of the Operators in Charge. When he made the announcement to the rest of the guys, he congratulated me on my commitment to the job and called me a valued employee. I'd nodded and smiled and pretended to be proud, but deep down I didn't believe I deserved the distinction. I didn't believe I deserved much of anything.

Mom was much more excited when I told her over our quiet Christmas dinner. "Oh, wow, Zoe, that's such good news!" She was practically beaming as she clapped her hands together and grinned at me.

"It's not that big a deal," I countered. "It's probably because I put in so many extra hours."

"Don't be silly. You work hard and they want to let you know how much they appreciate you. It's a compliment and you should be proud."

After dinner, Mom called Ricky. Before I could protest, she was saying, "Here, you need to talk to Zoe. She just got a big promotion at work."

I shook my head at her, but she passed the phone into my hands and waited expectantly while I said hello to my brother.

"So, are you running the plant now or what?" Ricky said. "How much more money you getting?"

"It's not like that," I explained. "It doesn't come with a raise. It's just a different title and it means I'm in charge of some of the day-to-day decision-making. It's because of all the extra work I do. That's all."

"Well, given how things went with Amir, I suppose you may as well be married to your job." He gave a short, barking laugh. When I didn't respond, he quickly added, "Zoe, that was a joke. I guess I should say I'm happy for you. Congratulations and all that shit."

Ricky had no idea why I hadn't married Amir. He'd never asked about it and even if he had, I wouldn't have told him the truth. But hearing him put it like that — saying I may as well be married to my job — struck a chord. Because he was right. I'd replaced the person I loved with a building made mostly of cement.

CHAPTER
NINE

·

FOR THE NEXT THREE YEARS, I slogged through the days that characterised my existence. The work at the plant was numbing and home was no more than a place to eat and sleep. There was nothing waiting for me there, nothing to rush back to. I continued to play around with photography though, and eventually being in my darkroom stopped making me think about Amir and his unbridled optimism. His belief in our future. His belief in me.

I had drifted, unknowingly, into a quiet acceptance of things continuing as they were, of my aloneness and detachment. Until Jason.

JASON HAD BEEN LIVING IN Dunford for close to a year before we met and if it hadn't been for Mom's neighbour, Mrs. Tisdale, dying, we might never have met at all. In her eighty-ninth year, Charlotte Tisdale still lived in the house next door to Mom — with that creepy bird, assuming it was still alive — although Mom had mentioned to me a few times that it was getting harder and harder for Charlotte to get around.

"She can barely make it up her front steps," Mom said. "She's going to have a fall one day. I just know it."

She didn't fall. She died sitting on her couch with a cup of tea on the table beside her and the only reason she was found so quickly was that her cleaning lady came by that same afternoon.

Mom didn't want to go to the funeral alone, and since I'd grown up next door to Mrs. Tisdale, I thought I should pay my respects. The service was held at the Baptist Church and afterwards there was a reception with tea and coffee and sandwiches in the basement. After about twenty minutes of sipping tea and murmuring polite expressions of sympathy in the church's low-ceilinged basement, I was ready to leave. Mom wanted to stay, so I made my way outside alone.

I was parked around the corner from the church, across the street from Stirling Automotive, and while I was waiting to turn left at the stop sign, a car came tearing up behind me and slammed into the back of my car. The force of the collision sent my car skidding into the middle of the intersection. Thankfully, there was no other traffic, because I just sat there, too stunned to move, not immediately understanding what had happened.

The driver of the car that hit me jumped out of his car and ran up to see if I was okay. I was shaken up, but I didn't think I was hurt. He returned to his car, which was quite damaged, and while I was gathering my wits, thinking about what to do next, he pulled around the corner, crumpled hood and all, and took off.

I watched him drive away in shock. Suddenly someone else was at my car door, asking if I was okay. "I saw the whole thing," this man said. "We've already called the police. He won't get far with his car like that." He helped me out of my car and led me to the waiting room of Stirling Automotive, where I sank gratefully into the chair he offered. "My name's Jason," he said.

When the police arrived, I explained what happened as best I understood it, and Jason gave a statement as well.

"If you want," he said, "we can pull your car in here to have a look at it. But if you have somewhere else you'd rather take it, we can call a tow truck for you."

"I guess I picked the right place to get hit, didn't I?" I joked. "I hope this isn't how you usually get your business."

Jason looked confused.

"From hit and runs in front of your shop," I clarified. "I was trying to be funny." I think I must have been borderline hysterical or something.

"Oh." He laughed unconvincingly.

He'd heard me give my name to the officer, but now I introduced myself to him properly. "I'm Zoe," I said, holding out my hand. "Thanks for all your help."

Jason seemed genuinely worried about me and his attentiveness was comforting. When he offered to drive me home, I accepted without giving it a second thought. My car didn't seem too bad, he assured me, but it might need a new bumper. He promised to get to it right away, and I was relieved to have someone else handling things for me. His eyes, when he spoke, were kind. Like Amir, but at the same time, not like him at all.

As it turned out, just as Jason had predicted, the man who rear-ended me didn't make it far at all. The police found his car three blocks away and the first person they talked to — the occupant of the house where the car had stopped — had actually taken the driver home, apparently believing his story about hitting a concrete barricade. So, in a strange twist of events, the same person who had rescued the driver was able to tell the police exactly where he lived.

When the police found him, he was obviously impaired. He was also on probation, which is why he had been so desperate to get away. I shared all these details with Jason after the fact, when I stopped by his shop to thank him for his help, bringing with me a Tupperware container of freshly-baked cookies. He invited me to sit and have a coffee with him, so we sat in the waiting area, the same place we'd first introduced ourselves, sharing coffee and cookies.

"Once your car is fixed, I guess you won't have any occasion to stop by with cookies," he said.

"I could always come back for the coffee."

"I'd rather share a real drink with you. How would you feel about going out sometime, somewhere a little nicer, to get to know each other?"

"I would like that," I replied. "Nothing against your waiting room."

WE ENDED UP GOING TO the newly-renovated, just-opened Crow's Nest, where we sat on the patio looking out at the Still River. I ordered chicken and Jason tried the steak sandwich. The evening air was cool, despite the glowing heat lamps, and at one point, Jason offered me his jacket. When I slid my arms into the sleeves, I felt a warm contentment settle over me. I hadn't felt that kind of sinking relaxation in years.

Jason told me about Parker, who was just starting kindergarten then. He touched briefly on his ex-wife, but didn't go into specifics.

"So, you're part owner of Stirling Automotive?" I asked, sensing it was time to change the subject. Previous marriages don't make great first-date conversation. I didn't want to get into the whole failed relationships thing.

"Originally, I just came on as a mechanic, but Gerald was looking for someone to pass the torch to. He's not ready to retire, but doesn't want all the hassle of running the place and I've always wanted to have my own shop, so it was a good fit. He's built up a pretty steady clientele, too."

Jason's hands were wrapped around his beer stein, and I wanted to reach for them, to feel his strong fingers gripping mine. I wanted to tunnel into his uncomplicated life, where things seemed so safe and simple.

ON OUR SECOND DATE, WE drove to Niagara Falls. As we were walking along the path at the edge of the escarpment, our hair and faces wet with the mist blowing off the falls, I was agonizing over whether or not I should hold Jason's hand. I had my camera slung around my neck, and was using one hand to stabilize it, but because of the crowded walkway, my other hand kept brushing up against his. It almost seemed like he was making a concerted effort not to hold my hand, so every time our hands touched, I moved mine away, too.

We walked in awkward tandem for a few more paces and while I was deciding what it might mean that he didn't want to hold hands with me, he suddenly took my hand firmly in his and said, "Is this okay?"

We continued down the path like that, holding hands, weaving through the stream of pedestrians and strollers and yellow ponchos, with the roar of water crashing down beside us and the spray from the falls making our hair damp.

Jason edged us over to the railing and we stopped to look out at the roaring spectacle of Niagara Falls. He was still holding my hand so I didn't take any pictures. I was afraid to let go of him. He leaned toward me, his lips parted just slightly and my heart raced. I lifted my head toward him, but just before he kissed me, his mouth skimmed past my lips and I realized he was saying something to me.

"Oh, sorry, I thought ..." I fumbled to cover my embarrassment, but his comment, whatever it was, died out completely.

"Oh! Did you —"

"No! What? Never mind. You were about to say something?"

He leaned his head back and laughed. "You thought I was trying to kiss you, didn't you?"

"For a second," I admitted.

"And would that be a bad thing?"

"YOU COULD STAY OVER, IF you wanted," Jason said casually. We were snuggled on his couch watching the credits to *Iron Man*. Neither of us made any effort to move.

We'd been dating for over two months, but things had been progressing slowly, so his suggestion caught me off guard.

"Are you sure?" I asked.

"You don't have to — I just thought ..."

"No, of course I want to! I only meant — I don't know what I meant. Forget I said that." We were sitting very close on the couch, but I could sense Jason shifting incrementally away from me. "Come here," I said, wrapping my arms around him and pulling him back in. For once, I wanted to be the one to take the lead. Also, even though I'd just asked it of Jason, I wanted to convince myself that I was sure.

CHAPTER
TEN
.

MOM FOLLOWED MY FLEDGING RELATIONSHIP with Jason closely, constantly asking me questions about him. With Christmas looming, she began making plans to have the two of us, and Parker, over for dinner.

"You're not going to take everybody else's shifts again, are you?" she asked.

Life had a different feel for me as the holidays approached — it was as if some of the magic had returned. Having someone other than my mother to shop for was a welcome change. I already knew what I was getting Jason, but somehow getting Parker's gift right seemed eminently more important.

I went to the mall in Leeville, passing the Leon's where I'd found Champ so many years ago, and made my determined way inside. I was feeling positive, but as I wandered past kiosks selling soap and calendars and personalized key chains, my confidence began to waver. I had no idea, really, what a kid his age liked to do. He was a quiet boy, and I'd seen him enough times to know that he liked books and puzzles, but he had so many of those already, I wanted to get him something special.

I walked into a hobby and games store, hoping something on one of the shelves would jump out at me. I finally settled on a model airplane kit, thinking it was similar to a puzzle in that it would require quiet concentration, but also because I could envision Parker and Jason sitting at their table, heads bent together, building the plane. I liked the idea of contributing to that future moment and intentionally or not, I wrapped a lot of hope around that model plane kit.

ON CHRISTMAS MORNING, I MADE my way to Jason's apartment so that we could exchange our gifts and hang out before heading to my mom's. It had worked out this year that Jason actually had Parker on Christmas Day, and Parker proudly showed me the presents he'd opened before breakfast. When I told him that I had one more for him, his face broke out into a beautiful smile. He reached out his hands eagerly.

"Just a minute, Parker," Jason said. "We have something for Zoe too, don't we? Why don't you grab it for her?"

Parker half-skipped, half-danced to the artificial tree by the window, and scooped up a tiny box, perfectly wrapped with an elegant bow. "This is for you," he said, setting the little package on my lap and looking up at me expectantly.

"Thank you." I reached into my bag and pulled out a slim gift-wrapped box for Jason, then handed Parker his present. He sat on the floor and immediately began ripping off the paper. When at last he had unveiled the model airplane kit, his face remained impassive. He turned the box over.

"What do you say, Parker?" Jason prompted.

"Thank you," he dutifully replied, but I could see from his expression that he wasn't even remotely excited about my gift.

"It's an airplane," I said. "You have to build it. You might need your dad to help you. I thought you could build it together."

He set the box down. "Open yours, Daddy!"

I could feel tiny flames of disappointment licking the edges of my mind. I had wanted Parker to be excited, but now that I saw him with the kit, I could see clearly that he was too young for it. He didn't even understand what it was.

Jason began slowly unwrapping his gift, revealing a thin, white cardboard box. He lifted the lid, where a scrapbook was nestled underneath layers of cream-coloured tissue paper. I had chronicled our first few months together, leaving a slew of empty pages — for our future, I told him, holding his eyes with mine. I had been so sure, back then, that I knew what I wanted.

I was strangely nervous about opening the tiny box on my lap. I tried to peel the tape off carefully, not wanting to rip the paper underneath, but then sensing Parker's impatience beside me, I tore the pretty wrapping off. I raised an eyebrow when I saw that I was holding a box from a jewelry store. As I lifted the hinged lid, my heart hammered erratically. I let out my breath when I saw a bracelet nestled on the box's satin lining.

"Oh, Jason, it's beautiful. I love it!" I leaned across the couch and kissed him, right in front of Parker.

WHEN WE GOT TO MY mom's, she was bustling about like an excited hen. She took our coats and shooed us into the living room where she had the fireplace channel on the TV and Christmas music playing too loudly. There were two bowls on the coffee table: one filled with mixed nuts, the other with Smarties.

"Who wants some eggnog?" Mom asked.

"I'll help," I said, standing up again, but Mom motioned for me to sit.

"No, no," she said. "You just enjoy yourself."

When she rejoined us, with a tray of drinks in her hands, she had this silly grin on her face and it reminded me of the way she had looked at Ricky's first wedding. Proud as a peacock. Maybe even a little smug. What had she expected for her children that these kinds of moments — generally quite normal — made her so happy?

She had prepared for this visit with the same attention to detail as when Ricky used to return for the holidays, first from Leeville and later from Toronto. The kitchen table was covered with the red and green checkered tablecloth and was already set for four with Mom's wedding china. Two tapered candlesticks stood like sentinels on either side of her Christmas centrepiece: a glass bowl filled with floating candles and sprigs of holly.

"It smells great in here," I said, inhaling the rich scent of poultry and gravy as my mom opened the oven to baste the turkey.

"I have a little something for Parker," Mom said, straightening up. "Shall we open that now? Dinner will be ready in an hour, and I'll need to do some last-minute prep before then."

As it turned out, she had a little something for each of us, even though she'd already given me a gift the day before. I didn't have anything else for her, and I didn't want Jason to feel awkward either about not having something to give Mom, but, as I was deciding what to say, Jason pulled a small package from beside his shoes, wrapped in silver paper, and graciously handed it to my mom.

When Mom saw the set of four intricately hand-carved coasters, each one representing a different biblical scene from the nativity story, she looked up, her eyes wide.

I reached out for a better look at the coasters. Each miniature scene had been etched with extraordinary precision: Mary riding on the donkey with Joseph at her side, under a sky of tiny sculpted stars; the shepherds with their sheep in the field, gazing at the new star in the east; the three wise men holding their gifts of gold, frankincense, and myrrh; and, of course, the manger in the stable, with baby Jesus lying on a bed of straw, Mary and Joseph kneeling at his side.

It was obvious Mom loved the coasters. Her gift for Jason didn't exactly have the same wow factor, but I could tell Jason was pleased enough with his new slippers. "She loves giving slippers," I told him.

It was Parker's gift, though, that left me wondering why I hadn't had the foresight to think of it myself. While he had looked at the model airplane kit from me and set it aside with disinterest, he was clearly thrilled when he unwrapped Mom's present: a box of Lego. He began playing with it immediately and I was reminded of my own sizable collection as a child. Where had all those bins gone? At some point when I was in high school, Mom had cleaned out Ricky's room where I'd been storing my stuff and I supposed she had moved everything to the basement, or maybe she'd given it away. Seeing Parker sitting on the floor, absorbed by whatever he was building, I pictured him at my house, surrounded by my old bins of Lego, as content on my living room floor as I'd always been as a child in my room sorting through my collection. Somehow, watching Parker play with his new Lego kit made my own childhood seem less tainted.

"DON'T BE NERVOUS. MY parents will love you."

"I'm not nervous," I said. "How much do they know about me?"

Jason laughed. "Everything. At least everything I know."

I kept my eyes trained on the road. We were an hour away from Haliburton and from me meeting his parents for the first time. Parker had finally fallen asleep in the back seat after keeping up a constant stream of chatter for the first two and a half hours of driving. The closer we got to Jason's hometown, the more jittery

I became. Our relationship was still so new and if his parents didn't like me, I was worried that he would suddenly see me differently and break things off. I knew he was close with them, and I imagined their opinion of me would weigh heavily with him. I didn't want to go back to being alone. I couldn't face a lifetime of solitary nights filled with white noise and regrets. Or of taking Christmas shifts at the plant because there was no one to miss me at dinner.

Gina and Terence welcomed me warmly. They lived in a condo apartment overlooking Head Lake, which was completely frozen over, and the view from their living room window was stunning. I tried to imagine what it would be like in the summer, with the sun reflecting off the water instead of the cold glare of the ice and snow.

"It's nice to meet you, Zoe," Terence said, shaking my hand enthusiastically.

"It's nice to meet you too," I replied.

"You can call me Terry. We're not all that formal here."

Parker ran off down the hall to the spare bedroom, where the three of us were going to be sharing a room. Gina had made him a bed of cushions on the floor.

"I hope that's okay," she said to Jason. "We don't have any other extra space."

"It's perfect. Zoe and I plan to be very chaste."

I looked at Jason, mortified. I was afraid to see his parents' reaction, but they were both smiling. "Not that you'll have much say in the matter," Terry said to Jason, before turning away to pour us drinks.

THE FIRST TIME JASON AND I were alone in the apartment was when his parents took Parker to the library for a bird-house-building event. As soon as they left, Jason walked into the kitchen where I was at the sink finishing the lunch dishes. He wrapped his strong arms around me and began pulling me toward the bedroom. My hands were covered with soap bubbles, but I didn't resist. We tripped over Parker's cushions on the floor and collapsed on the bed together, laughing.

"They might only be gone an hour," Jason said, climbing under the heavy blue and white striped duvet. "Get in here!"

Obediently, I followed him. Part of my mind was still on the dishes sitting in the sink — if they were still there when his parents returned with Parker, it would look suspicious. "I need to finish the dishes before they get back," I said.

"Zoe! Are you seriously thinking about the dishes right now?"

Jason had taken off his shirt and under the cover of the duvet was undoing my belt. As his fingers fumbled with my buckle, I finally stopped thinking about the dishes. Perhaps because we were in his parents' house, or because we knew we had only a short window of time — whatever the reason, that frantic tumble under the duvet was one of our better love-making sessions. Looking back, it probably paved the way for our other rushed couplings, watching the clock, waiting for the knock at the door that would signal Tammy's return with Parker. The anticipation of a possible interruption gave us a sense of urgency and excitement. We used to do that a lot, at the beginning, squeeze the most out of short windows of time, sometimes making jokes about leaving enough time to finish the dishes.

WE WERE MORE SECURE AFTER that visit to Haliburton. It was as if now that we had both met each other's families, our relationship became grounded in a way it wasn't before. I know I felt better after obtaining Gina and Terry's seal of approval. When we were driving back to Dunford, Jason turned to me in the car and said, "They liked you. A lot."

"You think so?" I asked, keeping my eyes straight ahead, while my heart thumped joyfully.

"I know so. My mom must have mentioned it to me a dozen times. How you were so sweet with Parker, how you automatically helped out with things like cleaning up, and on and on. My dad liked you, too. I could tell."

I felt a sweeping sense of contentment wash over me as we drove between the walls of towering rock that lined the road.

"So it's settled," Jason continued. "We all like you." He reached over and put his hand on my leg, just above my knee. "Me especially."

I couldn't look at him. My eyes were filling with tears and I didn't want Jason to know that I was on the verge of crying. I placed my hand over his, hoping that small gesture said what I couldn't say out loud because the words were lodged somewhere behind a sharp lump in my throat that felt as much like pain as happiness.

THESE MEMORIES TWIST AROUND ME, like tangled sheets, as I try desperately to sleep on Wednesday night. I've spent too much of the day drifting in and out of consciousness and now my mind is fighting me. Thoughts of Amir dance around the solid reality of Jason, and although there is an aching weariness settling over my bones, my body can't relax for the worry pounding and pounding against my skull.

Jason's hesitation on the phone last night doesn't mean a thing. I know that he loves me, but that thought does nothing to calm me. Because I am afraid that when he knows the truth about me, his love, like the storm-blown petals of a tulip, will droop and falter, before dropping off completely.

CHAPTER
ELEVEN

·

ALL OF THE FEARS THAT have been skirting around the edges of my consciousness morph into ugly monsters as I lie in the dark; they circle around my worn-out body and tear at my mind. Everything that's happened in the last few days — the case being re-opened, Mom's heart attack, the accident at work, me being sick — it all becomes larger than life. A hopeless sort of dread washes over me as I fight to remain rational and to quell my racing thoughts.

When I do sleep, my dreams are interspersed with confusing and disturbing incidents that involve Amir. In my more wakeful moments, I can't decide whether I'm hoping to run into him again or not, and if I am, then what does that mean? Knowing he's in Dunford has shifted something in my gut. Mom's message continues to play in my mind, *"Guess what I just found out?"* And in my more twisted hallucinations, Mom marches Darius into my living room. His head is hanging in shame, but when he steps to the side, there is Amy Nessor, standing on my carpet, smiling. Mom looks so proud. Then Amir is in the room, too, with his arm around me, and for a moment, I am overcome with the rightness of the whole scene. Amir. Sweet little Amy. Everyone back together. And I am relieved. So relieved.

Then, just as suddenly, everything is wrong again. Amy Nessor, even though she is standing on the carpet in front of me, is unmistakably dead, and Jason is in the room too, staring at Amir whose arm is wrapped possessively around my waist. I know it's Jason I should go to, but I can't because Amir's grip is like a vice, locking me in place.

Mom is gone. Where did she go? Why would she disappear right when I need her? I am casting about the room, searching for her, when I tumble back into consciousness, back into the equally troubling mess of my real life.

I lie awake in the pre-dawn hours trying to come up with a plan. Should I see if it's possible to reschedule my interview? Surely being as sick as I am is a reasonable excuse. Bruce can vouch for the fact that I'm legitimately ill. Even more pressing though is the need to talk to Jason. But I can't talk to him, not really talk to him, until I know what's actually happening with the investigation, and despite the message I left last night for Ricky, he still hasn't bothered to reply.

Will the police want to question me again? Whatever information Darius has given them, they must know by now that I was lying all those years ago. Or at least withholding key information. Will I be considered an accomplice? I can already see the headline: *Nine-year-old deliberately misleads police in investigation of missing six-year-old.* But I didn't mislead them, did I? I told the police everything I saw. I described the car over and over again. I looked at countless pictures of different vehicles and pointed out exactly which models looked like the one I had seen. Why couldn't they figure it out? Both Darius and his dad had driven the car all over Dunford, in plain sight of everyone!

As the initial investigation wore on, days turning into weeks, even I convinced myself that it must have been a different car I had seen on our street. I wanted to believe it so badly, and if the police had given Darius's dad's car the all-clear, then they must have had a good reason; I let myself be swayed, comforted by the certainty that I was wrong about the car. Wrong about everything.

Who would have thought that after twenty-nine years, Darius would talk? As I go over the scene one more time, from that long-ago afternoon, my childish suspicions coalesce into an ugly certainty. I was right about the car. I knew it. I always knew it.

In an attempt to soothe myself, I repeat certain truths over and over. I didn't see my brother in the car. I didn't lie to the police. I didn't lie to anyone. I was only nine. I was just a kid — a scared and confused little kid.

I close my eyes and try to quiet my turbulent thoughts. What I feel, as I lie in my tangled sheets, is absolute despair. And tiredness. I am tired of running from Amy's ghost.

What is Ricky doing right now? He must be taking stock of his options, hiring a lawyer. Does he think he can still get away with it? I remember him talking to Darius on the phone, telling him to convince Jeremy to lie about where they were the night Amy went missing. Does he think he can lie his way out again? He doesn't know about me, though. He doesn't know what I heard and what I saw. He doesn't know that I know. Or that I have carried the guilt of that knowledge like a boulder around my neck for the whole of my life.

I drag myself out of bed, but don't make it further than the couch, where I sit listlessly, waiting for whatever's going to happen next. I get up once to take an Advil, but I don't have the strength to keep moving. My legs feel slippery; the walls in my living room tilt and sway, as if the entire room is balanced on a knife tip. I keep my phone beside me, turn on the TV, and somehow, I end up dozing. Perversely, when I wake up, my stomach is grumbling. I eat a small bowl of cereal, but the Cheerios sit like lead bullets in my stomach. How much time do I have? Days? Hours?

It's been three days since I first saw the news, and I know something has to give soon. I keep the TV on. The police must know something that they aren't sharing.

I dial Ricky's number again and am caught off guard when Brenda answers. I must have called the house by mistake. What is she doing home, anyway? She should be at work. Does she know, too? Is she also sitting in front of the TV or the computer, waiting for her whole world to cave in?

"Hi Brenda," I say. "It's Zoe. Is Richard around?" I can't keep the urgency out of my voice. Ricky normally isn't home during the day either, so asking for him feels senseless. Like I'm playing at something.

There's a slight pause before she answers. "I don't know where he is. He took off." Her voice is hard, angry. Then she says, "You knew all along, didn't you, Zoe?" The censure in her tone is obvious, so instead of replying I just sort of grunt. She lets out an exasperated huff, then hangs up and I'm left holding the phone to my ear, the sudden silence on the other end echoing with her disappointment.

Her reaction is like a prelude for how it's going to play out with everyone around me. They will drop away, one after another. Jason will wrap his arm around Parker's skinny shoulders and turn from me, silently and sadly. Just like Amir, he will simply fade away, disappearing into the unreachable shadows.

The thought of losing Jason right now is worse than everything else. The prospect of being fired from my job, even of facing criminal charges — they don't wrench at my heart in nearly the same way as the thought of Jason and Parker being cut from my life.

If Brenda knows, if Ricky has gone MIA, then this is it. And right now, I don't know if I have the strength to face what's coming.

I'M CLUTCHING A HOT MUG of coffee, wondering if I can stomach any food for dinner, when my phone rings. The sound startles me and my heart lurches. I still haven't called to check on Mom. But it's Jason's name that pulses on the screen, backlit and insistent, begging me to answer.

"Hey," I say, my voice coming out gravelly and hoarse.

"How are you doing?" he asks. "You sound worse."

"I am," I admit.

"What are you going to do about your interview?"

"Maybe I'll feel better in the morning," I say. As if anything will be better in the morning.

"Here's hoping," he says. But his voice is flat. He sounds upset.

Normally, I would try to find out what's bothering him, but I can't summon up the energy to ask what's going on. I should keep talking — I have to come clean with him, I know that. He deserves to know the truth before the investigation blows my life wide open. Blows our life wide open.

Tomorrow, I'll go in for my interview, sick or not, then I'll sit Jason down and confess everything.

PART
FIVE

CHAPTER
ONE
·

I FIND IT HARD TO believe that Ricky has disappeared. Does he really think he can hide? He can't be that stupid. My breathing becomes short and shallow as I contemplate all the places he might have gone. Any thoughts of trying to eat something, of shoring up my strength, have left my mind. Food seems irrelevant. How dare Ricky run now. I will help the police hunt him down, if need be.

As I'm contemplating the ways I want to get even with my brother, a car door slams nearby and I hear footsteps approaching my front door. I stand up, expecting the worst, my pulse racing. But when I go to the door, I'm startled to see that it's Jason who is standing outside.

"I wanted to check on you," he says. Something is off about him. I'm trying to decide what to do now that he's here when I realize what it is that doesn't feel right. He isn't making eye contact with me, or not proper eye contact; he won't look at me for more than a few milliseconds at best.

"What's wrong?" I ask. I've been thinking about him so much in the last few hours and now that he's here, all I want to do is fold myself in his arms, but I stand across from him awkwardly, my arms hanging stiffly at my sides.

Does he know? Or does he at least suspect? While I'm waiting for him to reply, my phone rings. It's Mom. I have to pick up. What if she's having another heart attack? What if something else has happened? There's too much going on right now. I motion for Jason to come in. "Sorry," I say as I lift my phone to my ear.

"Mom? Is everything okay?" A stupid question, given the circumstances.

"Did you know Amir was in town?" she squawks, loud enough for Jason to hear.

I turn away from Jason slightly, just enough so he can't see the expression on my face. "Yes. I actually ran into him yesterday."

"Did you talk to him?"

"Just for a minute. Jason is here," I say pointedly. "Are you okay? I haven't had a chance to talk to you since you got out of the hospital."

"I'm fine. It was just a little blip. I suppose you've seen the news?"

Blood rushes in my ears. "Yes." My voice is almost a whisper. "Mom, can we talk later? I just need to —" I am acutely aware of Jason's proximity. He's sitting on my couch waiting patiently for me to finish. I can see him out of the corner of my eye; his hands are folded on his lap and he's watching me.

When I hang up and turn to face him fully, he looks back at me with a mixture of concern and confusion. I am tempted to cup his face in my hands and kiss him, but I'm too sick for that, and there's something in his expression that warns me off. He looks vulnerable and uncertain, but also sad.

"What's wrong?" I ask again, perching beside him on the couch, leaving more space between us than I normally would.

"Nothing," he says.

"You seem upset."

Jason looks away. He fidgets with his hands in his lap. When he turns to face me again, his eyes are filled with resignation. "It's just that after Sunday — when you made it clear you had no intention of us moving in together — since then, you've been ... so distant."

"I've been sick," I remind him.

"I just thought — it kind of feels like you're breaking up with me."

"What? No, Jason! Please don't read too much into what I said on Sunday. I didn't even really mean it. I was having a weird day." I don't tell him the whole truth. Not yet.

"Yeah, but since then, you haven't returned my calls and ..." His eyes pierce mine for a moment. "Zoe, you didn't even tell me your mom had a heart attack! I found out from someone else that she'd been in the hospital."

"I'm sorry. Things have just been weird the past few days —"

"So you keep saying."

"Jason, you don't understand." But I don't know what else to say. I don't know how to reassure him. My head is throbbing. "I've just been so sick. My mom was home again before I really knew what happened. I didn't even visit her in the hospital. I haven't talked to her, either, if that makes you feel any better. This was the first time we've spoken since it happened." I gesture to my phone on the table in front of us. Suddenly, him coming here to confront me like this seems unfair. I am so tired, and as easy as it should be to reassure him right now, how can I tell him there's nothing to worry about when that's all I've been doing for the past three days? "You know I'm sick," I finish weakly.

He slumps his shoulders. "Okay," he says.

Can't he see how tired I am? "Can we talk about this later? I just, I really can't do this right now."

He looks surprised. And hurt. "Of course," he says, standing up.

He holds my gaze for a second too long before turning away. When he walks to the front hall, I notice what he's wearing. He dressed up for me. I picture him standing in front of his closet, choosing an outfit for this awkward conversation, a conversation he probably rehearsed hundreds of times in his head over the past few hours. Bracing himself to find out whether or not I was ending things.

I'm trying to think of something to say to ease his mind, to lessen the hurt in his eyes, but before I can come up with anything, he's out the door and walking down my front steps.

I need a minute to think. I want to go after him, to call out to him before he gets in his car, but I just stand in the hall, watching him go.

After he is gone, I sink onto the couch, exhausted. Then I close my eyes against the pounding in my head. I have been waiting for something to happen. For everything to fall apart. But this? In the face of all the fears looming in my periphery, Jason's misunderstanding seems almost insignificant. And, yet, the look he gave me as he walked out the door feels like a knife in my chest. He knows there's more going on than me being sick. It's as if he can sense an impending blow, but doesn't know where to look for the source.

When my phone rings again, I assume it's Jason, that he wants to ask another question, to convince himself of one last thing.

But it's not Jason. It's my brother.

"You've been looking for me?" he says, his voice sounding as tired and drained as I feel.

"Where are you?" I say. "I talked to Brenda. You told her?"

"Yeah." A pause. "She would have found out anyway. She's pissed. She kicked me out."

"She told me she didn't know where you went." My voice sounds petulant, like I'm a little kid again.

"She didn't."

I slide down the wall until I'm sitting on the floor. "What are you going to do?"

"I don't know." There's a long sigh on the other end of the phone. "I guess I'll have to find a new place. I don't think Dee Dee exactly wants me to move in."

Why the hell would anyone, let alone Dee Dee, want to help him? "They're going to find you," I say.

Silence. Then, "Who's going to find me? What are you talking about?"

"The police."

Ricky actually snorts. "The police?"

I don't know what to say, so I stay silent, pressing my back against the wall. I let my head fall back until it's hitting the wall, too. I stare at the ceiling, at a small crack that starts in the corner, creeping outward until it splinters in two, like a fork in a stream.

"Zoe?" Ricky's voice has an edge to it. "What do you mean the police will find me? Did Brenda say something about the police?"

Anger flares through my whole body. "Stop with the fucking games, Ricky! I know what you did! I've always known! I saw her get into the car." I lower my voice. "It's over."

There is a long silence. "Zoe," Ricky finally says, "what the hell are you talking about?"

"Don't pretend you don't know."

"Is this about the girl that went missing on our street? Mom told me they re-opened the case, but what does that have to do with me and Dee Dee?"

"Her name was Amy, Ricky. Amy Nessor. And I saw her get in Darius's car, remember? I saw you guys drive away with her and I never told anyone. Ever." I am crying now. Long, shuddering sobs that make my ribs ache.

"Zoe," Ricky says, "what the fuck is wrong with you? You think I —"

I hurl my phone across the room and watch as it smashes against the doorframe to the kitchen. I can't listen to another word out of his mouth.

My head is throbbing, my legs are so weak I can barely stand, and my eyes feel swollen and sore. Everything hurts. I drag myself to my room and drop onto my bed where I simply shut down. I don't let myself think.

I wake to the sound of Champ's claws pattering against the hardwood floor. My room has grown dark and I blink in confusion. Then I remember that Champ is dead and I realize in that same moment what the tapping sound is. It's Amy Nessor, rapping at my window with her little dead fingers, begging me to help her. My heart lurches in terror. The sound gets louder, more insistent, until I realize it's not coming from my window at all. Someone is knocking at my front door.

I stagger out of bed. What now? If this is Ricky, I will kill him. I'm shaking as I approach the front door, still in my clothes, which are rumpled from sleeping.

It's Gary, standing on my front steps in full uniform. I step back, and because it's Gary, give him a brief nod, intended as a greeting. I don't trust myself to speak. I don't know what to feel, so in that instant, I choose to feel nothing.

"Zoe," he says, and my former friend's face is so full of sympathy I almost collapse against him. I'm surprised they sent him, of all people. Maybe the police are hoping, because of our history, that I'll be more cooperative. I motion for him to come in and watch as he closes the door gently behind him.

I start to say something, but the words get stuck in my throat.

Instead I stare at him helplessly, feeling the brittle threads of my life snapping one by one.

"Zoe," he says again. "There's been an accident."

"An accident?" I repeat dumbly. "Where?" I am imagining some kind of catastrophe at the plant, while at the same time a slow, seeping relief spreads through my veins. This isn't about Amy.

"On Snyder's Road, coming into town. Richard's car —"

"Richard?" I interrupt. "My brother, Richard?" My head is spinning. I can hardly make sense of what Gary is saying. I put a hand on the wall to steady myself.

"It's pretty bad, Zoe. He's been airlifted to Jefferson Memorial Hospital."

"Okay," I say. My mind is a whirlwind of confusion. "I need to find my keys. Does my mom know?"

Gary lays a gentle hand on my arm. "Zoe. It would be better if someone else drove you."

"I can drive," I answer automatically.

"Let me call you a cab," Gary says. "I would take you myself, but I'm still on shift."

I am about to argue, to insist that I can drive myself to the hospital, when what Gary is saying finally registers. And I wonder, for just a second, if Ricky's accident wasn't an accident at all. If this was his way of running from the truth for good. But why was he running back to Dunford?

CHAPTER
TWO

·

JEFFERSON MEMORIAL HOSPITAL IS A monstrous brick building. My cab driver, Leroy — he told me his name, but otherwise didn't speak to me during the forty-minute drive to the city — drops me off at the front entrance just before midnight. I stagger inside, unsure what to do or where to go. I spent most of the ride in a dazed panic, only half registering my surroundings as Leroy drove out of Dunford and along the dark highway. I didn't bring Mom. I didn't even call her. I want to see how bad it is before alarming her. The last thing I need is for her to have another heart attack.

At the first counter I come across, I ask for help. There are two people sitting at a desk, wearing uniforms of some sort, and after typing Ricky's name into a computer, one of them tells me he's in the Intensive Care Unit. A nurse is summoned to escort me there. She walks briskly and I have to scurry behind her on my shaking legs. We arrive at a waiting room outside the ICU doors, and when the nurse turns to face me, she eyes me carefully before asking if I am sick.

"Me?" I say, confused. "No, I'm here to see my brother. Richard Emmerson. He was in an accident."

"If you've had a cough or fever in the last twenty-four hours, we can't let you in the ward," she explains.

The back of my neck is sweating and my hands are shaking. "I have a cold," I admit. Can this nurse see how feverish I am?

She purses her lips and nods at me. "Someone will be out to speak with you, but I can't let you in," she says. "Wait here." She disappears through the doors that lead into the ICU. Within less than a minute, she returns. "I told the staff at the desk that you're here," she says. Then, without so much as a backward glance, she walks away, leaving me alone in the waiting room.

A different nurse emerges from the ICU and establishes my relationship to Richard. "I can't let you see him, but I will come out to notify you if anything changes," she tells me. "If you need to contact us, use this." She indicates a phone mounted beside the ICU doors. "It connects straight to the desk."

At first, I pace around the small waiting room, counting the chairs to distract myself. There are fourteen in total and all of them are empty. There's a TV on the wall, tuned to a news station, but the sound has been turned off. I am too wound-up to watch it anyway. Eventually, I collapse into one of the plastic chairs, holding my aching head in my hands. I am sitting like this, folded over myself, when Brenda arrives.

She nods at me before being led through the doors into the ICU where I am not allowed to go. Eventually, Brenda returns to the waiting room, white-faced, with a doctor close behind her. I try to stand up, but I'm shaking so badly I have to sit again. Brenda's eyes are red-rimmed and teary. She's looking somewhere beside me, as if she can't bring herself to look at me directly and I feel something in my chest breaking apart.

It is the doctor who speaks. Richard is in a coma, he explains. At his words, Brenda shakes her head slowly, although she must have already had a chance to digest this information. The doctor is still talking, still explaining. He's saying something about a medically induced coma, giving Richard's brain a chance to heal. Then he starts going on about bleeding and swelling, severe trauma. His words wash over me, a meaningless spray of information.

Brenda is crying and I realize she has only come here, to the waiting room, so that I am not alone to hear this news. I finally stand up and move closer to her, giving her an awkward hug, more of a sideways embrace. The doctor continues talking. "His vitals are strong. If the swelling goes down, there's a very good chance he will survive." He pauses. "But brain injuries are unpredictable. He could come out of this with no side-effects or he could have permanent damage. You need to be prepared for many different eventualities."

"Of course, of course," Brenda is saying.

"So you think he's going to live?" I say, and a small spark of hope ignites somewhere deep in my chest. I have often wished violent deaths upon my brother, but obviously I never really meant it. Only I didn't know I didn't mean it, until this moment now, when I am flooded with relief.

"If the swelling continues to decrease, his odds get better and better."

I nod. Brenda follows the doctor back into the ICU and I go back to my plastic chair where I lean against the wall and close my eyes. I will stay the night, I tell myself and, in the morning, I will go back to Dunford to pick up Mom and bring her here, so she can be with her son.

I sit in that chair for hours, slipping in and out of consciousness. No one comes to talk to me, no one checks on me, which makes me think nothing has changed. Not for the better, but not for the worse, either.

As I'm rubbing my eyes, my attention is snagged by the now-familiar image of Amy Nessor's face on the silent TV. I struggle to read the ticker at the bottom of the screen. There's been an arrest. My gut clenches. The picture of Amy's face is replaced by grainy footage of a man in an orange jumpsuit being led somewhere. I squint at the screen. Whoever it is, he's too old to be Darius. I look around the waiting room, searching for a remote control or some way to turn on the sound. I need to hear what they're saying about this guy in the jumpsuit. Who is he? What does he have to do with Amy's case?

The ticker continues to spit out the details: *Marcus Daley, formerly of Port Sitsworth, confessed to the murder of Amy Nessor, whose body was discovered almost 30 years ago less than 900 yards from her house in Dunford. Daley, in inmate at Collins Bay Penitentiary, was two weeks away from being released after serving a 12-year sentence for armed robbery.*

My thoughts fly off in a hundred different directions. I am trying to connect this man to Darius and Ricky, trying to make sense of the words ticking across the screen, but before I can even fully register what I just read, the news switches to footage of an earthquake in Nepal. *Four hundred missing*, the ticker types out. I don't see what comes next because I am on my feet, staggering down the hall, away from the ICU doors. I can't tell if I'm feverish or flat-out delirious. I make my way back to the same doors I came in on the main level of the hospital.

"I'm coming back," I say to the women at the desk. "I just have to get my mom — my brother, he's in the ICU. I'm not allowed to see him, but if there's any change — will you call me if there's any change? His wife is with him. Can you tell her where I am if she's looking for me? There's a phone up there. I was supposed to use the phone to tell them."

I know I'm not making any sense, but one of the women calmly asks for my number and writes in on a blue Post-it Note, promising to relay my garbled message to the nurses in ICU.

"I'm coming back," I repeat.

I step outside to call a cab from my cracked phone. The morning is lit by a weak, watery light, as if the sun can't be bothered to shine properly while Richard lies on a hospital bed, unconscious. It's too cold to wait for my taxi outside, so I turn to go back in and as I pass through the glass doors, I catch a glimpse of my reflection. I look like an addict, coming in off the streets. Desperate and hungry and haunted.

I'm leaving my brother behind, and as the full weariness of a night without sleep hits me, that one small spark of hope I felt at the doctor's words balloons into something bigger as it melds with the news about Amy's case.

Marcus Daley. Port Sitsworth.

I nod off during the ride back to Dunford, and as soon as I arrive at Mom's house, I can see by her face that she knows something is wrong. I tell her about Richard's accident, emphasizing the more promising details from the doctor's prognosis.

"Was he coming to Dunford?" she asks. "What was he doing on Snyder's Road?" She is surprisingly calm. I watch her closely, alert for any signs of heart trouble.

"I don't know," I admit. "I don't know what he was doing." But the last words I spoke to my brother are ringing in my ears. I accused him of killing our neighbour. Was he coming to see me? To set me straight? Why did Brenda kick him out, if that wasn't what he just confessed? Then the truth hits me like a two-by-four to the face: he told her about Dee Dee.

"You need to have a shower," Mom says. "We can't go anywhere with you looking like that. Were you at the hospital all night? Have you eaten anything?"

I don't argue because my brain has gone numb. It's just like Mom to put everyone else's needs before her own. She must be dying to get to the hospital, to see Ricky, but she's still worried about me, making sure I'm okay. I take a quick shower, then put on my same dirty clothes, and when I come out, Mom has set out a small breakfast for me. I take a tentative bite of buttered toast and wash it down with a swig of coffee, gripping the hot mug gratefully.

"They wouldn't let me see him," I say. "Because I have this cold. Brenda is there, though."

Just like when I was little, Mom rests the back of her hand, cool and reassuring, against my forehead. "You're burning up," she says. "Finish your toast, then we'll go."

"Did you see the news about Amy? About the arrest?" I blurt out.

Mom nods. "That was odd, wasn't it? For that guy to confess now, just when he was about to be released? I think he wanted people to know what he did. Then again, some long-term prisoners don't know what to do when they get out, so they commit another crime just to go back. Or in his case, admit to one. I'm just glad he's been locked up all this time. I hated to think whoever killed poor Amy was running around loose."

"How do they know it was really him?" I press. "Couldn't he just be saying he did it?" I think back to the blue car parked in front of our house and Amy Nessor climbing into the back seat. Could it really have been this guy all along? This Marcus Daley?

Mom doesn't answer right away. She must be able to guess at how Amy's murder has haunted me, although she has no idea how it shaped my life. Or maybe she's thinking about Ricky and not paying attention to my questions at all.

"He had her braid," she says. "It was buried in a lock box beside the shed in his mother's backyard."

This piece of information is still sinking in to my fog-filled brain when my phone rings. The sound jolts me back to the present. I glance at my splintered screen anxiously where a number I don't recognize pulses back at me.

"I think it's the hospital," I say, my mouth going dry. I answer the phone, turning away from Mom's fear-filled eyes. My voice comes out as a rasp and I have to clear my throat to repeat myself. I am trembling, but it has nothing to do with my fever.

"Zoe?" A clear, bright voice says. "It's Amir."

CHAPTER
THREE

·

AT THE SOUND OF AMIR'S voice, I sink into an even thicker bog of confusion. There is an awkward silence before I am able to speak.

"I thought you would be at work," Amir confesses. "I was kinda hoping to leave a message." He gives a light laugh and I remember how his eyes used to light up whenever he laughed.

I am halfway down the hall to the bedrooms, but I can still sense my mother's anxious presence in the kitchen. "Amir ..." I say. My head is swimming with half-formed thoughts, with emotions I thought I'd buried long before. "I'd love catch up, but Richard, my brother, was just in an accident and ..." *I need you.* I close my eyes, trying to shut out the image of collapsing into Amir, into his familiar arms and the happiness they once promised.

"Oh! Oh god! I'm sorry. I hope everything's alright! I didn't mean to —"

"He's in a coma," I say. I don't know why I'm telling him this. *I was wrong. I was wrong. I was wrong.* "I just came home to get my mom. I have to go back. I told the hospital I'd be right back."

When I return to the kitchen, Mom is watching my face, her eyes wide with worry.

"It wasn't the hospital," I say. "But we should go."

MOM OPTS TO DRIVE, AND I let her, because I am so exhausted. My eyes close as we hit the outskirts of Dunford. I am tired, but also lulled by the comfort of Mom's presence as she guides the car so capably toward Jefferson Memorial. As always, she is unflappable in a crisis. How could I have forgotten that? My head is swimming with Marcus Daley's confession and the strangeness of Amir calling and an overarching, pounding fear for my brother. It's a relief to feel myself drifting off, letting go of reality even if just for a minute. When I open my eyes, we are turning into the hospital parking lot.

"No change," I am told, when I pick up the phone outside the ICU to inquire about Ricky's status.

Today is supposed to be my interview with Crystal Clear Solutions, although no one from work has called to check in with me. Is anyone expecting me to show up given that I've been off for so many days? Is Bruce wondering right now where the hell I am? "I thought you'd be at work," Amir said. What on earth prompted him to call? He must know I have a boyfriend. Which reminds me, shouldn't I tell Jason about the accident? Shouldn't I be collapsing into his arms right now? Was Amir just being friendly or was there something else, something more to his call? The look on his face the morning I told him I couldn't marry him comes back to me in a rush. The disbelief, the confusion, and then the pain. But I only broke off our engagement because I thought — I pull out my phone, frantic to find out more about Marcus Daley. I don't understand. Confusion and anguish pound in angry waves against my skull.

There is a yellow bar spreading across my cracked screen, making the display next to impossible to read. I set my phone aside in frustration just as Mom walks over to me carrying two Styrofoam cups.

"Coffee. From a vending machine," she says. "Best I could do."

I sip the tepid coffee, waiting. But for what, I don't know. For someone to come out and tell me that my brother will be fine. For the news about the arrest in the Amy Nessor investigation to make sense.

After a while, Mom turns her attention to practical matters. "Has anyone spoken to Erika?" she asks. "She might want to bring Leah. Someone should call her." Maybe sensing my confusion, mistaking it for something else, she offers to do it herself.

I almost agree. It's tempting to hand this whole situation over to my mom and let her take care of things. To lean back in this hard, plastic chair and just close my eyes. "I'll call her," I say. I stand up and move into the corridor, where the light from the windows mixes with the light from the fluorescent bulbs in the ceiling, making the hall too white. Too bright.

Erika is flustered and upset when I tell her about Richard. I imagine part of her distress is really on account of Leah. Like me, Erika's probably wished her fair share of punishments on Richard. Except she didn't harbour angry accusations of false crimes. She didn't turn him into something he wasn't, and herself in the process.

Next, I call Bruce. He is all reassurance and understanding when I tell him where I am. He'd already made arrangements, he tells me, to have my shift covered for today and my interview has been moved to next week. "I took care of it for you. Wasn't sure when you'd be back."

"I don't know what's going to happen," I say.

"Don't worry about anything here," Bruce says. "Just do what you need to do and take care of yourself. Is someone with you?"

"My mom. My brother's wife is here, too."

As I make my way back to the waiting room, I consider stretching out on the floor. I so want to put my head down. But when I turn the corner, Brenda is coming through the ICU doors and all thoughts of sleep vanish as I scan her face.

"Still no change," she says. She looks haggard, the skin under her worried eyes sagging.

Mom steps forward and enfolds Brenda in an embrace. I think back to my conversation with Brenda, when she was so angry with me and I thought she was talking about the Amy Nessor case, but all along she was talking about Dee Dee. Here she is, holding vigil at Richard's bedside, right after he confessed to her that he was having an affair.

"You must be exhausted," Mom says, and at first I think she is talking to me, but then realize that of course she is talking to Brenda. "Have you had anything to eat or drink? What can I do to help?"

The TV in the waiting room flashes to the image of Marcus Daley in his orange jumpsuit. I cannot wrap my head around the simple fact that Ricky wasn't involved in Amy's murder. The thought that my brother is innocent floats through my brain, along with another thought, much more insistent: he has to wake up.

CHAPTER
FOUR

·

LATER, MANY, MANY DAYS LATER, Ricky remains unresponsive, though his body is not still and quiet, like I expected it to be. Stretched out beneath the bleached white sheets, his limbs twitch and jerk, and every so often a soft moan escapes his lips. With each fretful sound or movement, my heart thuds expectantly, but he doesn't open his eyes. He doesn't see me sitting beside him.

So I keep waiting.

I am better now and have been permitted to sit beside his bed with all its beeping equipment. In this noisy quiet, I play back the conversation I had the other night with Ricky's friend Jeremy regarding that long-ago Tuesday in October when Amy Nessor went missing. Jeremy was incredulous that I ever believed Ricky to be involved. I remember all too well Ricky's own disbelief on the phone when he pieced together what I was accusing him of. Right before he got in his car to drive to Dunford. He must have been more upset with me than I realized, which makes sense. It says something to know your kid sister thought you capable of abducting and then murdering your six-year-old neighbour. Though even now, with the truth staring me in the face, I wonder if I will ever forgive him for all the things I once believed, and if he will have the chance to forgive me for believing them in the first place.

MOM AND BRENDA TAKE TURNS beside him. We have rented a room at the Still River Inn, which is not on the river at all, but just down the road from the hospital, directly across from Lion's Gate Cemetery. It's like a joke of sorts, to stare out at a grave-yard, while your brother is fighting for his life. We use the motel room as a home base between visits. A place to sleep and keep a few things when we can't get all the way back to Dunford or, for Brenda, Toronto.

But right now, it's me beside Ricky. And while I'm attuned to every flutter of his eyelids, I am also preoccupied with the missing minutes and the hours of his life the day that Amy Nessor disap-peared. Jeremy did his best to describe what he remembers, but it was so long ago, and while that Tuesday has haunted me forever, it left a much fainter imprint on Jeremy's life. And probably Ricky's, for that matter.

Ricky was with Darius and Jeremy that night, in Darius's father's 1969 Ford Thunderbird, a model quite similar to Marcus Daley's 1967 Chevrolet Impala, a detail that will forever torment me. They weren't in Leeville watching a movie at all, which I already knew because I'd heard Ricky telling Darius to lie about it, only I had the reasons all wrong.

"After school we went to my house to smoke a few joints," Jeremy told me. "Then we drove to Boelen to hang out at the arcade. We weren't even in Dunford most of the night. Sometime later, I can't remember how much later — maybe an hour, maybe two or three — we convinced some guy to buy a case of beer for us. We took it out to the Boelen pier."

I can imagine them there, three underage teenagers drinking

beer behind the lighthouse at the end of the pier all the way over in Boelen, while somewhere between Dunford and Port Sitsworth, Marcus Daley was strangling Amy and I was answering a battery of questions about seeing her climb into a blue car.

"When the beer was gone, we got bored. Someone had the bright idea — it was probably Darius — to goof around with this fire trick. We bought four cans of aerosol hairspray from a convenience store and snuck into the abandoned mill. Ricky lit up the first jet of hairspray. We were drunk, probably still high, and we thought it was the most amazing thing we'd ever seen. Home-made fireballs. But then one of the cans caught on fire in Ricky's hands, so he threw it to the ground and we ran like idiots from the building. We thought the can was going to explode. We kept waiting for it, for the big boom, but nothing happened, so we just left."

My guess is they were laughing when they got back to the car; meanwhile, in Dunford, police were combing our neighbourhood for clues and Amy's mom had to be escorted back to her own house.

Somehow, miraculously in hindsight, Darius drove the three of them back to Jeremy's house and they spent the next few hours playing video games and smoking more pot in Jeremy's basement, oblivious to the tragedy unfolding on Lindell Drive. By the time Ricky walked home, after being gone for over six hours, there was only one police car left on our street.

"I think the police car freaked him out," Jeremy admitted. "Because of the pot. But he told me later that he relaxed when he realized it wasn't in front of his house. Then he found out your neighbour girl had gone missing. I think that scared him, you know, because of you. Because it could have been you."

I remember his reaction. I didn't think his fear had anything to do with me.

"Later," Jeremy said, "I think the next day, we found out that the Boelen Mill had burned down. That really freaked us out."

That burning can of hairspray that Ricky dropped didn't do nothing after all, it started a fire that blazed out of control while Darius, Jeremy, and Ricky were driving back to Dunford.

"I mean, the mill was a wreck of a building to begin with, it was slated for demolition, but we all knew we'd be in huge trouble if we were caught. Ricky said it would kill your mom if her son was charged with arson. It was his idea to make sure we all stuck to our original story about being in Leeville that night. Obviously, none of us wanted to get caught."

It's hard for me to reconcile these facts with the vague, half-formed — sometimes fully-formed — suspicions I've carried with me for almost the whole of my life. I guess there had always been a small part of me that wanted to believe in my brother's innocence. I'm still trying to convince the grown-up version of me it's actually true. And yet another part of me still resists, even knowing the facts. Almost every decision in my life has hinged on the knowledge that my brother is a monster. And that I protected him. I have carried that shameful secret around for so long that I have formed my life around it. I have lost so much, and justified it all, because of that single stupid belief.

And if that one thing is no longer true, then I am afraid to ask myself: what else in my life isn't either?

CHAPTER
FIVE
·

RICKY OPENED HIS EYES THIS morning. It was only for a few seconds and I wasn't there to see it, but Mom was. Although Ricky looked right at her face, apparently he made no sign of recognizing her. According to Mom, Ricky simply stared at her briefly, then closed his eyes again. Still, it's something. Dr. Hooverston says it's a good sign. And since I am sitting with Ricky now, I am praying that he will have another small moment of wakefulness while I am at his side, no matter how short that moment is.

I very much want the chance to look into his eyes and tell him I know the truth now. I want to see him for who he is, not who I've always believed him to be. I want to say I'm sorry. I'm sorry for believing the worst of him. I'm sorry that he might have been driving to see me when he had the accident. In all likelihood, though, the next time he opens his eyes, he will be alone. Or it will be a nurse leaning over him. Mom and Brenda and I spend hours with him, but none of us can maintain a constant vigil. I have returned to the plant after taking a short leave. My interview with Crystal Clear Solutions turned out to be a mere formality — just like Jason kept trying to convince me. And, while I spend as much time in the evenings at the hospital as I can, in the end, even I have to go home to sleep. We've tried to establish a schedule of sorts, to increase the odds of someone being with Ricky if he wakes. *When* he wakes.

Jason has come to the hospital with me several times. We haven't discussed the conversation we were having about our relationship the night of the accident, although I know it will come up again. He's giving me space right now, but we can't go on like this indefinitely. Amir has messaged me too, inquiring about Richard and I can't make up my mind about whether or not I want to see him. He's only in town short-term and I feel like a window is closing; at times the thought is suffocating. When he's gone, whatever flicker of our past lives is currently shimmering in my periphery will go with him. A big part of me is terrified, because I don't want to live with any more regrets. I have too many as it is.

Right now, I am talking to Ricky, as we've been encouraged to do. I am trying out what it would feel like to ask my big brother for advice. "Amir is in town," I tell him. "He's mentioned meeting for coffee, just to catch up, but I don't think Jason would like that. I was just getting ready to tell Jason that I'm ready for us to live together, which is a big step for me. For us. I think he wants to marry me. Or he did. But then I messed things up."

I should feel relieved, whispering these words to my brother, admitting out loud that I have a decision to make.

I keep talking. I tell him that when he's better, he might be my best man. "But you're still a jerk," I assure him. "Brenda has every right to hate you, yet she's here every day, so you can't be all bad. At least not as bad as I used to think. But you already know that. I hope you do."

And then I start crying. Not the silent tears I've shed so often in recent weeks, but huge, wracking sobs that shake my entire body.

"Come back," I choke out. "Come back."

I'm not sure who I'm talking to anymore. On the surface, it's obviously my brother. But I can still see Amy Nessor climbing into that car and I think I might be crying out to her too, because I want so desperately to save her and to save myself, to save the little girl I used to be before witnessing an act that made me believe the worst of my brother. That made me believe the worst of myself.

I STOPPED FOLLOWING THE CASE. It's in all the papers and on every news station and website, but I stubbornly turn a blind eye. When I am not at the hospital or at work, I hide away in my dark-room, finishing the final prints for Parker's collection. I am not completely immune to the details as they emerge, however. I've seen some of the headlines and Mom cannot stop herself from letting certain particulars slip. I know, for example, that Marcus Daley had a dog with him in the car, a great big lab, when he encouraged Amy to climb in. That dog must have been the shadowy figure I mistook for a second person. Apparently, he told Amy he was taking her to see the dog's puppies, or at least that's what he said in his long confession. I also know that before going to jail for armed robbery, he lived with his mother who described him as emotion-ally stunted and needy. "But he was a good boy," she was quoted as saying. "Most of the time he was a good boy."

"He couldn't go back to his mother when he got out of jail," Mom told me, "because she'd just moved into a seniors' home. I guess he couldn't cope with being on his own. And maybe he knew, deep down, that he deserved to stay in jail. That that's where he belongs."

"His mom didn't know anything about Amy? She didn't suspect anything, all this time?"

I had once made excuses for my own mom, but was less willing to make them for Marcus Daley's. I still faulted Mom, to some degree, for failing over and over to acknowledge what I saw as Ricky's shortcomings; yet, I found it impossible to believe that Marcus's mother could be so willfully blind when it came to her own son. That she could maintain he was a "good boy" even after finding out he'd strangled a little girl.

"By the time the police were looking for Amy, he'd already killed her and driven back to Port Sitsworth. As far as his mom knew, he'd never left the house."

I don't want to know the rest of the details. I have already wasted too much of my life imagining them.

I wonder if when Ricky wakes up and sees me, he will notice that I am different. That, despite the uncertainty with which this accident has blindsided our family — that despite everything — I am less afraid.

ACKNOWLEDGEMENTS

.

It's hard to know where to begin. There are so many people who, somewhere along the line, played a role in my journey with this novel. I want to offer a heartfelt thank you to everyone who offered encouragement, feedback, advice, information, or simply a listening ear. You know who you are.

I do, however, need to recognize a few individuals by name. When I first began piecing together the details of this story, one of my grade seven students, Jake Randall, acted as my research assistant for car-related information. Joseph Kuriger gave me a tour of the Dunnville Water Treatment Plant and Peter Clarke did the same at the Kitchener Water Treatment Plant; both were extremely generous with their time and about answering follow-up e-mail questions. I am indebted to Monica Pyear and Matt Cain for reading an early draft and offering valuable insights that helped shape the current story; as well as to the wonderful women from my soccer team/book club (Tina Butt, Laura Martin, Karyn Hynes, and Missy Cowburn) for reading a much later version and discussing it at one of our book clubs like it was already a real book. Later, those same amazing gals sent support in the form of wine and

M&Ms. I also received crucial encouragement from my writing group (Kate Jenks, Kayleigh Platz, and Robin Cecily) who in the later stages of the game fueled me with bourbon, uplifting notes, and more chocolate. Lana Button offered inspiration at a critical juncture, which, strangely enough, included requiring me to watch *Flashdance*. Nicole Pilgrim-Shier shared insights into the world of photography and provided me with samples from some of her early practice assignments in the darkroom. She also took my author photo.

At the end of the day, though, I don't know where I would be without my mentor, Merilyn Simonds, who continues to offer support and guidance, and who, when she agreed to take me on as a mentee, truly made me think I might have a shot at this whole writing thing. Of course, I am also deeply grateful to my editor, Marc Côté, and to the entire team at Cormorant, for believing in this story and for making my dreams of becoming a novelist a reality.

Finally, and most importantly, a huge thank you to my family — Hannah and Jacob, who never complained about having to "find something quiet to do" while I worked, and Scott, who encouraged me in so many ways from the very beginning and who believed in me long before I believed in myself.

We acknowledge the sacred land on which Cormorant Books operates. It has been a site of human activity for 15,000 years. This land is the territory of the Huron-Wendat and Petun First Nations, the Seneca, and most recently, the Mississaugas of the Credit River. The territory was the subject of the Dish With One Spoon Wampum Belt Covenant, an agreement between the Iroquois Confederacy and Confederacy of the Ojibway and allied nations to peaceably share and steward the resources around the Great Lakes. Today, the meeting place of Toronto is still home to many Indigenous people from across Turtle Island. We are grateful to have the opportunity to work in the community, on this territory.